KF LEE

Awakyns

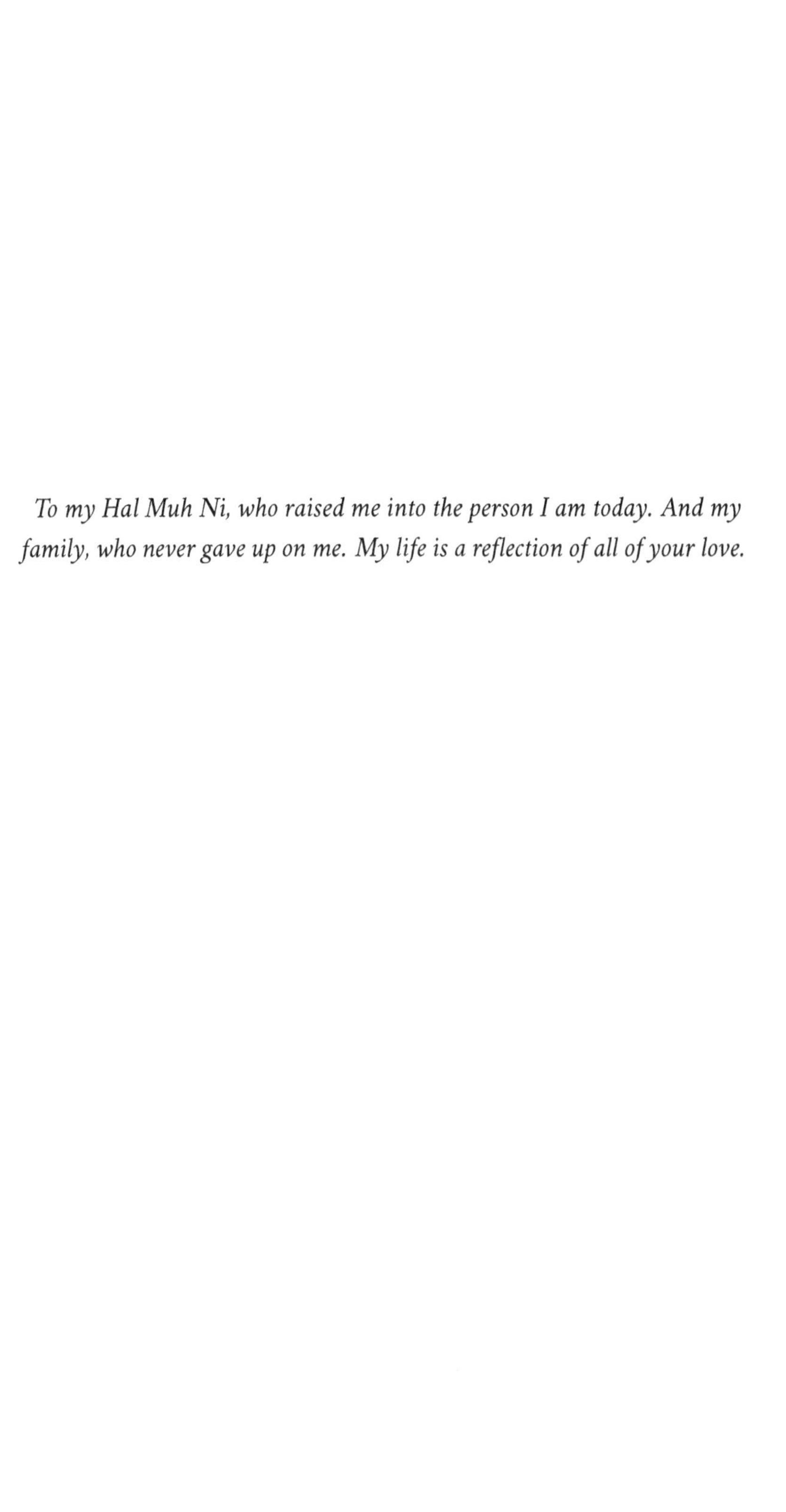

To my Hal Muh Ni, who raised me into the person I am today. And my family, who never gave up on me. My life is a reflection of all of your love.

"Each book you read not only teaches you something new, but also opens up different ways of thinking about old ideas."

— James Clear

Dear Reader,

Thank you for taking an interest in "Awakyns". I am thrilled to introduce you to the world of Awakyns and Judanites. Each page that you read makes my dream into reality. From the bottom of my heart, I am grateful for you engagement.

Sincerely,

KF Lee

Prologue

Kishinev - Bessarabia Governorate,
 Russian Empire; 1903
 (Jewish Ghetto)

"Kill 'Em All!" the rioters hollered in unison. Each syllable carried the vile contents of their hearts. "Kill 'Em All!"

The hateful shouts drew Jairus to the window. He peered out the soiled pane. Torches in their grasp, the rioters marched down the alleyway. The open flames illuminated the darkness. Some of the rioters carried hunting rifles, while others held pitchforks or garden hoes.

Jairus squeezed the hilt of his Roman broadsword on his hip to ease the tension that grew inside of him. His hand grew numb. For the last few decades, he had witnessed the hopelessness that humanity had become. Evil seemed to have taken a stronghold in the minds of men. Could his fellow Awakyn brothers and sisters keep the balance between good and evil?

A mob of townsmen broke through the door of the unpainted clapboard house from across the street. Shouts of protest mixed with the screams of victims. Jewish families cowered in the streets as rioters invaded their homes. The Jews looked no different from the townspeople who assailed them.

Windows shattered as rioters threw rickety wooden furniture into the streets. One man poured pig lard over the broken contents, while another man dropped a torch in the middle of the pile. The flames burst upward.

Jairus turned away from the window as a howl of wind sounded between the walls. He scanned the empty room, studying the sun-faded outlines of where portraits once hung and the floor where furniture once occupied. The frigid gust howled between the cracks in the wall, which stood no chance of keeping the freezing night air out or retaining the heat inside. The same dilapidated construction that had become a staple of Jewish ghettos across Europe.

Jairus had been Jewish once, a long time ago. He knew too well the pain and sorrow of the Jewish diaspora. A people without a homeland. Still, he observed the shanty walls covered in vibrant wallpaper and the floor, which seemed to have been cleaned daily. A total contrast to the building facade. Jairus could envision the happiness and laughter shared by the family that once lived here. How could the resiliency of humanity make a desolated place feel like home? With love, anything is bearable because it keeps hope alive.

The pine floor creaked behind him. He swiveled around as he pulled his broadsword from his scabbard into a defensive position. The moonlight reflected down the golden-hued blade. A lone figure dressed in dark clothes with a derby cap pulled low on his face appeared before him.

"Peace be with you, Jairus." The dark-clad figure removed the cap from his head, exposing his handsome face gifted with high cheekbones.

"And also with you, Dao-Ren." Jairus sheathed his sword and clasped Dao-Ren in a hug. "I feared you weren't going to show."

"I thought twice about it." Dao-Ren crossed his hands in front of him.

"There's too much going on to stay in one place."

Jairus studied Dao-Ren's brown eyes. "I understand."

"Why have you been looking for me?" Dao-Ren asked.

"I have a favor to ask."

Dao-Ren's eyes narrowed.

"I need you to hide the boy."

"I'm not a Watcher, Jairus."

"He's the last of his lineage." Jairus stepped closer to Dao-Ren. He saw the sorrow that exuded from the man's eyes.

"I'm sorry." Dao-Ren turned away.

"Do it for Soraya?"

"Don't bring Soraya into this."

The tone of his voice ended all conversation. Jairus placed his hand on Dao-Ren's shoulder. "Sorry, brother. You're right."

Dao-Ren hesitated. "Why me?"

"I believe you're the only one who can protect him. You're off the grid."

Dao-Ren faced Jairus. "I'll do what you ask of me, Jairus."

"Thank you, brother."

Jairus rushed to the back of the room and pressed the wall with both of his hands. He pushed the panel to the right, opening into a tiny crawl space. A five-year-old boy with wavy brown hair that hung above his honey-green eyes sat cross-legged in the cramped space.

Jairus held out his hand, "Come, Benjamin, it's time to go."

The boy crawled out of the hole, got up, and dusted himself off. Jairus squatted down to the child's height. "You see this man?"

The boy stared up at Dao-Ren.

"He will take you somewhere safe." Jairus grasped his hands over the boy's shoulder.

Benjamin returned his gaze to Jairus. "Why can't I stay with you?"

"I'm sorry. You're not safe here," Jairus replied.

Tears gathered in the boy's eyes. He threw his small arms around

Jairus' neck.

Jairus held Benjamin an arm's length away. He wiped the tears from the boy's cheeks with his thumb. "Remain strong, Benjamin, and grow up to be an honorable man."

The boy nodded, though he probably didn't grasp the magnitude of the words.

"Always listen to your heart." Jairus tapped Benjamin's chest.

The boy wiped his tears with the back of his hand.

Jairus smiled before kissing him on both cheeks and saying a quick blessing over his head.

"Jairus, we must depart before the Russian soldiers surround the ghetto to break up the riot," warned Dao-Ren.

Jairus stood and lifted Benjamin off the ground. Dao-Ren accepted him with his right arm. Benjamin held onto Dao-Ren's neck.

"Go in peace, brother," Jairus said.

"And may peace be upon you." Dao-Ren bowed his head before he disappeared into the night. The only sign of their departure was the open window.

A cold draft gusted through the open window, carrying the scent of death. Jairus unsheathed his sword and snatched his round golden shield off the table. With his feet shoulder width apart, he dug into a defensive stance. He lifted his shield over his head. The windows on the second floor imploded from all sides of the house, sending glass shards everywhere. Debris pelted his shield.

Hooded beings crept through the shattered windows.

Judanites.

A man in a mink coat with soft brown, wavy locks that framed his chiseled face strode toward Jairus. The other human figures fell behind their leader. The moonlight danced off his honey-green eyes.

"My old friend, Jairus, it's been far too long since we last saw each other. I hope this time won't be the last," threatened Jacques. "Just give me the boy."

Jairus inhaled deep, letting his spirit course through him and setting fire to his muscles. He stepped back and stood on the balls of his feet. "Jacques, I ask you and your minions to repent and God will have mercy on you."

Jacques harsh laughter twisted the night air. "Kill him." Jacques flicked his ring-laden hand in the air. "The boy is near."

Judanites howled together.

Jairus positioned his sword and shield in front of him. Judanites rushed him from all angles. Jairus' sword collided with steel as he blocked an ax with his shield. Jairus parried to his right and swung down, cutting the first Judanite across his chest. A bright bluish-black light burst from the slash then the Judanite exploded into ashes.

Using his shield to clear the way, Jairus pushed forward. The narrow room made it difficult for the Judanites to overwhelm him with sheer numbers. Jairus had a touch of hope. Two Judanites leapt into the air with feline grace, and their swords were wielded high. Jairus jumped back and slung his sword at the Judanite on his right. The sword pierced her stomach. The wound flashed a bluish-black light. Her sword clunked to the floor.

The other Judanite landed directly in front of Jairus. He swung his scimitar. Jairus blocked it with his shield, then tumbled to the ground in a roll and snatched his sword off the ground. The Judanite attacked, and Jairus lunged forward, plunging his sword into his opponent's heart, bluish-black light. Ashes littered the ground.

Jairus straightened up and viewed Jacques with a scowl on his lip, standing by the far window. Jairus sprang toward him. Jacques watched with amusement. Alarms went off in Jairus' mind. The blade of a sword arched toward Jairus. At the last moment, Jairus raised his shield to block the blow, exposing his underside.

A Judanite, concealed behind the doorframe, stabbed his sword upward through Jairus' armpit into his heart. He clenched his jaw. Not from the pain, but from the hatred that came from the Judanite. He stumbled backward and felt his spirit leaving his body. His shield dropped from his grasp. He reached for the embedded sword, but the effort was futile. Cold hands restrained him.

A calming sense came over Jairus. He'd given Dao-Ren enough time to escape. He raised his head high as Jacques picked up Jairus' sword. The stars twinkled brightly through the shattered windows.

"Lord, receive my Spirit," exclaimed Jairus before feeling the bit of metal on his neck.

Chapter 1

Present Time

A subtle stench of death saturated the cool winter night air. Dao-Ren knew a mass of Judanites had converged within the city limits of Los Angeles. This imperceptible malodor of Judanites couldn't be detected by humans without MaNa.

But Dao-Ren was no longer a human. He was something more.

An Awakyn.

Dao-Ren moved easily through the crowded boulevard. Shoppers didn't pay him any attention when he walked past them. He had mastered the art of being inconspicuous through his early years of immortality. All it took was the proper clothing selection. His slim-fit jeans and a black wool pea coat over a plain gray t-shirt did the trick. No unusual graphics or bold colors to distinguish him.

He donned a dark-blue baseball cap low over his head to mask his eyes. It was not to cover his East Asiatic features. The world had become a smaller place than the one he was born into, and being East Asian on the streets of Los Angeles was the norm. Yet people were drawn to the depths of his eyes—pain recognizes pain, and sorrow begets sorrow like two kindred spirits. He wanted to appear ordinary. It was the fastest and quietest way to get things done without any unneeded attention.

He had lived up to his given name, Dao-Ren. In Chinese, *dao* means path," and *ren* means "endure." With much remorse, he had endured plenty in his path, more than most would have ever experienced in ten lifetimes.

Numerous retail establishments occupied the buildings along Abbot Kinney Road. Each storefront displayed its wares through large windows. Christmas shoppers came and went, carrying their purchases in oversize bags.

The sun faded behind the horizon and cast a reddish glow over the city. The modern storefronts switched on their signs, which brought illumination to the coming darkness. Dao-Ren quickened his pace. Evilness tended to emerge at night, when Judanites came out to prey on humans.

Judanites forced him to remain attentive to his surroundings at all times. His duty was to protect humans. A height of six feet allowed him to observe without attracting undue suspicion. Upon rising from the dead, his five senses had been enhanced four times beyond those of any mortal man. He analyzed everything within his visual scope and earshot.

Just ahead two lovers touched each other lightly. To his right, a baby boy cooed in his stroller. The infant's mother conversed on a cell phone about a late dinner and pushed the stroller with her free hand. The musky odor of a large man trudging laboriously behind him reached his nose.

Where Judanites were concerned, nothing can be missed. They used all temptations and deceitfulness to turn a person's spirit to Satan.

A young man in overalls stapled posters promoting a nightclub to a telephone pole. Dao-Ren scanned the flier. "A Night of Blood and Lust." A male face with elongated canines dotted the center flier. Dao-Ren shook his head. It was implausible for him to wrap his mind around the idea of romanticizing vampires. Everywhere he looked, the media expressed this fascination with vampires, from books to television shows to blockbuster movies. If people only knew vampires were not mere myths, then perhaps the allure and admiration would cease to exist.

Vampires were not lovers, friends, or even monsters. They were worse.

They were Judanites.

The rapid clicks and bright camera flashes grabbed Dao-Ren's attention from across the street. A group of paparazzi descended upon a young couple exiting a furniture store. He recognized the two actors. Their fresh faces were plastered on every national entertainment outlet.

"Are the two of you moving in together?" a reporter shouted at them.

The actor covered his head with his trucker jacket and pushed through the crowd, never looking back.

"Is it true that the two of you are expecting a child?" someone yelled over the others.

Multiple photographers impeded the dark-haired starlet's path. Separating her from her boyfriend. Her face flushed to a reddish hue as her lips pressed together. She looked from side to side, trying to find an escape route.

"Did you secretly get married in Las Vegas last weekend?" asked another, sticking a microphone in front of the woman's mouth.

She swiped the reporter's hand and forced her way through the mass of paparazzi. She took off across the busy boulevard, not bothering to look down the street. A city bus barreled down her path. People on the sidewalk shouted warnings of danger, which caused her to stop and glance up. Fear froze her. The bus brakes screeched in protest, metal grinding metal.

Dao-Ren bolted toward her, and at the last possible moment, pulled her into his arms. The bus sped past, spinning her ponytail into a whirlwind. He swiftly carried her to the curb between two parked cars. Her eyes were wide with fright, and she shook uncontrollably, but physically, he saw nothing wrong with her. She opened her mouth to speak, but Dao-Ren raised his index finger over his lips. He then leaned her back against a car bumper.

The sounds of approaching voices pulled her attention away from Dao-Ren. He took this opportunity to take his leave. He slipped back into the steady flow of passersby on the sidewalk.

No one noticed him.

It wouldn't be long before he arrived at his destination, a café. He peered through the establishment's front window, unobscured by the white stenciled letters scrawled across the glass. He had come to make sure a specific someone was safe.

Inside, customers purchased their desired flavor and roast of ground coffee beans from the barista at the register. Pastries and sandwiches filled the grate shelves inside the glass counter. Customers brewed their own coffee according to their preferences using the different coffee brewing machines on the center island.

Some of the customers took their coffee and meal to the rear area, where tables and chairs were set up. The café catered to a mixture of customers, from college students typing away on their laptops to the artsy crowd doodling on tablets.

Through the crowd of patrons, Dao-Ren located the person for whom he searched: Malayah Vega—May. She sat by herself at the far corner table, engrossed in an art magazine. Her espresso sat momentarily forgotten in her hand.

The overhead lights reflected off her long, silky brown hair that cascaded down her oval-shaped face. Her perfectly arched eyebrows floated above her rich hazel-green eyes. A small, pointy nose gave birth to full, red lips that moved silently with the words of the article she read. Her skin had a light olive complexion, like that of her ancestors from the Mediterranean. The slight movements of her body displayed the gracefulness of athletic discipline.

Dao-Ren had known Malayah since her birth in Eugene, Oregon, twenty-four years earlier. It was easy to forget how fast humans tend to age and mature. He has not given her much thought in the last sixteen years, but he saw how much she has grown from the child he once saved in a car wreck to the woman she had become.

The strangest part of this encounter was the strong stirring in his spirit that he never felt towards her. This was something new. He sensed the feeling of loss in her spirit. How much had she endured because he couldn't save her parents from the car accident? There was such longing in her soul. His spirit yearned to be close to her and protect her from all the evil and hardship this world would throw at her. This realization rocked him to the core. It had been centuries since he felt this strongly for someone—a feeling he thought he would never feel again.

He stepped away from the window and leaned against the red stucco wall. He refocused his thoughts on the reason why he returned to Los Angeles. He had to remain rational if he wanted to protect Malayah. At all costs, Judanites must not find out who she really was.

Suddenly, a breeze from the north carried a strong scent of Judanites. Dao-Ren turned in that direction and scanned the pedestrians walking by. He fell back into the crowd of shoppers, never giving Malayah another glance. The best way to protect her was to keep his distance from her. There were Judanites who hunted him to settle an old score. They were here, calling for him with the serial murders committed by the Exorcist Killer. He came to put an end to these senseless murders and find out why they chose this city where May resides.

***

May glanced up from her magazine and saw the stranger with a dark-blue baseball cap move away from the front window. Recognition startled her. Her heart raced, and her breathing became short and choppy. It was her guardian angel, the one who had rescued her from the deadly car accident that claimed her parents.

She burst to her feet, and the wooden chair squeaked against the floor. Her thigh bumped into the table, spilling her espresso.

"You okay?" someone asked.

She didn't answer, dashing out the front door. Pedestrians blocked her view. She headed in the direction where she saw him leave, searching for the dark-blue cap in the crowd. He was nowhere in sight. Doubt clouded her mind. *Was he even there in the first place?* She exhaled her disappointment, which was quickly replaced with anger.

This had to stop, she told herself. It had been going on way too long. Over the years, she had chased after any man who resembled her angel. She tried to convince herself on numerous occasions that he was only a figment of her imagination. Someone she had conjured up in her moment of need and fear of loss.

Despite all of her attempts to forget him, the result was the same. It was useless, her feelings and emotions for her angel rushed back tenfold when she saw anyone that remotely resembled him. Even in her dreams, he was there, watching her with his captivating eyes. He dwelled inside of her.

How could she escape that?

Now she was upset with herself. It had been months since her last episode. She blew out a long stream of air. Even so, it might not have been him. The baseball cap fell so low over his eyes, she couldn't get a good look at him. *Stop this!* She had to get it through her head that she was only a child when she was in the car accident that killed her parents. She had to accept the hard truth that being thrown from the car had saved her life. By chance, she had survived. No divine intervention saved her. Her angel was not real.

She took a moment to steady her emotions. These episodes needed to end before she went insane. Maybe Kat, her best friend, could set up an appointment with her psychologist.

A hand touched her shoulder. May pivoted around, swatting the hand off her shoulder with her forearm. A step backward gave herself enough room to face her attacker. *Uncle Bernardo.* A sign of relief escaped her.

Bernardo held up both of his hands in the air. "I come in peace," he said.

"You're late." She gave him a hard look.

He paused. "I got caught up with work, but are you alright? I've been shouting your name since I spotted you out here."

"It's nothing, Unc." She smiled. "Just lost in my own thoughts."

"Are you sure?" Bernardo questioned. "You know that we can talk about anything." He touched her shoulder.

"It's nothing. Really." She met his eyes.

His eyes never wavered.

"It's getting cold out here. Let's go inside." She leaned into Bernardo and hugged him. She knew he wouldn't let this issue go. And the way she felt right now, she was not in the mood to answer his probing questions that were to come.

Chapter 2

Lust ignited inside Stacy Smith. She kept her sights on him, hoping to catch his attention. The tall, athletic guy stood alone by the edge of the dance floor. He looked so out of place with his tailored slacks, a navy blue button-down shirt, and a burgundy leather jacket. His ears, neck, and hands were iced out with diamonds and gold jewelry. It reminded her of a young Korean chaebol heir she saw in K-dramas.

Her attempts to lure him to the dance floor, failed. She let the straps of her halter-top fall halfway down her shoulders as she started to dance closer with her friend, Lisa. She felt his gaze on her. Their eyes met. His lips curled up, and his intense gaze burned desire through her body. She tossed her hair back and ran both hands over her locks. This felt so good.

When she looked back, he vanished. Disappointment thumped in her chest. She scanned the club and caught him by the exit door with a smirk on his face. He motioned with his finger for her to follow him.

Lisa tracked Stacy's gaze. Before her friend might say anything, Stacy took off after him. She ignored the warning bells sounding in her head. Her wanting threw precaution out the window of good sense.

Stacy exited Les Tres nightclub onto Sunset Strip. No one seemed to be outside in the cold. A lone figure turned into an alleyway. She hurried after him. The searing infatuation that boiled inside her kept her warm against the freezing wind.

An arm snatched her around her waist and yanked her into the darkness. His strong arm spun her around, and he locked his lips on hers. He shoved her back against a brick wall while she straddled his hips with her legs and kissed him harder, trying to devour his slippery tongue.

He broke free from her lips and started to lick his way down to her neck. "You're mine," he said. His tone alarmed her, but before she could pull away, she felt his sharp teeth pierce into her neck. Her body convulsed with fear. She twisted and turned. He tightened his grip on her shoulders. Surprisingly, there was no pain—a drowsiness came over her. Yet fear made her fight on. She tried to scream. He chomped down on her larynx.

Hot, sticky blood trailed down her throat and onto her chest. She made one last futile attempt to escape, reaching up and pulling on his well-styled hair. He pressed harder into her neck and slammed her back firmer against the wall, squeezing the breath out of her. She plunged her thumb into the soft tissue of his right eye. It was not enough. Her thoughts began to fade.

***

Ricky drank for another five minutes to make sure there wasn't a single drop of moisture left in her body. He tasted the sweet vitality of her spirit enter his being. Blood wasn't the main reason why he drank from his victim. It was to siphon the essence of his victim. Her spirit fueled his immortality, and her blood carried nutrients to his decaying body.

Nevertheless, this feeding wasn't for need. It was for another purpose. After the last drop of fluid, Ricky let the body flop to the ground. A special enzyme in his saliva healed the puncture wounds on her neck as if she had never been bitten. All Judanites had this ability.

He waited a moment for his right eye to heal. When his vision cleared, he then straightened out Stacy's corpse in the alley and ripped off her halter top with one swift motion of his hand. With the torn shirt, he wiped the red splatter spots off her breast. He wished that he could have toyed with her a little bit longer before he had to kill her. *What a shame.*

He discarded her top with a flick of his wrist toward the dumpster and pulled out a box cutter from his pocket. The razor sliced easily through her skin and muscles as he carved out the symbol he wanted on her abdomen. When he was satisfied, he stuffed the surplus skin into her mouth. He stood up to his full height, put the box cutter back into his pocket, and brought out his cell phone.

"Ricky." A sweet, sensual voice called out his name.

He turned to look in the direction of the voice. From the shadow, Jacqueline strode toward him. Her dyed blonde hair was tied back into a French braid that displayed her beautiful, innocent face. Ricky smiled, knowing fully well that nothing about Jacqueline was innocent.

She paused next to him and examined his handy work. "Very good, Ricky," she said, regarding him with dark eyes. "For this, you deserve a kiss."

Ricky bent down and kissed Jacqueline on her small mouth. He grabbed her backside, but she shoved him back with authority. He wanted to lash out at her insolence, but he thought twice about it. Her size contradicted her ferocity.

"Make the call," Jacqueline ordered.

Ricky dialed the three numbers and put the phone to his ear. "I just witnessed a man snatching a woman off the street into an alleyway. I think he's going to kill her!"

Chapter 3

Unc's brow furrowed, and his sights remained steady on May's face—the same intense gaze that intimidated the most hardened criminals in Los Angeles. May matched his scrutiny with her own straightforward stare. "You don't have to look at me like that, Unc! I'm really okay," May said.

Unc sipped his coffee. "Please tell me you didn't have one of your episodes again of seeing your guardian angel."

May turned away, she felt her cheeks flush.

"You promised me that you would go see a psychologist if you had another episode."

"And I will. I was thinking the exact same thing. I'm getting tired of it too."

Unc reached over the table and patted May on the hand. "Good, then maybe you can meet a nice man."

She rolled her eyes and hissed through her teeth.

"But everything is up to you," Unc said.

May reached out for her espresso. The cup was empty.

"You want another one?"

"No thank you. I've had enough."

May took this moment to look her uncle over. She tilted her head back to study him. He looked exhausted, with large, dark bags under his eyes. His hair had become grayer at the temples, and thinned at the top of his head. His scalp shone through. Deep wrinkles lined the edges of his mouth and eyes. There wasn't much to laugh about in his line of business. He looked much older than forty-six. Twenty years with the FBI would do that to a person.

"Why are you looking at me like that?" Unc asked.

She smiled. "I was just admiring how handsomely you've aged."

He huffed. "Where did you learn how to segue the attention away from you so smoothly?"

"A wise old man once told me. A compliment and a direct statement can make an elephant forget," May said.

Bernardo shook his head. "I'm regretting it."

May laughed. "With great power comes great responsibility."

"Don't misuse it." Bernardo smiled. "But I do feel my age every time I see you. It seemed like only yesterday that you came to live with me as a little girl. And now look at you, a grown, beautiful woman."

May had come to live with Unc when both of her parents had died. At first, she was hesitant to go live with him because he resembled her deceased father too much. They both had thick, curly brown hair, wide shoulders, and stood six feet and three inches. It was hard at first, but in due time, she had come to appreciate Unc's resemblance to her father. It felt as if her father was still here with her.

"Oh, I'm sorry, May. I didn't mean—"

"It's okay," she said. She had moved on from her parents' deaths.

"Anyways, how's your artwork coming along?" He said it too quickly.

May smiled. "It's great. I got booked to showcase my first exhibition at the Museum of Contemporary Art on the third Sunday of January."

"That's amazing. I'm so proud of you. You had me worried when you changed your major from journalism to fine arts. But when I viewed your sculptures for the first time, I knew you had a special gift." He nodded his head in thought.

"Thank you." She pointed her finger. "But you better be there on time."

"I'll try my best to make it on time. If not, I'll stop by."

"What do you mean, try?" She threw him an accusing glare.

"If I can wrap up this present case, I'll be there on time." He gave her a weak smile.

Though he hadn't mentioned it, May knew he was talking about the recent serial murders, which the media dubbed the Exorcist Killer. Already, four bloodless bodies with a religious symbol carved into their flesh had been discovered.

"How's the case coming along?" she asked, aware that Unc rarely talked about open cases.

He sighed. "Like chasing the wind, there's nothing concrete to go on."

"I'm sorry to hear that. Hopefully you'll catch a break soon."

Unc's cell phone rang, and he accepted the call. "Bernardo." A pause. Then his jaws clenched. "I'll be right there."

Chapter 4

Bernardo jostled his way through the spectators that had gathered in front of the police barricade. He pushed forward toward a uniformed LAPD officer and flipped open his FBI credentials. "Agent Vega."

A reporter must've heard Bernardo announce his name. She stepped in front of him and began to bombard him with questions. Bernardo bumped past her and slipped under the yellow police tape. He made his way to a group of detectives in street clothes.

The closer Bernardo got, the louder his partner, Daniel Thornton, became as he rambled on about USC football. No matter how dire a crime scene, Daniel could always guide any conversation to USC football. He never missed an opportunity to share that he almost made the team as a walk-on place kicker.

Daniel's booming voice didn't match his five-foot-five-inch height and one hundred forty-pound frame. This job had taught Bernardo that most things weren't always what they seemed to be. Everyone had secrets. Always prepare for the unexpected for human nature was unpredictable.

Daniel's tan face and beach blonde hair came into view. He stood next to two plain-clothed detectives.

"Ah, you finally decided to show up," Daniel said.

The two detectives turned their attention to Bernardo. He extended his hand to the burly African-American man with the low haircut, who looked to be around Bernardo's age.

"I'm Agent Vega."

"I'm Homicide Detective Charles Bradley of the LAPD." He shook Bernardo's hand firmly. "And this is my partner, Detective Tessa Richards."

Bernardo focused his gaze on Tessa, a tall woman around six feet in height. Her mid-length auburn hair was tied in a ponytail that showed off her deep-ocean blue eyes, and her defined jawline. He liked her immediately. He shook her hand, and she gave him a pleasant smile.

"What do we have?" Bernardo inquired.

"Follow me," Tessa said.

Bernardo followed a few steps behind as the two detectives spoke. Daniel bumped his elbow on the Bernardo's arm when the detectives seemed out of earshot. He leaned in and whispered to Bernardo. "Man, that Detective Richards is a real ball-breaker. I couldn't get her to laugh for anything."

"It's okay, Daniel. Only a special few get your humor," Bernardo said, patting Daniel on the back. "Plus, I don't think it is time for jokes." Bernardo increased his speed to catch up to the detectives.

A topless corpse came into view in the alleyway. CSI technicians were combing the vicinity with their ultraviolet lights and chemical apparatuses, searching for any type of evidence. Bernardo crouched and studied the body with his eyes. The victim's face was unscathed, and she was topless from the waist up. There appeared to be no visible signs of any physical altercation, minus the dark smear marks on her neck and breast area that seemed to be dried blood.

Why would the killer carelessly forget to wipe the blood off after making the painstaking effort to drain her body completely of fluids? It didn't make any sense unless some blood had accidentally spilled on her while he drained the body. The only visible wound Bernardo saw was the symbol carved into her abdomen, which had no trace of plasma around it.

Bernardo inspected the wound. The killer had cut out a symbol of the Islamic Crescent Moon. Straight and precise, just like the wounds carved into the other four victims. The only difference was the location and the religious symbol.

This was the same killer.

Bernardo noticed that the victim's miniskirt was raised past her hips, which exposed her lace, pink undergarments, still intact. Most likely, she hadn't been sexually assaulted, even though her left garter was pulled down below her mid-thigh and her fishnet stockings had tears in them. He scanned the crime scene and found her stilettos by the brick wall.

"Here," Tessa said, handing Bernardo a pair of latex gloves. He stared up at her as he accepted the gloves. "Thank you." He pulled on the gloves as Tessa read from a notepad.

"Stacy Smith, 26-years-old. She lived in Torrance and worked at a small computer firm in Culver City called New Tech."

Bernardo lifted Stacy's left hand and observed that she still had her watch on her wrist and that her index fingernail was broken. There was also some type of substance under her thumb and middle fingernail. "Time of death?"

"The coroner estimated the time of death to be anywhere between an hour or so ago. He won't know for sure until he can get her back to the lab. We did get a 9-1-1 call from a male witness around 20:43 hours. The caller claimed that he had seen the victim get assaulted. He wasn't here when we arrived. We're searching for him now."

"What time did you find the body?"

"21:03 hours."

"Any other witnesses?"

"We're looking now."

Bernardo examined the victim's other hand. "What's your assessment of this, Daniel?"

Daniel studied the corpse. "I believe it's the same killer as the other four victims. It follows our working hypothesis that we gathered from the other victims and their crime scenes. Just by our observation, we can see that there are no outward signs that the victim's hands or legs have been bonded. This indicates that the killer must have used some type of anesthetic to subdue the victim, but I'm sure there won't be any trace of chemical drugs in her system like the other four victims. A toxicology screen would support this."

Daniel knelt beside Bernardo. "Also, I don't see any type of needle marks or other outward puncture wounds that could've been used to drain the blood. Logically, this means that the killer had covered the puncture wound with the carved-out symbol. Still, it doesn't answer the question of how he drained a whole human body in several minutes."

"How can you surmise that the killer didn't kill the victim first and then drain the blood?" questioned Tessa.

"That's simple. The other four victims died from exsanguination and excessive blood loss. Serial killers rarely ever change MO," Daniel stated.

"Did anyone find her shirt and bra?" Bernardo questioned.

"On top of the dumpster," Detective Bradley informed.

Bernardo scanned the area around the dumpster. "That makes sense."

"What's your insight so far, Agent Vega?" Tessa asked.

Bernardo returned his sights to Stacy. "The murder happened right here in this alley. The perpetrator lured the victim here." He examined the miniskirt. "I want officers to question the nightclubs down the Strip to locate any potential witnesses."

Detective Bradley nodded and got on his radio.

"What makes you think the murder happened here?" Tessa moved next to Bernardo.

Bernardo could smell the light, flowery scent that swirled around her. "Because of the state of her clothes. You can see scratches near the backside of her leather miniskirt." Bernardo pointed it out with his finger. "There are gaps between the scuff marks. That indicates that she wasn't dragged here on the cement because the markings would have made a more uniform mark. These marks seem more consistent with the shape of the wall near the dumpster." He nudged his chin towards the wall.

"Taking into account that her body had no physical wounds or marks." Bernardo kept his eyes on the corpse. "But seeing that her skirt is hiked up and her stockings are only torn around the inner thighs." Bernardo motioned with his finger. "Makes me think she might've been intimate with the killer before she died. The killer had her pinned up against the wall with her legs wrapped around his waist."

"So you think the killer met her somewhere around here," Tessa inquired. "How you know that it wasn't someone she knew."

"I don't," Bernardo said. "But if we believe this was the Exorcist Killer than I highly doubt it she knew him." Bernardo understand that Tessa was playing the devil's advocate.

"Maybe the killer was a john and drove Stacy here," Tessa said.

"Could be, but she wasn't dressed for the cold." Bernardo scooted over to see another angle of the body.

"She could have left her coat in the car." Tessa stood next to Bernardo.

"Why would she solicit herself when she had a job?"

"Maybe she needed extra money," Tessa interjected.

"Why this alley then? No prostitute would go into a dark alleyway with a john." Bernardo lifted Stacy's lifeless hand. "What do you make of this mark on her hand?"

Tessa leaned over and squinted her eyes. "Is that an ink stamp when you enter a club?"

"I believe so," Bernardo agreed.

"Can you read it?"

Bernardo raised the hand a little bit higher. "No, it looks like it washed or sweated off."

"So you think the killer met her in a club and seduced her here?"

"I assume it could be. That's why she has no personal belongings with her. She left it behind in the club." Bernardo looked up at Tessa.

"And now, explain how the killer drained all of her blood?" Tessa said.

"Your guess is as good as mine." Bernardo's raised his brows.

"I think it's a vampire," Daniel quipped.

Both Bernardo and Tessa stared at Daniel.

Detective Bradley returned with a somber face. "We found a witness who claims that she went to the club with Ms. Smith."

***

Dao-Ren watched Bernardo and the other detectives from his position within the crowd of spectators. They approached a young woman whose face was obscured by makeup. Bernardo introduced himself and the female detective, named Tessa Richards. Dao-Ren could hear their conversation. The young woman's name was Lisa Hill. Her eyes were wide and flicked back and forth between the crowd and the police scene. She explained that her friend, Stacy Smith, had run after an Asian guy while they were in the club, Les Tres. Lisa crossed her arms over her chest.

When Dao-Ren first heard about the serial murders of bloodless corpses with a religious symbol carved into their flesh. Which the media outlet had dubbed as the "Exorcist Killer". He had to investigate. Now, he was one hundred percent certain that Jacques and Jacqueline were the masterminds behind the Exorcist Killer's murders. They groomed someone who resembled him to commit these murders. They knew Dao-Ren would show up to put an end to the killings.

Clearly, Jacques and Jacqueline had lured him here, but for what purpose? Almost a millennium had passed since their last encounter. The time when Jacqueline had viciously mutilated Dao-Ren's Spiritmate Soraya. Jacqueline had hung Soraya's naked, decapitated body upside down with a sword embedded in her chest. Soraya had perished because of his failure to protect her.

Dao-Ren surveyed the immediate vicinity for any signs of Judanites. Their peculiar stench was strong, which indicated a large number. What are they planning? This was more than getting him to Los Angeles. Was it about Malayah? He was confident that the Judanites didn't know about her. If they did, she wouldn't have been drinking coffee tonight.

Time would reveal all. Everything in darkness comes to light. Until then, he must stop these senseless murders. He'll notify Jacques and Jacqueline of his presence and see if they'll remain hidden.

"Can you describe the guy to one of our sketch artists?" Dao-Ren heard Bernardo ask.

"Yes, I can. I'll never forget his face," Lisa said.

"Why's that?" Bernardo asked. "Did he have a certain distinguishing mark?"

"No, he just had this strong attraction." Lisa dropped her eyes to the ground. "I was jealous when Stacy ran after him."

"It's okay. One of our agents will be with you soon to drive you down to the field office."

Lisa shivered in the cold, or was it uneasiness? She looked at Bernardo with wide eyes. "Will Stacy be there?"

<h1 align="center">Chapter 5</h1>

Five dead bodies in two weeks, all the victims completely drained of blood, the only visible wound was the carved religious symbol made by the Exorcist Killer. What's his motive? Nothing made sense of the murders or the crime scenes. There wasn't any plausible connection between the bloodless victim and the religious symbol cut into their flesh. There were no dots to connect.

Bernardo rose up from his desk and walked over to the bulletin board, where the team had pinned up the information about the Exorcist Killer. He reviewed the list of victims and their photographs for the hundredth time.

Victim #1: Shontella Williams, African-American female, Baptist, age 21. College Student. Found in Glendale, CA. The symbol of the Chinese Yin-Yang carved into her left pectoral.

Victim #2: Jerry Font, Caucasian, male, Atheist, age 63. Retired. Found in Santa Monica, CA. The symbol of the Buddhist Wheel of Life carved in his right pectoral.

Victim #3: Shaheed Carter, African-American, male, Muslim, age 19. Unemployed. Found in South Central, CA. The symbol of the Jewish Star of David carved in his upper chest, beneath the neck.

Victim #4: Giorgio Falcon, Hispanic, male, Catholic, age 31. Construction worker. Found in Gardena, CA. The symbol of the

Crucifix carved into his solar plexus.

And now.

Victim #5: Stacy Smith, Caucasian, female, Protestant, age 26. Computer technician. Found in West Hollywood, CA. The symbol of the Islamic Crescent Moon was carved into her abdomen.

Different genders, races, ages, social backgrounds, and religious denominations. Only the carved symbol on victim #4 matched his religious beliefs. Possibly more out of coincidence than as planned. There wasn't any direct connection to the victims, except that they all seemed to be random.

The first three murders had occurred in a thirty-six-hour span. No traces of evidence were found. It seemed as if the bodies had fallen out of the sky. The media had gobbled it up. A week after that, victim number four was discovered. This time, a witness claimed she saw an East Asian male about six feet tall and around one hundred and eighty-pounds walking away from the body as he wiped his mouth. The witness didn't see the man commit the murder or drop the body off.

Now, five days later, victim number five had popped up with multiple witnesses all claiming that they saw an East Asian male with Stacy. Bernardo had brought Lisa Hill and two other witnesses down to the Los Angeles FBI field office on Wilshire Boulevard to give statements and to create a sketch composite of the suspect they had seen with Stacy Smith. They had been with the sketch artist for the last thirty minutes. A sketch should be finished any minute now.

The only lead on the suspect being an East Asian male would be tedious at best. Los Angeles County alone has about a million East Asian males. Even if they narrowed the search down to the characteristics of six feet in height and one hundred eighty-pounds in weight, it would still result in thousands of individuals. That didn't even include the illegal immigrants.

Bernardo had a nagging feeling that the Exorcist Killer wanted to be seen this time. No scraps of evidence were found at the first three crime scenes. No fingerprints, no hair strands, no DNA—nothing. Why go to the trouble of covering his tracks in the earlier murders to being so careless in the latter ones? Unless he wanted to be seen.

The 9-1-1 call that reported the assault on Stacy Smith was from a prepaid cell phone. There was no way to trace the phone back to the buyer. Bernardo's intuition told him that the Exorcist Killer had made the call himself. If it was his intention to draw national attention, then he had gotten his wish. Reporters from every major network, from CNN to Fox News, reported on the Exorcist Killer.

Someone had leaked to the media that Bernardo was the case agent in charge of the Exorcist Killer, and his phone had not stopped ringing yet. As long as he had been an FBI agent, he had never spoken with the media, and he wasn't about to start now. The FBI had a press/media department for that.

Bernardo went back to his desk and read the profile of the Exorcist Killer that the agents in Quantico had created using their profiling database and programs. The profile was more useless than the evidence they have gathered so far. That was saying a lot to Bernardo. A computer program could never out-investigate a real person.

Still, no one had come up with a plausible explanation for how someone could possibly have drained a full-grown human body completely of blood in several minutes or less. The carved symbols weren't anywhere near any vital arteries, nor were there any other open or punctured wounds located on the victim's bodies. The victim didn't just bleed out. Their blood had to be pumped out or sucked out. Hypotheses were thought up from far-fetched to crazy and all were determined to be implausible. It perplexed even the coroner and medical experts.

This was the first case in his twenty-year career that had eluded

Bernardo. No connections or leads. Only what the Exorcist Killer had wanted them to find. A thought occurred to him. He rolled his swivel chair to his computer and tapped a key. He double-clicked on the Google icon. He typed in "bloodless corpses" in the search engine and pressed enter. Numerous sites and articles popped up on the screen. Most of the information was rubbish about myths and legends about vampires.

An article about a "Catholic monk and bloodless corpses" grabbed Bernardo's attention. He clicked on the hyperlink and began to read. The article was about a monk named Luke Kafka of the Franciscan order, whose dead body was discovered in a burned house in Syria in 1942. The local firefighters had found the decapitated body in the basement of the house with a sword embedded in his chest through his heart. No bloodstain near his body or on his person. An eight inch dagger with the symbol of an almond blossom imprinted on the handle was clenched in his dead hand. The mystery of Brother Kafka was that he had been born in 1714, yet his body was neither mummified nor decomposed.

The article stated that the house that Brother Kafka's body was found in was said to be haunted. Local legend had spoken that the house was haunted by demons, and those same demons transformed into gorgeous people at night to lure potential victims into the house. Whoever entered the house supposedly came out cursed. The victims would die from a mysterious illness.

Bernardo clicked on the image of the dagger with the almond blossom symbol imprinted above the handle. He examined the photograph. The curved blade looked plain and ancient, a Middle Eastern design. He zoomed in on the almond blossom symbol. The symbol was a simple three-flower stem.

Bernardo leaned back in his chair and locked his fingers behind his head. He must be more tired than he had thought to go off down this rabbit hole. Daniel and his notion of vampires. Bernardo needed to get some sleep.

And like that, he made an odd connection. He rose and returned to the bulletin board. He reviewed each murder victim and the location of his or her carved symbols. If you brought all of them together into one picture and connected them with lines, they made a crude outline of an almond blossom or a cross.

Was there a connection here? Bernardo couldn't fully form the idea in his mind. He dropped his head and massaged his temples with his hands. It was time to go home.

"Excuse me, Vega."

"Yes, Brad," Bernardo said, looking up at the young agent.

"We've got a sketch of the Exorcist Killer." Brad handed Bernardo the composite and studied it.

No, it couldn't be—this face bore an eerie resemblance to May's angel. She had drawn and sculpted numerous pieces of artwork of him throughout her life. He didn't like this coincidence at all. The warning intuition burned in his gut. He would need to speak with May soon. He didn't want her to have an episode and chase after this guy if she saw him by chance.

"Send a copy to the LAPD, to Detective Charles Bradley and Detective Tessa Richards. Leave a message that I will get back to them sometime this evening. Email a copy to Daniel and tell him to verify the sketch with the witness from victim number four."

"Got it," Brad said, and he walked away.

Bernardo returned his sight to the sketch. He couldn't shake the nagging suspicion that he was looking into the Exorcist Killer's eyes. It worried him that without more substantial evidence, it would be difficult to smoke out and apprehend the psychopath before he killed again.

Chapter 6

May splashed water over her face from the chic bathroom sink. She hoped it would wash away her angel's handsome face from her memory. She kept reflecting back to the man in the baseball cap. She tossed and turned all night, trying to shake the thoughts of him. The face she viewed yesterday was the same face she had seen sixteen years ago. But he should've aged. It couldn't have been him.

She dried her face with a towel and stared at her reflection in the mirror. With her hair tied in a ponytail, her bangs fell loosely above her eyes. She stared back at her hazel-green eyes, the ones she had inherited from her mother. Sometimes, if she concentrated hard enough, it would seem like her mother was staring back at her. She missed her.

May replaced the towel on the rack and stepped into the nude-colored hallway. Her bare feet felt cold against the stone tiles. Her apartment had been renovated from an old Spanish-style storefront, which she had remodeled to her taste. The ground floor became her art studio, and the second floor was her apartment. She considered this a gift from her parents, who left a very sizable inheritance and life insurance in her name. Money would never be an issue.

Prints of famous artworks by Titian, Leonardo Da Vinci, Jan Vermeer, and Paul Cezanne decorated her walls. She enjoyed viewing each scenic print each morning and basking in the beauty of the scenes before her. This was her unique way of meditating. She would change out the prints every month, showing that her taste and flair for the arts had no particular time period. She cherished the artwork of the Middle Ages, with their mastery of the Gothic and Romanesque styles. She admired the intricate designs of Islamic carvings and the mysticism of Asian paintings. She studied the Renaissance period, filled with mannerism and self-realization. A touch of her love for all art styles could be seen in her own works.

She paused in front of the Paul Cezanne print, the "Mont Sainte-Victoire." The outlines of the mountain range combined with the subdued hues of the woodland in their straight geometric forms, reflected her current mood. Nothing was concrete. Her reality seemed surreal. It was as if she were holding on to something that she wasn't totally sure was tangible. Why couldn't she have the normal dilemma of waiting for a guy to call her?

She headed out of the hallway that opened into the spacious living room. The rich aroma of freshly brewed Colombian coffee greeted May's nose. Her roommate, Kat, must be awake and making her morning cup of coffee. May smiled as she followed the scent, looking forward to joining Kat for a chat over a warm cup of joe.

The kitchen and the living room shared the same space. The kitchen was positioned at the far end of the living room. She stopped dead in her tracks. A total stranger with trim blonde hair sat at the dinner table, drinking coffee out of her favorite mug. May's smile faded as confusion washed over her. She glanced around, trying to make sense of the unexpected presence in her home. Her heart raced, wondering how this stranger had managed to enter without her knowledge.

"Who the hell are you?" May spoke, her voice trembling with a mix of fear and anger.

The stranger looked up from his coffee, his expression calm and nonchalant. He smiled, flashing perfect white teeth. "I'm Todd, a friend of Kat's."

"Where's Kat then?" May asked, her voice still filled with apprehension.

Todd's grin widened as he casually replied, "She's probably still sleeping." He kept his gaze on May.

"Good morning," Kat said in her singsong voice. She walked past May from the other side.

May followed Kat with her eyes. She wore a lace bra and matching panties. Her bra barely covered her enhanced breasts. Kat's golden hair was twisted back in a bun that displayed her striking features of high cheekbones and large doe eyes. May noticed the newly hot-pink dyed streaks in Kat's hair.

Todd shifted his sights to Kat's well-toned derrière, as she poured herself a cup of coffee.

"Catherine Leah Dorr!" May exclaimed in disapproval.

Kat turned, and her face reddened. "Didn't I tell you to leave before my roommate woke up?" She slammed down her cup, splashing coffee on the counter. "Get out." Kat rushed over to Todd and pulled him out of his seat. She shoved him all the way out the door and slammed it in his stunned face.

May pinched her face, and her nostrils flared in anger as she watched Kat walk back into the kitchen. Kat didn't dare make eye contact with her. She grabbed May's coffee mug off the table and washed it under the double steel sink. She dried the mug with a paper towel and poured a fresh cup of coffee. She stirred one scoop of sugar the way May liked it.

Kat faced May and held out the mug as a peace offering. May just glared at her. Kat struck out her bottom lip in a sad puppy-dog expression and batted her eyes. May snatched the cup out of Kat's hand and took her customary seat at the dinner table. Kat sat down next to her.

"May, I'm sorry. I know how much you hate it when I bring a guy home without your permission."

"Then why do you keep doing it? You know I hate strangers in the house."

"I just got caught up in the moment." Kat smirked.

"You went to the gym last night," May said.

"I know. Todd is my personal trainer. One thing led to another, and we ended up here in my room."

"Why couldn't the two of you go to his place?" May glared at Kat.

"He lived farther away."

May shook her head. "I understand that you got caught up in the moment, but it's important to respect my boundaries. Next time, please consider finding another place to spend time with your personal trainer."

"You're right." Kat stirred her coffee.

May saw the new fleur-de-lis tattoo on the inside of her forearm. "It might be time for you to find your own place."

Kat's mouth dropped, surprised by May's suggestion. "You think I should move out?" she asked, her voice tinged with uncertainty.

May sighed, realizing the weight of her words. "I just think it's important for both of us to have our own space and independence."

Kat looked at her wide-eyed. "Why are you so upset? I said I was sorry."

"I'm just tired of it all." May sighed, her frustration evident in her voice. "It's not just about this one incident, Kat. It's about the constant cycle of recklessness and poor decision-making. I worry about you."

Several seconds ticked. "This isn't you." Kat tilted her head back. What's going on, May?"

"Nothing." May glanced down at her coffee.

"May, don't tell me you had another episode." Kat leaned forward with concern. "You know you can talk to me about it, right? I'm here for you."

May had nothing to say.

"May!" Kat called out.

"What?" May looked up, holding back the tears.

"Are you alright?" Kat reached across the table and touched May's hand.

"No, I'm tired of chasing a shadow of a ghost." Tears fell.

Chapter 7

Dao-Ren nudged open the imposing bronze entry doors of the Cathedral of Our Lady of the Angels on West Temple Street. New World images of the Virgin Mary interspersed with multicultural icons decorated the door. He swiftly slipped into the canyon-like interior of the cathedral. It reminded him of a Buddhist temple—airy and sparse. Natural light filtered through the translucent curtain walls of thin Spanish alabaster, which illuminated the holy sanctuary in a mystic glow. One hundred and thirty-five human figures were woven into the tapestries that lined the nave wall: the Holy Angels.

Dao-Ren made his way to the underground entrance of the mausoleum. He entered the maze-like corridor and traveled down it. When he approached the end of the corridor, he sensed an attack.

A saber blade sliced toward his head. He bobbed his head back. The blade missed his neck by an inch. He reached behind his back and unsheathed his twin Chinese writer's knives from under his jacket. The knives had long blades with serrated topsides that were the size and length of a machete.

The saber arced up toward his face. He blocked the strike with the knife in his left hand. He then circled the knife around the saber blade and dipped forward, sliding the knife down the saber's blade to the crossbar. Dao-Ren twisted his hip and slammed the attacker against the wall. He placed the edge of his free knife under the attacker's throat. The handsome, rugged face of Gasper de Portola grinned up at Dao-Ren. Dao-Ren released him.

"Peace be with you, brother," Gasper said.

"And also with you." Dao-Ren hugged Gasper.

"After all these centuries, I still can't sneak up on you." Gasper smiled.

"You must control your anticipation. It was as thick as your head, my old friend."

"Maybe next time."

Dao-Ren laughed. He regarded Gasper for a second, and like all of his Awakyn brothers and sisters, Gasper didn't look older than twenty-eight years old. His face had that angelic glow that humans find attractive. It was his spirit shining through. Awakyns were a spirit with a body and not a body with a spirit. They were immortal.

Gasper stood a few inches taller than Dao-Ren and still carried the authoritative aura of the governor he used to be when he was a human a few centuries ago. A time in his past he didn't care to look back on. Gasper motioned with his hand to follow him. He led Dao-Ren into a catacomb with a large marble tomb at the center. The tomb had intricate engravings of Jesus' life on the outer perimeter walls, with a glorified scene of angels praising God on the top lid.

Gasper placed his open palm on top of the left corner angel's chest. A green laser light scanned his hand. The whole tomb shifted to the side, revealing a metal staircase.

"Guest first," Gasper said, pointing the way with a sweep of his hand.

Dao-Ren paused to study the top surface of the tomb. No visible sign of the hand scanner could be seen. He descended the stairs that opened into another corridor. Artificial overhead LED lights bounced off the white marble like a mirror, giving the threshold a heavenly glow. The tomb slid shut with a depression of air behind them.

"We have over 150,000 square feet of space. This site is fully equipped with the latest technology. It could take a 9.0 magnitude earthquake. The walls are five feet thick and reinforced with steel beams." Gasper slapped the wall.

"All of you have done well. This place will work out great for us," Dao-Ren said with a slight bow of his head.

"Come, the others are waiting."

Together, they headed down the corridor, side by side. The only sound that could be heard was the low hum of lights and the drone of the central air system. The corridor forked into two ninety-degree hallways, a left and a right.

Gasper pointed to the left. "The sleeping quarter, kitchen, entertainment, infirmary, and training grounds are down that way."

Dao-Ren nodded.

"And to the right are the transportation area and the command center." Gasper took the right and led the way down the hallway. Dao-Ren trailed. A steel door appeared on the right. Gasper halted and pressed a button on the side keypad. The steel door slid into the wall. "This is the transportation area."

Dao-Ren glanced inside the spacious garage. A fleet of different types of vehicles, from sport cars to SUVs lined the space. There were two rows of street-legal sport bikes in the back.

Gasper pointed with his finger toward the tunnel at the far back. "The tunnel is about a mile long, and it leads to the other exit onto Highway 101. The exit is well hidden and hard to notice. No one will accidentally find it."

"Which vehicle have you prepared for me?"

"The Audi should be suited to your standard." Gasper grabbed a key fob from the wall key rack.

Dao-Ren accepted the key and pocketed it.

Gasper pressed the close button, and the door slid shut. They moved further along the hallway until a second steel door appeared in front of them at the end of the hallway. The door slid open, and Omarosa stepped out.

Omarosa stood there with an expressionless look, her eyes fixed on Dao-Ren. Her beauty was uncompromising, with a high forehead, thick lips, and a strong and sleek physique.

Dao-Ren didn't dare lock eyes with her. His closest Awakyns brother and sister were probably still upset with him for leaving decades ago without a word. He noticed that her hands were balled into tight fists by her thighs. In the next instant, she rushed at him. He could only hold his position. He was lost as to what to do next. Gasper stood to the side of him quiet and of no help.

Omarosa swung her fist, missing Dao-Ren's face. Her arms wrapped around his neck and pulled him into a long awaited hug. Dao-Ren let out a sigh of relief and embraced her.

"Know that I'm still upset with you. It took you sixteen years to let me know you were alright," Omarosa admonished.

"I'm sorry, Rosa. I should've been more considerate."

"I accept your half-hearted apology." Omarosa kissed Dao-Ren on each side of his cheek. "Now come, we've got much work to do."

Dao-Ren smiled. Omarosa was the most dedicated Awakyn he knew. She had pledged to herself to be ever vigilant against Judanites, ever since Judanites had wiped out her entire native village in Northern Africa. They all entered the command center.

An expanse of ceiling lights illuminated the command center. The familiar faces of Who-Dat, Rita, William Wallace, and Otis Bush stared at Dao-Ren. Who-Dat with his high mohawk and sharp facial features, rose from his seat, a grin plastered on his face. His tan skin looked so out of place in this artificial light. Who-Dat struck out his arm, and Dao-Ren clasped his forearm while Who-Dat grasped his. They both leaned forward until their foreheads touched in the traditional greeting of the Shoshoni tribe of the Yang-Na, the original native people who settled in the area now called Los Angeles.

Rita stepped forward and stood next to Who-Dat, her Spiritmate. Spiritmates were two people who confessed their love and spirit as one and became husband and wife. The red dot at the center of her forehead, combined with her piercing dark eyes, gave her a mystic aura. Dao-Ren hugged her in a welcoming gesture.

Someone snuck up behind Dao-Ren and wrapped him in a tight bear hug, lifting him off his feet. His deep laughter shook Dao-Ren. After a few seconds of intense pressure, Willie released Dao-Ren. He faced his bear-size brother. He couldn't help but laugh at Willie's new hairstyle. He no longer had the tangled locks of a Scottish highlander. He had an expansive Hollywood flare with styling gel. His vibrant blue eyes shone with glee.

"I never thought Sir William Wallace would go mainstream."

"It's a new time and place. We all need change." Willie smooth the sides of his hair with his palms.

Dao-Ren chuckled. "Don't tell me you're sweet on someone."

A look of pure joy appeared in Willie's eyes.

Otis Bush strutted over in his designer clothes and his million-dollar smile. Dao-Ren stuck out his hand. Otis's caramel colored hand slapped Dao-Ren's and brought him into a dap-hug. Otis was the newest Awakyn to this post. He answered the call to rise in Harlem, New York, twenty-two years ago.

"Dao-Ren, come check out our new center," Who-Dat said.

On the far side of the room, a whole computer screen with smaller monitors around its top and side perimeters made up the wall. Independent computer stations were positioned in rows and columns throughout the whole center.

"Dao-Ren, meet our newest member, Thelma." Who-Dat spoke like a proud father and opened his arms out wide in a circle.

"Hello Dao-Ren," a soft animated voice said as a digitalized female's face appeared on the large screen.

"Hello, Thelma," Dao-Ren said to the virtual face.

"Thelma is the fastest AI computer in the whole world. ChatGPT is a calculator compared to her. The FBI and NASA would be amazed by Thelma. She checks all the internet and communication links to find any unusual occurrences that are common with Judanite's tactics. Then she'll alert us, and we'll send a team to investigate."

"Very impressive, Who-Dat. I've seen your ingenuity implemented across the globe. The Holy Council has made sure of that," Dao-Ren said, "—but where's Ariel?"

Who-Dat tapped a few keys, and a display of Central America appeared on the main screen with red dots scattered around the region. The image zoomed into central Mexico as a red dot blinks. A profile of Ariel pops open on the side bar.

"She's in Mexico investigating the Swine flu. We have evidence that the Judanites mutated the influenza virus. She'll be back in a week or so. But I can call her up on video if you would like," Omarosa said.

"It's okay. I'll catch up with her when she returns."

"Good thinking, Dao-Ren. You know it's inevitable. She's going to rip your head off. Get all the days you can, because when she finally catches up with you, peace will be an afterthought," Gasper said.

Everyone broke into laughter.

"And what's going on in LA?" Dao-Ren asked.

"Thelma alerted us when the first bloodless corpse popped up. Gasper, Otis, and Willie investigated each murder and crime scene. No Judanites could be tracked or located. As you know, their stench is strong around the city. Yet, for some reason, they're staying low and out of sight. We haven't seen any recently," Omarosa explained.

"It's Jacques and Jacqueline," Dao-Ren stated.

Omarosa stepped up closer to him. "How do you know that?"

"Because they carved those same symbols onto Soraya's body after they killed her."

The center went silent. Dao-Ren had never mentioned Soraya's death. Only he and Ariel knew how Soraya perished.

"Jacques and Jacqueline have called me here. I'll let them know I've arrived."

"How? We can't even find one Judanite," Gasper said.

Dao-Ren nodded. "Simple. The police."

Chapter 8

It was always best to slowly shape the stone into the desired vision. May lined the tracer in the direction of the grooves on the stone. She tapped the top of the tracer with her hammer and guided it to her wishes. Chunks of rock tumbled to the floor. She stepped back to get a better view of the angel forming out of the black marble. The sculpture stood seven feet tall with proper proportional dimensions.

This was May's last piece to complete for her main attraction, "Heaven's Guardians," at the Museum of Contemporary Art. It had taken her five years to complete. Altogether, there would be a total of twenty-two pieces to showcase.

Now and until the day of her exhibit, she'll be spending the majority of her time in her studio. She was pressed for time to finish her last statue. It would be tough, but she would meet the deadline. She had fashioned and equipped her studio with every material and tool necessary to complete the job.

The single obstacle impeding her progress was mental. She couldn't get into her zone to bring the marble into form. Her episode from last night placed her in an agitated mood. She couldn't concentrate on her work. She even tried to calm her nerves by selecting the soft Lofi beats on her playlist. Nothing seemed to ease the frustration that bubbled inside her.

She spun to the west side of her studio, where her completed works were lined up. Each one was detailed with artistic precision. It was there that her guardian angel stood at the center of "Heaven's Guardians," looking powerful and handsome. Could he possibly have been a figment of her imagination? As much as she tried to convince herself that he was a dream, deep down, she knew without a doubt that he was real. The eyes she chiseled into the marble were his eyes, which she witnessed that night when he stared down at her. There was so much intensity and suffering in those eyes that no eight-year-old could have possibly imagined it. This fact was the only hope that gave her faith that he existed at all.

From time to time, when all was quiet, she could hear his strong voice and picture his handsome face with those sorrowful brown eyes. Sometimes she remembered him better than she did her own reflection.

The recollection of that horrific night was never too far from her consciousness. Little minutiae things would trigger those painful flashbacks. It was like tiptoeing through a minefield; anything could set it off. It could be a certain way a person laughed, like her father used to, or a style of pearl necklace that her mother used to favor.

In a heartbeat, she would be eight years old again, sitting in the back passenger seat of her father's car. Her sophisticated father, Leonardo Vega, Professor of Literature at Oregon College, was driving in his dinner blazer and gold-rimmed glasses. And her beautiful mother, Erin Vega, Professor of History at Oregon College, dressed in a crème-colored evening gown embellished with her pearl necklace, sat in the front passenger seat.

They were coming back from a late dinner party. May was having a terrible night. The boy she had a crush on had punched her in the stomach after she kissed him on the cheek. She felt so hurt that tears couldn't find their way out of her little heart. She stared at the falling snow through the window, vowing to never fall for another guy again.

Love could be so cold.

November nights in Eugene, Oregon, were icy and frozen. The land before her was dark and unmoving. All trace of light hid out until morning. They were halfway home when May heard her mother's dreadful scream pierce her lonely thoughts. A scream she could still hear to this day. Her father's car fishtailed on the black ice on the road, whipping the rear end from side to side. May clutched the door handle with both of her hands as the car spun out of control. That was the last memory she could recall of the accident.

May didn't know how long she had been unconscious. She might never know. It didn't really matter. She first heard his strong, powerful voice, which encouraged her to believe that she could heal herself. His voice penetrated into the depths of her consciousness. The forcefulness of his words resonated in the deepest part of her spirit. It had strengthened her faith to believe that the impossible was possible. She fully trusted him, as only a child could.

The pain came hard and fast. A pain so intense that nothing else seemed to matter. Even so, his voice was more powerful than the pain. She heard him and held onto his encouragement. Then, out of nowhere, warmth blossomed in the center of her chest and exploded throughout her damaged body.

Her upper body shot upward from her waist, inhaling her first new breath. The frigid air frightened her and sent a cold shiver down her spine. Warm, attentive hands guided her to lie back down on the frozen pavement. She glanced up at those sad eyes that examined her with concern. She had never seen eyes that deep. Deeper than any ocean, its depths dominated by sorrow. She loved him at that moment.

And through the years from then to now, he became more vivid to her. She could see the details of his handsome, symmetrical face with thick eyebrows and an average nose and mouth. Short stubs of facial hair dotted his chin and upper lips. His cheeks cuffed under his cheekbones when he smiled down at her. He placed his jacket over her. "Malayah, stay here so I can help your mother."

She felt disgusted about forgetting her parents' welfare. She turned her head toward the direction he had gone. Fear and panic clenched her heart tight at the instant she viewed the disfigurement of metal around a telephone pole that once was her father's car.

He was already there, pulling back the steel frame of the car with his bare hands. How could any man be that strong? She quickly took notice of the yellow and red sparks of electricity spewing in the air. The exposed power line snapped in the frigid night, ready to strike. She watched silently as the sparks traced down to the ground. The road ignited from the gasoline runoff from the punctured fuel tank.

May screamed. Her rescuer pulled her mother out of the wreckage an instant before the car erupted into flames. The deafening explosion shook the ground at the same moment, he launched himself into the air with her mother wrapped tightly in his arms. The roaring flames brushed against his back, creating an image of fiery wings. It was then that she knew he was her guardian angel.

Her angel landed about thirty feet in front of her. He lowered her mother onto the frozen street and bent over to her ear. May could only imagine that he prayed the same encouragements he told her mere minutes ago. After a few spoken words, he laid his hands over her mother's chest. His lips moved rapidly in a chant. He returned to her mother's ear to whisper something again.

Nothing had to be said to know there was no hope alive. Her angel's head dropped onto her mother's still chest. He had swept her mother up into his arms and lifted her limp body, holding her so close against his chest that it seemed like he was trying to jumpstart her heart with his own. His face pointed skyward, and he let out the most tearful, soul-wrenching roar she had ever heard. The dam to his suffering ruptured, unleashing the sorrows that lurked beneath the depths of his eyes.

Sadness stabbed May in the heart. She knew both of her parents were dead. The sudden loss wrecked her more than the accident. For a moment, she could not breathe, and then her chest heaved with the first wave of tears that blurred her vision. She longed to be next to her mother. She had so badly wanted to tell her she loved her. Yet, she couldn't move—her body wouldn't respond.

Through the tears, May had seen her angel rise up from the ground. He began to head toward her. A spasm of tears had racked her, she felt so alone. She did her best to blink the tears away so she wouldn't lose sight of him. When her vision cleared, he was gone. She wanted to search for him, but her own eyes began to fail her. They started to close on their own.

When she woke, she felt disoriented. The room was unfamiliar to her, and there was an irritating beeping noise. Fright held her in place as confusion stirred her fears. She shifted and pushed herself up from the bed, scanning the room for something familiar.

A lone figure slept on a cushioned chair next to her bed. Unc. She didn't want him. She wanted her mother. She was about to yell for her, and then her memories awoke. Tears deluged from the sorrows of her heart. Her cries woke Unc and he came to comfort her. He hadn't spoken a word; all that needed to be said was the sound of tears.

A week later, May buried both of her parents. During that time, a local newspaper had written a story about how mysteriously Malayah Vega had survived a deadly car crash with no injuries to her body. Even though the clothes she wore that night were all in tatters and covered with her blood.

Soon after, May moved to Los Angeles to live with her uncle. He had given her the liberty to be who she desired to be. He had never pushed her in any certain direction. The one thing he forced on her was martial arts. His justification for this was that she had to learn how to protect herself from the world because it could be a cruel place sometimes. It was better to be prepared than hopeless. Through martial arts, she had discovered the inner reflection of herself that helped her cope with the loss of her parents.

Within the first month of living with Unc, May had her first episode. They were touring downtown LA when she spotted her angel, strolling down the opposite side of the street, holding hands with a young lady. May started to yell for him and dashed across the busy street. Angry drivers honked at her.

She caught up with her angel and grabbed his free hand. He peered down at her with a baffled look. It wasn't him. May backed up, her face flushed with embarrassment. He had spoken to her in a language she couldn't understand. Unc finally chased her down with a frown on his face.

Truth be told, May had never thought much about her episodes growing up. She would just brush off each incident. That was until her senior year of high school, when she learned her fixation on her angel was a problem.

The time had come when she had decided to share herself with her boyfriend of two years, Trent Blake. They had been making out in her bedroom, and she was getting lost in his touches. Until she caught a glimpse of the flicker of the candle flame, she had lit earlier. Her mind traveled back to the accident. The face of her angel appeared in her thoughts. He peered down at her lovingly.

All of a sudden, Trent's tender kisses burned like hot coals on her skin. She felt dirty. Her body convulsed, and her stomach lurched. She shoved Trent off of her and ran into the bathroom to throw up. When she came out of the bathroom, she knew their relationship was over.

Since then, May has never had another intimate relationship or taken a lover. She couldn't.

Now, she stood there, feeling robbed of the beauty of an intimate and physical relationship with someone.

May glared down at the leader of "Heaven's Guardians," whose sorrowful eyes were captured in stone. The anger boiled inside her chest. Her body became rigid and pulsed with rage. May cocked her arm back and threw the hammer with all the pent-up frustration she felt. The hammer clanged against his bronze breastplate, leaving a dent in the area by his heart. Tears flooded May's eyes, trying to drain the loneliness out of her own being.

The realization was clear. He wasn't her angel. He was her demon.

Chapter 9

"Don't make me tell you twice, you little ungrateful brat!"

Dao-Ren turned to the sound of the threat a block away. A beast of a man yelled at a little tangled-hair girl who stood by a young woman and a small boy. The man pressed two boxes of chewing gum into the girl's arms. They stood nearby the detailed wooden cross that marked the center of the Old Plaza, a part of the historic Pueblo de Los Angeles. Large groups of tourist strolled down Calle Olvera, the historic pedestrian only street.

The young woman intervened on behalf of the tangled-haired girl. She begged and pleaded in Spanish with the large man. Dao-Ren understood her clearly. Out of all the gifts bestowed upon him when he had awakyned, he treasured the gift of tongue the most. No matter what language a person spoke, he heard it as it was spoken, but his spirit discerned its meaning. It was the same when he spoke. He would speak in his ancestral language of Lolang, yet the person would hear it in his or her own language. All spirits shared a single language—the Word of God.

The man shoved the girl from the young woman's side. The girl's face trembled. She held her tears at bay. Her small hands squeezed the boxes of gum.

"Take your little brother with you!" The man pulled the little boy by the back of his jacket from his mother's arms. The boy fought to hold onto his mother's skirt. The mother grasped the little boy by his arms, trying to pull her son away from her husband. Tears poured down the boy's face. The man yanked the boy free and tossed him towards his sister. The girl crossed her arm over her little brother's chest, pulling him close to her side. The man then seized the woman by her upper arm and led her down the street in the opposite direction of their children.

Dao-Ren headed towards the two children down the street. Century-old abode buildings aligned the red brick street, with grapevines hanging overhead. Colorful clapboard stalls were erected down the center of the street that sold traditional Mexican handicrafts. He maneuvered his way through the busy plaza that was shaded by century-old magnolia trees.

"A pack of gum for 25 cents, five for a dollar," the girl announced to the passing tourist. She wore ripped jeans and a threadbare sweater that was thinner than an undershirt. Tear tracks left streaks on her dirt-covered face. The little boy wasn't in any better shape. His jacket was patched together, and his pants were two sizes too big. He clung to his sister's side.

The girl approached Dao-Ren. "How about you, Mister? A pack for 25 cents, five for a dollar."

Dao-Ren smiled. "I'll buy both boxes for a hundred bucks."

The girl threw Dao-Ren a quizzical look and stepped back from him.

"Please." Dao-Ren pulled out a hundred-dollar bill. "I didn't mean to frighten you. I just want to help you."

"Why do you want to help us? We don't know you."

"I'm feeling generous today."

"Whatever. Give me the money first."

Dao-Ren held out the hundred-dollar bill. She plucked it out of his grasp. Both she and her brother examined the bill, their eyes wide.

They looked at each other and smiled. She shoved the money into her pocket.

"Here." She handed Dao-Ren the two gum boxes. "Thank you very much, Mister."

"You're welcome." He accepted the box. "Can I ask you a question?"

She considered Dao-Ren with a wary stare. "Maybe."

"Is that a good restaurant over there?" Dao-Ren pointed to the Mexican restaurant.

"I wouldn't know I've never eaten there," she said.

"How does a hot meal sound to celebrate our deal?" Dao-Ren offered.

"I'm hungry, Tabitha," the little boy shouted, pulling on his sister's arm.

"Hush, Peco." She gave Peco a stern glare before looking back up at Dao-Ren. "You've already done enough for us."

"I hate to eat alone," Dao-Ren said.

Peco peered up at his sister as Tabitha studied Dao-Ren. "I'll accept your offer only if you pay."

"Of course." Dao-Ren gave a slight bow. "I wouldn't have it any other way."

Chapter 10

"Did you confirm the sketch with the other witnesses?" Bernardo asked Detective Tessa Richards.

"It took a little longer than I thought, but all the witnesses had confirmed the sketch as the individual they saw in Les Tres," she replied.

"Good." Bernardo held her gaze.

"Is there a reason why you came all the way here? I could've easily relayed all this over the phone."

"I was in the neighborhood." Bernardo twirled a cigarette between his fingers.

"I see." She grinned. "I didn't know you smoke."

"I don't. I quit twelve years ago. This case has my nerves up and running. And there's nothing quite like a little nicotine to take the edge off."

"I can think of a better way to distract you from the case." Tessa grinned.

"Such as?" Bernardo smiled and lifted his eyebrows.

"Korean BBQ."

"Love it. I wouldn't have it any other way."

***

Peco peered up at Dao-Ren with salsa smeared all over his mouth and grinned at him. Peco's front tooth was missing. Dao-Ren smiled. Peco gave up the use of this fork for the easy movements of his fingers. Dao-Ren handed him the aqua fresca to wash down his food.

The dinner crowd had packed into the small Mexican restaurant. The scent of chili peppers and cheese dominated the air. A quartet of Mexican musicians in decorative sombreros and matching black and silver costumes played their instruments, harmonizing a Mexican folk song.

Dao-Ren watched Tabitha use her fork to dip her quesadilla into a sauce and eat it. She cleaned and washed her face before dinner. She had been adamant with Peco about doing the same. She was very mature for being only ten years old. No child should be robbed of a childhood.

Earlier Tabitha told Dao-Ren that she grew up around Pueblo de Los Angeles, a tight-knit community. Still, the townspeople ignored her and her family's troubles. Not out of pity but to mind their own business. Even the manager had chased her off multiple times when she tried to sell gum in front of the restaurant.

The overweight manager had watched them with a suspicious stare since they sat down. Dao-Ren stood from the table and maneuvered through the crowded dining area. The manager looked straight ahead as Dao-Ren approached the hostess stand. The manager smiled under a large black mustache. His starched white dress shirt had a name tag on his left pocket that spelled "Emmanuel."

"May I help you with anything, Señor?" Emmanuel said.

Dao-Ren nodded. "Do you happen to know who Tabitha and Peco's parents are?"

"Yes, I do. And I must say it's very kind of you to buy them a meal. Their home life isn't very stable."

"Can you contact their parents for me?"

"I don't think that is wise. Their father, Roberto, is a real nasty drunk."

"How about their mother?"

"Oh, Isabelle is a saint. Love makes you act so foolish sometimes."

"Please, call Isabelle for me and tell her she can pick up her children at the house down the street."

Emmanuel tilted his head back and narrowed his eyes. "I'm sorry, Senor. There's no house down the street."

"I'm talking about the brown house where the Franciscan monks used to live."

Emmanuel's eyes grew large. "The House of Angels."

Chapter 11

The rhythmic trance beats vibrated off the plain storefront. A line of partygoers stood one block down from the entrance. Kat strutted in her Jimmy Choo shoes to the front of the line. She wasn't a celebrity, but she was a social media darling, invited to all the hippest parties in town.

May was surprised that Kat didn't shiver in an off-white silk cocktail dress by the winter breeze. She really fit the bill when it came to being "hot in a dress."

May followed Kat in a tight Dior sweater, a pair of custom jeans, and a Burberry coat.

The bouncer recognized Kat and waved them through. The loud, thumping sounds of EDM and warm heat greeted them. Colored lasers crisscrossed in the dim setting throughout the club. The décor of the interior was fashioned after a Roman bathhouse. Bare-chested male and female dancers gyrated on each other in shallow water. May shook her head.

What the hell had Kat dragged her into?

Kat held May's hand and weaved them through the partygoers. May kept her eyes open and alert. This wasn't her type of scene or crowd. May recognized some of the guests that graced her television. A young starlet with dyed blonde hair and freckles drained a shot of liquor and returned to making out with some guy. She saw a rapper with long, thick dreadlocks and bejeweled teeth smoking what appeared to be a blunt. On the dance floor, a beautiful bronze-skinned female singer danced with another dark-haired singer.

Kat led May to the private VIP section in the back. Kat stopped in front of a large booth with a lion face and a headrest in purple upholstery. Kat bent down to hug a short, wiry guy and gave him a peck on each of his cheeks. The guy's face looked familiar to May. However, she couldn't place a name.

"May, remember Billy Jacobs from high school?" Kat asked.

Yes, she remembered. The skinny guy with glasses who begged Kat for a date. A wish he never got. May waved to him. The next person Kat greeted stood up and scooted out of the booth to give her a hug. She lingered around his neck. May couldn't help but to study his attractive features. He had a sharp, chiseled face and a strong, angular jaw line, along with wavy brown hair. His nose was aquiline, his lips thin, and his eyes were like hers—hazel-green. He could've been a mythological Greek god.

"I told you, Jacques. You and May could pass as brothers and sisters," Kat said.

His wide-set eyes settled on May. She felt an awkward connection to him, almost déjà-vu like. But she was a prodigy with faces, and his would have been difficult to forget.

"I'm Jacques Saint-Clair," he said, his slight French accent apparent.

"Hi, I'm Malayah Vega."

Jacques enclosed May's hand in his and kissed the back of her hand. "A pleasure to meet you, Mademoiselle Malayah."

May wanted to trust him, but her intuition cautioned her. "Likewise."

He gave her a light grin. For a brief moment, his eyes reflected it: misery. There was more to Jacques than what he presented.

"Malayah, let me introduce you to my lovely wife, Jacqueline,"

Jacques said.

Kat made a sour expression. He bowed and arched his arm as if he were announcing a queen. May's eyes shifted to an East Asian woman who sat in the cushioned booth, her beauty was beyond perfection. Her features were small and proportional, enhanced by her ivory skin. She seemed delicate, and her body soft. She embodied femininity. May was very attracted to her innocent glamour. She wanted to etch Jacqueline in stone.

The woman's dark eyes fixed on May, and a small shiver went down her back. Jacqueline's eyes were like those of a predator, ready to devour any person, who dared to show any sign of weakness. It was there too in Jacqueline's demeanor that May had glimpsed in Jacques, pure malice, except Jacqueline didn't try to hide hers. She gave May a jeering smile, evident of the hatred she possessed.

"Next is my dear friend, Ricky."

May nodded and moved her attention to the person sitting next to Jacqueline. May saw him before she had ever laid eyes on him, his face was constantly in the back of her mind.

She couldn't believe what she saw before her—her angel.

***

What was a year or even a decade to an immortal? Time had become one steady flow, leaving a constant stream of memories in its wake. Dao-Ren no longer counted the days. He only marked moments and events in his life.

Moments were those joyous periods in his life he had spent with the ones he loved. There were only two. The times he shared with his wife Xin-Ji when he was still human and the sunset memories he shared with his beloved Soraya, his Spiritmate.

The rest of his life was cataloged by the events in which he had partaken. Dao-Ren reached out and touched a wooden support beam of the old adobe house. Its once-white walls had turned yellowish-brown with age. He could still smell the faint, flowery incense the Franciscan monks used to burn daily, captured in the semi-petrified wooden foundation.

One hundred and fifty years had passed since Awakyns had lived openly with the monks. Their life together had ended after the great battle with Judanites. Many Franciscan monks and Awakyns had lost their lives in the conflict. While mortal wounds couldn't kill Awakyns, humans would succumb. To kill an Awakyn, it took a pierced heart and decapitation, in that order. Even so, the myths of Awakyns persisted throughout the decades among the local residents.

They knew this house as the "House of Angels."

Somebody had paid a housekeeper to maintain the dwelling. The open ground-level room was sparse and ascetic. Three birch-framed twin beds were brought down from the second-floor dormitory. The beds looked as though they had been slept in. Dao-Ren viewed the few Christian-themed drawings on elk hide hung around the room. His eyes settled on the print of the Mona Lisa. He grinned in the memory of his old friend.

Dao-Ren heard the second floor creak above him as the water faucet shut off. The light footfalls of Tabitha and Peco caused the single naked light bulb to swing on its hook on the bottom floor ceiling. They raced down the stairs, laughing. They halted in their play, and fear crawled onto their demeanor when they noticed Dao-Ren standing there. He surmised that their loud playing would have infuriated their father. Tabitha hugged Peco close to her.

Dao-Ren smiled and nodded at them to continue. Neither moved, clearly unsure what to do.

"Rahhh!" Dao-Ren raised his arms in the air.

The kids jumped back, startled. They looked at each other and broke out into giggles. Dao-Ren roared again and chased after them. Their merriment filled the whole house with joy.

Out of nowhere, a glass bottle smashed against the front wooden door and echoed loudly in the room. Their fun ceased.

"Tabitha, get your ungrateful ass out here! I told you to do one thing, and you always seem to do something else. Come out now, you stupid girl," threatened Roberto.

Dao-Ren opened his arms, and the children ran into his embrace. "It's going to be okay. I won't ever let him hurt the two of you again. Be strong, God is on our side." He scooped Peco up and escorted Tabitha to one of the beds. Both children sat down on the same bed. He gave them a reassuring smile before he made his way outside.

Chapter 12

Bodies bumped and rubbed against one another on the dance floor to the melody of the music. Strobe lights flickered above them with a cool fog rolling out from the mist machine around the DJ booth. May danced with Ricky, and the more time she spent with him, the more it showed that he wasn't her angel. Plus, she had detected the same dark malice in his eyes as his friends. She had only agreed to dance with him to see if she could forget her own demon. A lost cause—the flaws of others only enhanced the perfection of her angel.

Ricky pressed closer to May. She took a step back, uncomfortable dancing that close to him. He moved towards her, and she raised her arms between them.

"I'm tired. I'm going to sit back down." She left before Ricky could give an answer.

Kat was seated in the booth between Jacques and Billy in an animated conversation. When May approached the booth, Kat gave her a knowing smirk. May ignored her and sat down. Ricky came and sat at the end of the booth, which blocked her exit to leave in a hurry. May searched for her orange juice on the table. The glass was empty.

"You want another drink?" Ricky asked.

"Yes, more juice would be nice."

Ricky signaled for a waiter. A waiter appeared to take the order.

May's curiosity got the best of her. She faced Ricky. "Have you ever been to Eugene, Oregon?"

"Yeah, a few times. Why do you ask?"

"I used to live up there, and you remind me of someone."

"Oh, I hope that's a good thing."

May shrugged. "The jury is still out on that one."

The waiter returned and placed a bottle of orange juice in front of her. She sensed Ricky's intense stare on her. It made her feel uneasy. She glanced to the side in the direction of the dance floor. She heard Ricky twist the plastic cap off the orange juice bottle.

"Malayah?"

"Yes." She faced him but scooted back.

"This guy I remind you of—did you know him personally?"

She didn't know how to answer the question. She saw him once, but he lived with her daily. "No, I don't know him personally. I met him briefly once."

"Kat told me that you sculptured statues that resembled me."

May clenched her teeth. She couldn't believe Kat had discussed her personal life with a complete stranger. May snatched the bottle of orange juice and drained half the bottle in one gulp to wash the bile down her throat.

"I sculpt," May said through her teeth. Her chest rose and fell.

"You seem upset. Don't be." Ricky pushed closer to her and placed his arm around her shoulder. "Kat talked so fondly about you that it made me ask her tons of questions." Ricky brushed his fingers on her cheek. "But meeting you tonight…"

May turned away from him. A nauseating feeling came over her. She bit down on her bottom lip to remain focused.

"…you captured me with your first smile," Ricky said.

What's he talking about?

Goosebumps rose on her skin from his breath before he kissed her on the neck. May pulled back and slapped Ricky hard across the face. He hissed through clenched teeth, but he stayed in place.

May pointed her finger in his face. "Don't you ever touch me again!"

Ricky snarled, his mouth rich with spit. "You'll pay for that."

May's vision started to blur. She shook her head to regain her composure. It didn't help much. She closed her eyes and took a deep breath. Something was wrong. She needed to get out of here fast.

She got her vision under control, and she peered over at Kat to let her know it was time to go. Kat was sprawled on the booth with her breast exposed, and was deeply tonguing Billy with his hand underneath her dress. May's stomach lurched. She swiped Ricky aside and rushed out of the booth.

The physical exertion caused her head to spin, and her balance was shaky. She steadied herself with her arms and forced her legs to move. The whole club drank from the fountain of lust. Man on woman, man on man, woman on woman, or any combination of the two.

May slugged through the partygoers, her feet heavy. Some of the guests began to bite and drink the blood of others. What the hell was going on? Human bodies on the ground reached out for her with their hands. She tried to circumvent their clutches and tripped on a table leg. Her arms didn't respond to brace her fall. All her energy had been weaned off. She was helpless against gravity.

Someone grabbed her arm and held her up. May fought with her last bit of strength. Her captor shouted her name, a voice she had once known in her youth. It couldn't be him. She concentrated and made out his face.

Trent Blake.

Her eyes closed.

***

Jacqueline watched a tall man carry Malayah outside the entrance. She was surprised Jacques let her go. Malayah did have an eerie resemblance to Mary, the Father's wife. Mary had been dead for close to two millennia. The only reference Jacqueline had to go on was the vision she had viewed when she drank the Father's sacred blood to become a Judanite. A part of the Father lives in all Judanites.

Even though, Malayah might be a descendant of the Father, Jacqueline still wanted to torture and kill her. Kat's words about Malayah's obsession with her angel were true. She witnessed how Malayah had stared at Ricky. Jacqueline knew the identity of Malayah's angel. The same person who once declared his undying love for her. The one for whom she had carried a child in her womb, the coward who had denied her in the end.

A strong arm enclosed Jacqueline's waist. He pressed his body against her back, and she leaned into Jacques.

"Malayah is the last of the Father's descendants," Jacqueline said.

"I believe so. Ricky couldn't drink Malayah's spirit to confirm it."

Jacqueline glanced to the side and saw Ricky sucking on Kat's chest. "I'm surprised you let her go."

"I didn't want Caiaphas to know."

Jacqueline heard the enmity in Jacques' tone. She twisted around and pulled Jacques closer to her. She peered over to her left and viewed Caiaphas indulging himself with two human males. She despised Caiaphas.

"I will capture Malayah tomorrow. Dao-Ren should be here by now. It made perfect sense that he would be the last Watcher," Jacques said.

"You won't go back on your word, right, my husband?"

"You have my word, my love. I'll capture Dao-Ren, and you'll carve out his heart. This will prove my love for you." Jacques gazed down at Jacqueline. "I love you."

"As I do you."

Jacques lips touched hers, and she felt his passion grow below his belt. He broke away. "We must gain our strength. The days to come will be busy." Jacques motioned with his hand.

Two of his minions carried a drugged-induced human in each of their arms. Jacqueline touched the warm bodies filled with life. She opened her mouth wide, and her teeth elongated into fangs. She drove her fangs into one of the exposed necks. The skin popped and muscles tore until she tasted the metallic flavor of blood. She sucked deeper from her victim's throat.

She welcomed his spirit. Strength and vitality coursed through her body. She released him from her clenched jaw and wiped the blood from her mouth. The puncture wounds on the victim's neck healed before he dropped to the floor.

Not a scratch on him.

***

Dao-Ren stepped into the cold, cloudless night. A crowd of local residents had gathered along the sidewalk. Dao-Ren viewed the beast of a man, he had seen earlier that evening, Roberto. He carried a wooden bat in one hand and a bottle of brown whiskey in the other. Isabelle stood close behind Roberto. She hugged herself, and her eyes were cast down, red and puffy from crying. Dao-Ren stared into Roberto's face, whose eyes were narrow in angry slits. The scowl on his face enhanced the lightning-shaped scar down his cheek. He shifted his bat to his shoulder and took a gulp of liquor, his eyes never faltered from Dao-Ren.

"Gusto en conocerte, Roberto," Dao-Ren said. "Y tú también, Isabelle."

Isabelle peeked up for the first time, most likely surprised to be acknowledged in her native dialect.

"Where are my children? You perverted bastard!" Roberto demanded, stepping closer to Dao-Ren.

"Your children are safe."

Isabelle cast a worried glance before craning over Roberto's shoulder to see if her children were near.

"Go to them, Isabelle," Dao-Ren said.

Roberto locked his jaw. "How dare you order my wife?"

"If it's her wish to be with her children, it's her God-given right."

"She has no right except what I allow," Roberto spewed.

"Mommy!" Peco ran from the house. Dao-Ren intercepted him with his arm.

"Mommy, please!" Peco fought against Dao-Ren's hold. His arms stretched out wide for his mother. Isabelle beelined to her son.

"You bitch." Roberto hurled the bottle at her. It twirled in the night air, marked straight for Isabelle's head.

Dao-Ren dashed towards Isabelle and snatched the bottle from mid-air. Isabelle dropped to her knees to embrace Peco. Dao-Ren poured the rest of the liquor out of the bottle while watching Roberto's forearm muscles tighten up on the bat.

"Let's talk," Dao-Ren advised.

"I have nothing to talk to you about. I should call the police."

"If you think that's wise, go ahead." Dao-Ren discarded the empty bottle in the public trashcan with a flick of his wrist.

"Isabelle, grab those ungrateful children of yours and let's go."

"They aren't going anywhere with you," Dao-Ren said. "Isabelle, take Peco inside."

There was a brief pause before feet scampered away and a door slammed shut.

"Isabelle! Isabelle! Get out here now!" Roberto stomped after her. Dao-Ren stepped in front of him and impeded his advancement. Roberto towered over Dao-Ren. The musk of alcohol and sweat was thick on Roberto's dirty body.

"You're not welcome there," Dao-Ren stated.

"That's my wife and kids."

"You gave up your rights as a husband and a father when you placed alcohol before them."

"Who are you to make that decision?"

"God's will."

"Well, tell your God if he never took my knee away, I'd still be playing baseball. Matter of fact, give him this message for me." Roberto swung the bat with a two-handed grip. Dao-Ren jumped back, out of reach. Roberto's face burned a deep crimson shade and charged Dao-Ren, swinging the bat wildly. Dao-Ren bobbed and dodged each blow. On his last attempt, Roberto slipped and fell headfirst onto the curb. His head snapped back and remained still. Dao-Ren knelt beside Roberto and felt for a pulse. He picked Roberto up from the ground and carried him inside the house.

Isabelle watched Dao-Ren lay Roberto down on an empty bed.

"He'll be okay," Dao-Ren said.

Tabitha turned away, her lips in a tight pucker. Dao-Ren went to her and knelt down beside her. "Tabitha, please look at me."

She focused on Dao-Ren, and her eyes began to moisten.

"It's perfectly alright to be angry with your father. He deserves your anger and a hard kick to his butt."

She smiled and wiped her tears with her hand.

"You being angry with him doesn't make you anything like him."

"I want him to die!"

"No, you don't. That's your anger speaking. I see the goodness shining off of you like gold. You're a strong and loving person. And you have something your father doesn't possess."

"What's that?"

"Forgiveness. You have this strength, Tabitha. That alone makes you a better person than your father will ever be."

She wrapped her small arms around Dao-Ren's neck.

Dao-Ren stood and looked at Isabelle. "I'm sorry for the trouble I caused you."

"No, I prayed for this moment."

"Then I'm happy that I was able to help. But do you have somewhere safe to go?"

"Yes."

"You must leave tonight." Dao-Ren pulled out a large roll of money. "For the children."

After a slight hesitation, Isabelle accepted the money. Peco tugged on Dao-Ren's pant leg. "Mama says you're an angel."

"Peco," Isabelle said.

"Your mother is a smart woman. You should always listen to her."

"I will."

Dao-Ren rubbed the top of his head and acknowledged Isabelle. "It's time to go." Dao-Ren embraced each one and escorted them to the door. Then, he returned to Roberto, lifted him up, and exited the back door.

Chapter 13

The explosion of her father's car erupted in front of May. The ground quaked under the intense blast. Her angel landed on the frozen road with her mom wrapped in his arms. His face was pressed toward her mom's ear, telling her secrets that he wanted no one else to hear.

May longed to be with them. She felt her legs underneath her this time and ran towards them. Something wasn't right. She saw a massive hump on her angel's back and halted mid-stride. A puddle of dark blood formed beneath her mom. The angel leered, snarled. May gasped and stumbled backward.

It wasn't her angel. It was a demon.

And it wasn't telling her mom secrets, it was devouring her throat. Its black lips curled into a sickening grin, with her mom's blood dripping off its teeth. The demon's red eyes bore into May's psyche. May held her ground. She needed a way to get the demon away from her mom.

"I want to taste your precious blood." The demon's hissing voice strangled her eardrums. She had to cover her ears with her hands. It rose to his full eight-foot stature. Black scales covered its torso. It discarded May's mom to the side, as she was a piece of garbage. Her limp body thumped hard on the frozen road.

May watched in horror. Her mom's eyelids snapped wide open, and her eyes pleaded with May.

"Run, May, run!" Her mom's voice carried on the wind.

The demon lurched at May, his black tongue licking over his sharp teeth. May glanced at her mom one last time. Her eyes were closed, she was dead. She turned and fled into the forest.

Fresh snow blanketed the redwood trees. Nothing seemed to be alive. Only the stars led May to an unknown destination. She trod harder, sensing the demon's presence close by. Her heart pumped in her chest, sweat burned down her face, and a shadow cast over the moonlight. The ground trembled when the demon landed in front of May's path. She diverged to the right. He leapt to cut her off. Realization halted her. The demon had been toying with her, just playing with its food.

Fear took control. The ability to run evaded her. The demon strode hungrily toward her. She remained there, helpless. He snatched her up, his rotten breath washing over her. She thought of her angel as a last plea. Out of nowhere, a wave of immense heat rushed past May and sliced through the muscle-bound forearms of the demon.

May and the detached arms crashed onto the snow. Steam rose from the hot, black blood. She scurried out of its dead grasp and searched the area for somewhere to escape. A man with fiery angel wings extending from his back stood between her and the demon. Without hesitation, he struck down the demon with a blazing sword. The demon withered away to skin and bones.

May held her breath. The man turned to face her. She regarded his sorrowful eyes. Her angel.

"May, run into the light," he said, pointing to the brightness glowing in the distance. "There are more demons coming to try to capture you."

May didn't want to go. How could she leave him so soon? She wanted to fight with him so she could spend a few more minutes in his presence. The pleading in his eyes refuted any hopes of standing by his side. The thought of her own selfishness adding to his sorrow terrified her.

"You must go now. I'll come to you soon."

More demons crashed down from the pitch-black sky. He raised his flaming sword and attacked. He would protect her. She honored his wish and bolted toward the light. The light got brighter until everything became hazy, and her eyes burned. The brightness became too much. A flash exploded inside her mind, and then her eyes popped open. The light converged into one focal point.

It took May a moment to adjust to her surroundings. She was still partially lost in her nightmare. Her angel was there, and now he was gone again. Then it dawned on her. She had no idea where she was. She tried to think back and connect the dots on how she had gotten from the club to here. Her memory drew a blank.

May's eyes darted everywhere in the room. She noted the ceiling done in a Romanesque design of straight lines and subtle curves. A small crystal chandelier dangled above her. She looked down and saw she was lying in a queen-size bed with goose down pillows and a thick beige duvet tucked high above her chest. A glimpse beneath the duvet revealed she still had clothes on. She sighed with relief.

May sat up and studied the room. A nightstand to her left had a room service menu on top of it. "Four Seasons Hotel Beverly Hills" was stenciled in gold. How did she get here? She didn't know, and she didn't want to find out. The demon in her nightmare was fresh on her mind.

Hushed voices sounded outside, and adrenaline pumped through her. She pushed herself off the bed and onto her feet. A wave of nausea hit her. She had to steady herself with deep breaths. The voice came nearer. May searched the immediate area for a weapon. She snatched the brass reading lamp off the nightstand. The doorknob turned.

Whoever came in first was going to find out she played cleanup on her high school softball team. It might work better if she hid behind the door, adding an element of surprise.

Too late, the door swung open. May lifted the lamp high. A tall, broad-shouldered man stepped into view, the dim light cast a shadow over him.

"May, what are you doing?"

The voice stunned her. It couldn't be him. The chandelier lights came on. May squinted at the brightness. Her mind didn't want to believe who she saw. Trent Blake stood there with a worried expression. She let the lamp drop from her hand onto the plush carpet. Trent made it to her with a few long strides. An older Middle Eastern man in a cotton blazer, toting a brown leather satchel, followed him.

"I'm so relieved you finally woke up," Trent said.

May stared at him.

"You've been sleeping for over fourteen hours."

May sat down on the side of the bed, exhausted. Trent came and sat down next to her. She noticed his hair was longer than it used to be in high school, and he had a day growth of hair on his chin and cheeks. His face had become more angular and defined. Yet his deep blue eyes still held the same exuberant confidence for life. A quality she had come to admire during their relationship, which made him a superstar quarterback.

"This is Dr. Behrani. I called him when you wouldn't wake up."

The doctor set his brown leather satchel down on the table and unclasped it. He retrieved a stethoscope. He gave a reassuring smile.

May smiled back.

"Are you allergic to anything?" Dr. Behrani asked.

"No."

He flicked a penlight into her eyes.

May turned away from the light.

He nodded his head. "And now say aah."

May opened her mouth.

He inspected inside her mouth. "How do you feel?"

"I have a headache, and I feel very weak."

He felt around her throat. "Have you taken any illicit drugs lately?"

"Of course not."

He looked at her with a stern gaze, and May stared back at him. He blinked. "You're severely dehydrated, from what I can tell. Seems you've been drugged. I won't know for certain until a toxicology test can be performed."

The orange juice Ricky had opened for her came to mind. Anger smothered the shock.

Dr. Behrani produced a bottle and shook out two pills onto her palm. "It should help with the headache."

Trent brought her a bottled water.

"I'll show myself out," Dr. Behrani said and left.

"Thank you, Trent," May said.

His lips lifted into a shy smile. A smile she remembered so well.

"I'm glad you decided to wake up. I was on the verge of calling Uncle B before I fetched the doctor."

"I have a hard time remembering how I got here."

"You don't remember anything."

"Not much." May stared at her feet.

"I got up to leave the club when everyone started getting sexual with each other. I saw you stumbling through the crowd. And when I reached you, you passed out in my arms, so I brought you here."

"I think one of Kat's friends spiked my drink."

"That says it all. I don't know why you're still friends with her."

May couldn't look at Trent. "Please, Trent. Don't talk about Kat."

"I'll bet she dragged you to that porn party."

Indignation rose in May. "And why were you there?"

"For your information, I had a Thursday night game against San Diego. Some of my teammates coaxed me into coming out to celebrate our victory." He sighed. "Look, I don't want to argue with you about Kat."

She nodded her head in agreement.

"Good." Trent said.

A few seconds ticked by. "It's good to see you, Trent. It's been a long time."

He held her in his gaze. "Too long."

"I heard you're getting married. No more People Magazine's top 50 bachelors.

"I am. She's wonderful. Her name is Jacqueline."

Chapter 14

Dao-Ren stationed himself at the center of the room and lowered himself onto the floor, folding his legs in lotus style. He reached behind his back and freed both of his Chinese writer's knives. The sixteen-inch blades reflected the final hour of sunlight. It shimmered with a soft golden hue. The blades had been re-casted with a special mixture of transitional metals and iron ore called MaNa metal, which was perfect for dispatching Judanites. The handles were woven with aged leather, and each had an amber orb pommel.

These knives had been Dao-Ren's steady companions for the last seventeen hundred years. They were never too far from his side. Destiny had made sure Dao-Ren wielded these knives. It came at a time when blood needed to be shed. A part of his past he wished he could forget, but only his memories drew him back with all the attached emotions.

The first day he held these knives was in battle. He was a prisoner forced to kill the enemy. He had slashed, stabbed, and killed the soldiers in front of him. The mental wounds of his massacred family and the blotched death sentence of a thousand cuts had fueled his ferocity. The fury had rushed out of him in the deadly waves of his knives, and blood flowed in its wake.

With each life he took from that day forward, he lost a little part of himself. His hands would always remain bloody. It had been a sacrifice he was willing to make. After his wife Xin-Ji's avaricious father sold her into slavery, she was still alive. Two armies stood between her and him. Nothing except death could stop him from marching to his Xin-Ji. A trail of blood marked his journey, which always ended in death.

He cleared his mind and placed a knife on each side of his leg. He enclosed the tips of his index fingers at the top of his thumbs to form a circle. He rested the backs of his hands on his knees. He closed his eyes and welcomed the peace of darkness.

***

Not too many travelers or employees bustled around the Bob Hope Airport. Trent had just left on a charter plane. He was flying back home to his Jacqueline, and not the one she meant last night. A picture on his phone confirmed it. *Thank God.*

May headed back to her car when her eyes caught something by the newsstand—a wanted picture of the "Exorcist Killer" on the front page of a local newspaper. A face she recognized so well. She purchased a paper and snapped it straight to the article. There was a fifth victim, and multiple witnesses had identified an East Asian male with the victim. May studied the sketch, and her chest tightened. In the image, his forehead and nose were too large, and his lips too thick, but she couldn't deny the fact that it was Ricky.

Kat.

May grabbed her iPhone and selected Kat's number on the menu. Her hand trembled more with each ring. She had a terrible feeling about this.

"Hi, you've reached Kat's voicemail. Right number, wrong time."

Beep.

"Kat, where are you? Call me back ASAP when you get this." May ended the call and sent a text message.

Panic settled in. Her heart raced. She counted to ten then reversed her count.

Okay, today was Friday, and it's four thirty. That meant Kat was preparing for her aerobics class, and she wouldn't be done until six. If she didn't call by six thirty, May would try to call her again—or alert authorities.

Think positive.

May dropped her chin forward and rubbed her temples to alleviate the headache. She rotated her head back and forth to ease the stiffness in her neck. She looked at the watch, she had time for a run. She knew that she shouldn't go for a run but it would really help her to relax, Plus, Pan Pacific Park was on the way home, and she had fresh jogging clothes in the trunk of her car. A thought hit her, and she fumbled for her phone.

A text message from Unc: Call me.

She chose his number, and it went straight to voicemail.

"Hey Unc, I wanted to tell you that I met a guy last night who really resembles the Exorcist Killer."

Chapter 15

The bile in Bernardo's stomach churned when he thought about how this pencil pusher was running the Los Angeles Field Office. Just the sight of the tall, lanky man with his high forehead and beak-like nose got on his last nerve. The high nasal voice of Ernest Graham droned on about the Exorcist Killer. They were in a status meeting with the assistant director of the FBI Criminal Investigation Division, the Los Angeles mayor, and the chief of police.

Assistant Director Steve Blair twirled his pen and looked to the side. Mayor Hector Navarre texted on his phone. And Chief Alex Porter nursed his coffee and viewed something on his phone.

Bernardo could only blame himself for Graham getting the Special Agent in Charge position. Bernardo had passed up on the promotion, uninterested in sitting behind a desk all day.

Headquarters had sent Ernest Graham from Quantico to lead the LA field office. He had very little field experience. Most of his twenty-two years of service came from being a technical expert in criminal profiling. No one in the field office trusted him. He reported any infraction, no matter how trivial it was, to investigative services. He didn't understand the notion that—bending the rules wasn't breaking it. Most field agents probably went beyond protocol to solve a case.

Bernardo felt a sharp kick to his shin. He peered up at Tessa, who stared straight at him. She closed her eyes and tilted her head like she was nodding off to sleep. A light chuckle cracked from Bernardo's throat. Everyone glanced his way. He grabbed his glass of water. Graham threw him a reproachful glare that made him look like a rat that smelled his own ass.

Bernardo returned his attention to Tessa. She had a sly smile on her face. He could still taste her lips on his from the other night. The tannic taste of red wine on her mouth was addictive. He never felt this much desire in his life. He wanted her in every imaginable way.

This was the first woman for whom Bernardo fell head-over-heels. Even the woman he almost married never made him feel the way he felt about Tessa. He had been more dedicated to his job than to a relationship. All his passion and drive went into his cases, which left nothing for his personal life.

He had given up on the idea of love a long time ago, and now it might be staring back at him with ocean-blue eyes. Even after one date, the idea of being with Tessa seemed so right and natural. He hoped that she felt the same way about him; if not, he would enjoy his time with her.

"Vega!" Graham said.

Bernardo looked up and saw Graham's flushed face.

"Could you join us and share your insights into your investigation?" Graham asked.

Bernardo stood and headed to the podium with his notes and files. He faced his audience. "The information that Agent Graham shared with all of you are the facts and data we have collected so far in this case. The sketch composite of the Exorcist Killer." He pointed to a drawing posted on the wall. "We've gathered from three witnesses who saw Stacy Smith, our fifth victim, with the suspect at the nightclub, Les Tres.

"With the assistance of LAPD, we cross-referenced the sketch with the other witnesses that were present at the nightclub that night.

And unanimously, the clubbers identified seeing him there. We also showed the sketch to the sole witness of victim number four, Stephen Falco. To reduce the fallacy of agreeing with the sketch, we showed the witness six different sketches of East Asian males. She picked the last person seen with Stacy Smith."

"Has something changed since my briefing this morning? There weren't any witnesses who had seen victim number five leave with the perpetrator," Assistant Director Blair said.

"You're correct. We have no witnesses who actually saw the victim leave with the suspect. We did gather some forensic evidence from the last victim. We have some hair strains that are consistent with Asians. Also, the technicians found a substance under the victim's fingernails that appeared to be human remains. It's still inconclusive at this present moment."

"What do you mean it appears to be human remains?" Mayor Navarre asked.

"The test results of the substance came back as decomposed human flesh," Bernardo informed.

The mayor shifted in his chair.

"When we apprehend the suspect, we can test the hair sample against him." Bernardo added.

"And how does the chief forensic scientist explain the bloodless bodies?" Assistant Director Blair inquired.

"We're still working on that. We know from the other bodily fluids found in each victim's bodies indicated that the time of death occurred an hour or so before we discovered the bodies. No large amounts of blood were found on any of the victim's bodies or around the immediate crime scene. No unnatural marks were on the victims except for the religious symbols that were carved into their upper cavities. There's no logical connection between the victims and their carved symbols."

"Any leads on the suspect?" Chief Porter asked.

"There's nothing strong to go on at this moment. We've got lines taking in information from the public. There's a $50,000 award for his capture or arrest."

"Anything else?" Chief Porter queried.

"We believe the suspect called 9-1-1 after he murdered victim number 5. We can do a voice analysis of the suspect against the 9-1-1 recording. Then we can place him on the scene."

"Very well, but what do you assess the killer's motive to be?" Assistant Director Blair asked.

"I believe the killer is sending a message to someone saying. I'm here, come and get me."

Graham shot to his feet. "That's preposterous!"

Bernardo tightened his fist. "It might very well be. But we've eliminated that he's not after sexual gratification, nor does he have the God complex, or any of the other motives you know so well from your profiling days. This might very well be new data you can input it into the NCIC."

Graham ground his teeth, and his face turned red.

"Are there any more questions?" Bernardo inquired as he scanned the room, only to be met with silence.

"Very well, I thank all of you for your time." Bernardo grabbed his materials and exited the room. He headed towards his desk. He was going to break Graham's neck soon.

"Wait, Vega," Tessa called out.

"Yes, Detective?"

Tessa nudged her head at the exit. "Let's grab some dinner."

"Let me get my jacket."

"Bernardo!" Brad shouted, running down the hall.

Bernardo turned.

"I think you should look at this. We just got a call about the Exorcist

Killer. The caller sent a picture off her camera phone." Brad handed Bernardo an enlarged photo.

Bernardo studied the photograph. "When was this taken?"

"The caller said around 3 o'clock this afternoon."

Bernardo glanced at his watch 17:41. "Did she give his whereabouts?"

"134 Olvera Street, in the downtown area. She said she saw him enter the house in the late afternoon and never saw him come back out."

"This is a go!"

Chapter 16

If someone had drugged May, then Kat likely experienced the same thing. May's lungs expanded to take in the cool air. Sweat trickled down her face underneath her beanie. May prayed that Kat would answer her voicemail soon. She felt terrible for leaving her there with Ricky. If he turned out to be the Exorcist Killer and had done awful things to her... *No, stop it!* She shouldn't be thinking like that. Kat was all right and safe.

May focused straight ahead and kept a steady pace on the dirt trail. The evergreen trees around her stretched their trunks high into the sky. Their leaves had shed and carpeted the forest floor in yellow, brown, and red. This peaceful setting did nothing to mollify May's distressful mood. She increased her pace.

Even though May had been duped, she should've been more careful. She was the responsible one. Kat depended on her. It had always been that way since they had become fast friends at the age of ten. When the other girls in fifth grade had picked on Kat, May was the one who stood up to those bullies when she didn't even know Kat yet. They were complete opposites. May played sports, and Kat was into beauty pageants. She wore jeans, and Kat donned dresses. In the balance of things, they had complemented each other. Their relationship had grown into a true sisterhood.

Yes, Kat could be irresponsible and naïve at times, but they didn't know her like she did. They didn't see when Kat nursed two stray dogs back to health and found each one of them a new home, despite the fact that Kat was allergic to dog hair, or witnessed her resiliency when things didn't go her way. Her motto was, "It happened, can't change it, learn to change the way you look at it."

The sun dipped behind the top of the tree lines. It caught May off guard. How could she totally lose track of time? It frightened her that she was quite a distance away from the parking lot. She patted her pockets. No phone. It must be in the car. She pressed her lips together and gave a slight shake of her head. She was never this careless. At least she remembered her keys. She slipped the pepper spray bottle out of the keychain case and held it in her hand with her index finger on the spray button. She took off on a run as nightfall pursued her.

***

Dao-Ren had Malayah in his thoughts. He saw the fortitude and strength that burned brightly in her eyes and exuded from her spirit. The same essence his beloved Spiritmate Soraya once had. A person he couldn't protect, just like he had failed his wife Xin-Ji. The sorrows of those moments were ever present in his mind.

How could he have thought it would have been different with Soraya? He should've known better. Life had never shown him fairness. His father's words echoed loudly: "Dao-Ren, your path in life will be to endure." And he had endured for the sake of love.

Since he first had became an Awakyn, he had roamed the earth, lost in his past. He had to make things right, and do what he had promised—protect the one he loved. Not until Soraya had entered his life did he return to the present moment. He could smell the cherry blossom in her thick brown hair. He had seen the love that reflected in her gray eyes when she looked at him. These anchors were no longer there to keep him grounded in the present moment.

Now, the power of these forgotten feelings and senses has been rekindled. Still, Dao-Ren wouldn't let these emotions forget the lesson he had learned. The pain of losing a lover was fiercer than loving that person. It was for the best to never meet Malayah in person.

The stench of Judanites assaulted Dao-Ren's nose at the same instant a fusillade of automatic weapons rattled outside. Bullets punctured their way in. The wooden beam structures burst into splinters. He remained seated even when bullets found it marks on him. Gunshot wounds couldn't kill him outright. Dust gathered around him with the crumbling of the abode walls and the cracking of the packed earth floor.

Three Judanites, dressed in full LAPD SWAT gear, barged into the room with swords held high.

"Repent and God will have mercy on you," Dao-Ren announced before he flexed his crossed legs, propelling his body into the dusty air. He slipped the shurikens from his belt and threw them with a flick of his wrist. Each shuriken found its target on the three Judanites exposed throats. Their bodies erupted with a bluish-black light, followed by a cloud of ash.

Dao-Ren landed in a low squat, his hands on his knives. Four Judanites rushed in, and he also detected movements upstairs. A hot-pink-haired Judanite swung her long sword. He leapt at her under her strike, and his knife sliced her stomach, bluish-black light.

He then tumbled to the ground, shot up with knives out in front of him, and made a clean incision on the next Judanite, bluish-black light. He pointed his knives downward and blocked a sword. He twisted his hips and arched his arm on the waiting Judanite's neck, bluish-black light.

Another two Judanites attacked at once. Dao-Ren parried their offense. He saw a third charge from the corner of his eye. He punched outward with the knives and pushed off the ground with his legs. The two Judanites backpedaled from his shove. Dao-Ren slung one of his knives at the charging Judanite's eye, bluish-black light.

Dao-Ren threw up his lone knife behind his head and impeded a sword blow. The sword tip grazed his neck. Dao-Ren spun low and around, stabbing the Judanite in his gut, bluish-black light. Dao-Ren dove and side-kicked up into the last remaining Judanite's chest. She slammed high against the wall. Before she could slide down, Dao-Ren flung his remaining knife and pinned her against the wall by her shoulder. A high-pitched scream resonated from her.

She tried to yank the knife free. Dao-Ren snatched a discarded sword off the ground and embedded it in her other shoulder. He retrieved his other knife and pressed it against her throat.

"Where are Jacqueline and Jacques?"

"You're dead, Watcher!" She spat at Dao-Ren's face.

Bluish-black light.

Dao-Ren grabbed his other knife off the ground and sprinted out the door. His pulse quickened. How did she know he was a Watcher?

Chapter 17

With the coming of night, the blue and red flashing lights on the light bar shone bright on the unmarked car as the high-pitched sirens wailed down Arcadia Street. The lead car screeched to a stop in front of Olvera Street. Bernardo hopped out as Daniel exited the passenger side. Other federal and LAPD vehicles pulled in behind them. A lead agent shouted at his subordinates to get the area secured.

Bernardo studied the scene. A boisterous crowd of residents had gathered and headed straight to him. Bernardo held up his hands to slow their progress and quiet them down. They were excited about something. He was able to discern enough of the garble of English and Spanish that was shouted his way. It had to do with gunshots being fired five minutes ago.

Bernardo flagged over a group of LAPD officers to deal with the growing crowd. In a methodical manner, they swiftly got the crowd under control. Daniel approached Bernardo with Tessa and Sergeant Roscoe, who was dressed in a FBI SWAT fatigues.

"Sgt. Roscoe, I want snipers stationed on both ends of the street." Bernardo pointed at the corner building. "I want your team to lead us down the street in the next minute. The residents claim that multiple gunshots were fired five minutes ago."

"Yes, sir." Sergeant Roscoe grabbed his walkie-talkie off his shoulder clip and spoke into the receiver.

Bernardo returned to his car and popped open the trunk with a remote. He tossed Daniel a bulletproof vest. They both strapped on their Teflon armor. Bernardo handed Daniel a Colt M4A1 semi-automatic rifle and took one for himself. He cocked back the slide. Tessa freed her Glock from her side holster.

The street was cleared of all pedestrians. A twelve-member SWAT team stood fully geared and ready with their H&K MP5 fully-automatic rifles. Bernardo and other law officers jogged up to the awaiting SWAT team. Bernardo nodded at Sergeant Roscoe.

"Form up!" Sergeant Roscoe said.

The SWAT team formed a V-formation with a single-point man. Sergeant Roscoe gave a forward hand signal, and the team moved into the street, guns aimed straight ahead. Bernardo fell to the rear with Tessa by his side.

Olvera was a pedestrian only street. No vehicles were allowed. Nevertheless, the street was clustered with wooden-framed stalls with merchandise stacked high. There were plenty of hiding spots. At least the streets were cleared of people, yet he could feel the curious stares of residents peeking out of their storefronts and home windows.

Sergeant Roscoe held up a balled fist, and the team halted. He motioned with his hand from side to side. The team split in two and positioned themselves on either side of the front door.

The air still smelled of spent gunpowder, and empty shell casings littered the sidewalk in front of a bullet-ridden house. If the Exorcist Killer was inside, he would have been mutilated. Who would send this type of force against him? Something strange was going on.

Two SWAT members from each side of the entrance tossed flash grenades through the shattered windows. A loud explosion sounded, and a bright flash followed. The SWAT team filed into the house. Bernardo shouldered his assault rifle, pressed his face to the stock, and trailed after them.

The numerous bullet holes in the house's facade allowed streetlamps to stream in and illuminate the structure. The rampage of bullets cracked the packed earth floor.

"Clear!" someone shouted to Bernardo's left.

Bernardo heard footsteps above him.

"Clear!" another shouted from upstairs.

Sgt. Roscoe approached Bernardo, his assault rifle pointed down. "All clear."

Bernardo nodded. The overhead lights clicked on. He took a step back as he surveyed the unusual items of swords, specialized Uzis with silencers, and black tactical SWAT uniforms.

The SWAT team exited the house to let the forensic team enter with their equipment. Bernardo grabbed some latex gloves from a technician and squatted down next to the pile of clothes. He lifted the heavy, double-edged sword that lay nearby the SWAT uniform and examined it. He didn't have a working knowledge about swords, but this one looked medieval and expensive, with gemstones embedded in the handle. The blade was razor-sharp. This weapon wasn't for show. He placed the sword back where he found it.

Next, he shifted through the discarded uniform with a pen from his pocket. The clothes were authentic SWAT-issued uniforms that appeared to be covered inside and out with ashes. It was difficult to obtain these clothes. Whoever got these uniforms had an inside connection to the LAPD. He would discuss this with Tessa.

A shimmer of light caught Bernardo's eye. He dislodged the object from the shirt. It was a shuriken, a Japanese throwing blade. He inspected the short, three-inch blade. It was crafted with a unique type of metal, a chrome color with a slight golden sheen. He noticed a faint three-flower blossom symbol imprinted at the end of the blade. He had seen this symbol before... *No, it couldn't be.* He would have to double-check, but he was quite positive that it was the same symbol on the dagger that was found on the bloodless priest in Syria.

"Vega."

Bernardo got up and pocketed the shuriken.

"I found the witness who had made the call, sir," Brad said.

"Did she provide any more information about the suspect?

Brad twisted his mouth. "…I'm not sure."

"Let me hear it."

Brad moistened his lips. "The witness's name is Alicia Arias. She said the suspect helped a young woman named Isabelle Cortez and her two young children flee from her alcoholic husband last night. Isabelle Cortez is Mexican, 5 feet 6 inches, dark brown hair and green eyes."

"Brad, have a typed copy of the witness's statement on my desk later tonight." Bernardo stepped away and retrieved his cell phone. The description reminded him of May. He turned his phone back on. There was a voicemail from May.

"Hey Unc, I wanted to tell you that I met a guy last night who really resembles the Exorcist Killer at a club with Kat. I'm okay but I can't get into contact with Kat. Call me when you get this. I'm going to take a quick jog at Pan Pacific Park. Love you, bye."

He viewed the log time: 16:39. Now it was 18:34. He selected May's number and let it ring.

Her voicemail came on.

"May, call me back now!"

***

Dao-Ren made a second loop down Venice Boulevard. He hadn't found any trace of May. He had just finished searching her apartment, and by the looks of things, no one had been home all day. Their toiletries and Kat's daily heart medication were still in their bathrooms. That meant they didn't take a trip out of town.

Where could she be? Had the Judanites taken her? Dao-Ren couldn't even fathom how they knew about her. The last Judanite he released tonight called him a Watcher. There weren't any more Watchers left.

No one was supposed to know about Malayah and her ancestry.

His inner sense told him they hadn't found her yet. Jacqueline and Jacques would've used Malayah to get to him. They would know he would've trade his life for hers. No one on earth knew Dao-Ren was a Watcher, not even the Holy Council. This was the main reason why he never stayed in one place for too long. He was determined to throw the trail as far away from Malayah and her family as he could.

Dao-Ren understood Jacqueline's hatred for him. She would disobey the master of the Judanites, the one they called the Father, for her own devious purpose. Moreover, Jacques would always comply with her every wish.

Dao-Ren turned right on Abbot Kinney, the street was crowded with people. His cell phone rang. Who-Dat.

"What you've got for me?"

"Agent Vega left Olvera Street in a hurry."

"Where's he going?"

"I locked into Agent Vega's federal car's GPS signal. I'm transferring it over now," Who-Dat said.

A map appeared on Dao-Ren's car navigation system.

"Got it." He slammed down on the pedal and shifted the gear.

Chapter 18

"Unc, what are you doing here?" May said.

"Are you okay?" Bernardo got closer to May. "I got your voicemail about knowing the Exorcist Killer. And when you didn't answer your phone. I came here to see if you're alright."

"Please, don't tell me something terrible happened to Kat." May held her breath.

Unc tilted his head back. "What's wrong with Kat?"

May sighed. "I haven't heard from her since last night."

"She's probably at a friend's house."

"I don't think so. She was with the guy that resembles the Exorcist Killer."

He steadied his gaze on her. "When was this?"

"Last night." Tears gathered in May's eyes. "You have to find her."

Unc opened his arms. "Don't worry, we'll find her."

She leaned into his embrace.

"Aww, isn't that sweet? A picture-perfect moment."

They turned towards the deep voice. A gang of five people headed directly at them. They moved incredibly fast. May recognized two of them from the club last night, the red-headed female and the bearded man. May shivered in Unc's arms. He gave her a quick glance, stepped in front of her, and drew his gun. He pointed the weapon at them.

"FBI, don't move!"

The gang members laughed.

"Don't make this hard for yourselves," Bernardo warned.

"How about I don't make this hard for you?" the bearded man said.

In a blink, he was an inch from Unc. Three quick bursts of gunfire sounded. Smoke rose out of the barrel of Unc's gun. The bearded man flew backward from the force of the bullets. He landed hard on his back. May clutched the tail of Unc's blazer. A chuckle erupted from the fallen man. The bearded man flipped back to his feet into a low crouch. He glared at Unc with a sneer. "Boo."

Rapid shots fired from Unc's Glock. He grabbed May's arm, and they ran in the direction of the forest. He stopped short of the trail. "Keep on running until you're safe enough to call the police."

"I don't have a phone."

Unc handed May his. She accepted the phone and stayed put, not wanting to leave him with these people. He released the empty clip and popped in a full one.

"Go, now."

"I love you." May said and dashed into the forest. She knew Unc's best chance was for her to call the police. She dialed 9-1-1 as she ran deeper into the shadowy forest.

***

Bernardo stood his ground and fired at the oncoming thugs. They must be on some type of powerful drug. He hit three of them with a chest shot, and they didn't stay down. They kept coming at him. Time to go for their heads.

The redhead lunged at Bernardo from her squatted position and landed ten feet away to his right. He squeezed the trigger in three quick pulls. The last one hit her dead center, on her forehead. She tumbled backwards on top of the ground. She used the momentum and rolled back onto her feet. She hissed at Bernardo. The bullet hole above her left eye was healing.

What the hell?

Another attacked from his left. He swung his Glock and released three shots. He hit the thug in the torso. The bearded man in front sprung from his spot at Bernardo. Bernardo twisted around and let loose two shots. His luck had run out, he missed. The bearded man chopped down on Bernardo's extended arm. He felt the bone snap in his forearm. The pain took him by surprise, and he dropped the gun. He tightened his jaw and bent down with the other hand to reclaim his weapon.

His fingertips grazed the gun handle when the redhead blindsided him with a backhand. The magnitude of the slap loosened his jaw. It was broken. She stood over him and lifted Bernardo by his throat, which choked off his curses. Her tiny hand squeezed tighter. Bernardo struggled for his life. He swung his good fist and connected with her chin. Her grip slackened. He inhaled a small victory of air.

It was short-lived. She flung him across the parking lot, and he slammed into the lamppost. His ribs took the brunt of the impact, cracking under the force. He felt lucky that he still had on his bulletproof vest. Even so, it did nothing to dull the excruciating throbbing pain. He tried to sit up, but his arm couldn't support the leverage to push his body up. He collapsed back onto the gravel.

The redhead peered down at him with a pleased smirk curled on her thin lips. Bernardo gave her the middle finger. She snatched him by his hair and forced his head back, which exposed his neck. He swiped the area with his eyes. He didn't see any of the other thugs. He hoped he had given May enough time to escape.

The redhead's face morphed right in front of Bernardo's eyes. The skin on her face stretched over her facial structure, which became more pronounced. Both of her top and bottom canines elongated an inch. *A vampire*. Bernardo wouldn't have believed it if he hadn't just battled this hideous beast.

Her head swung downward to his neck, plunging her icepick canines deep into his jugular vein. He experienced a warm sensation leaving his body. Even the pain faded away. The last of his strength was being siphoned, and it was more than his physical strength. It was something deeper inside of him. He knew it wouldn't be too much longer.

It could have been a dream. He was falling in and out of consciousness. He thought he heard a car skid to a stop. It didn't really matter anymore he just wanted to go to sleep. No worries, no problems, only peace.

Bernardo felt the jolt when he hit the ground. It awoke him. He opened his eyes, and his vision cleared enough to see the redhead levitating off the gravel. Then a bluish-black light exploded from within her, and she burned to ashes. He wanted to laugh about how bizarre this night had become.

Hands touched Bernardo, and he felt himself being leaned against the lamppost. May's angel came into his vision. He had seen enough drawings of him to know. He trusted those eyes.

"Where's May?"

He pointed toward the forest. He felt a brush of air before he succumbed to the falling of his eyelids.

Chapter 19

May kept running, not knowing which direction to go. Cold sweat rolled down her face, and she felt the tightness in her lungs. Each breath burned, and a small cramp stabbed her side. She slowed her speed. It's been a few minutes since she heard any gunfire. Maybe she was far enough away. She looked down at the cell phone in her moist hand. There weren't any signal bars on the screen. She shook the phone and lifted it to the dark sky. Unc depended on her. She pointed the phone each and every way, but there was still no signal.

"Malayah, where are you?" The bearded man was very close.

May's heart jerked inside her chest, and her mouth went dry. With a quick glance, she swept the area where she thought she heard the voice travel. She bolted in a full sprint in the opposite direction. The spidery branches tugged and scraped against her jacket. She had to slow her pace, the branches were too thick. She used her hands to swipe the branches away from her face. The forest ground was uneven with decaying vegetation and rocks. She stumbled a few times, but she managed to keep upright.

"Malayah, I smell your sweet scent."

May needed to find a place to hide. Her frantic pace caused her to trip on a gnarled tree root and fell face first. Her arms shot out to brace the fall. The cell phone flew out of her hand.

May scurried back to her feet, and her eyes searched the immediate ground for the cell phone. Her sights darted from side to side. Perspiration dampened her clothes. It was taking too long. A branch snapped to her right. She gave one last glance for the phone. She caught sight of an indentation at the bottom of a tree trunk—a spot where darkness gathered.

She went straight to it. It was a burrow. It was large enough for her to squeeze. She filled in the space and plopped down onto the soft mulch. Darkness cloaked her. Footsteps sounded right outside. It was more than one pair of feet. She scooted herself all the way back and pulled her knees to her chest to get as small as possible.

Dry leaves and twigs crunched around her. May muffled a cry with her hands over her mouth. The seconds ticked by. The cracking sounds of twigs became more distant. The howling wind and the rustling of leaves were louder than the footfalls.

"I can feel it, coming in the air tonight. Oh, Lord." Unc's ringtone filled the night.

May's survival instincts overrode her thoughts. She scrambled out of the burrow and took off in the direction she had come from. Something hooked the back of her jacket. She unzipped her jacket and slipped free from it. She kept her legs pumping, moving further from her pursuers. Branches and bushes scratched her face and bare arms. She ignored the stings. She was determined to put distance between herself and them.

Her nightmare from last night had become a reality. The urgency of the situation drove her onward. *"Run, May."* She heard her angel's voice warning her in the back of her mind, and she listened. Moonlight was her only illumination. A fallen tree thirty feet away blocked her path. It was too high to hurdle over and too long to run around.

She planted her feet to stop, her left foot rolled underneath her. A sharp pain streaked through her. She hobbled on her good foot as she tried to step with her injured feet.

"There you are, Malayah," the bearded man said.

May held onto the fallen tree and faced her pursuers. There were four of them.

"We aren't here to hurt you. We just want to talk." The bearded man halted ten feet in front of May.

"About what?"

"Jacques wishes to speak with you about your family," the bearded man said as they inched closer.

May narrowed her eyes. "Why?"

"Jacques will explain everything."

"Stop!" May shot her palm out.

They paused.

"Where's my uncle?"

"Your uncle is safe with our friend. They're both waiting for you in the parking lot." The bearded man said, lifting both of his hands. "I'm sorry, I frightened you earlier. I was just being an ass." He took a step toward May. A direct beam of moonlight lit his face. She saw the evil lurking behind his smile.

He reached for her arm. She pulled her arm back. Her damaged ankle went out from under her. She crashed to the ground. They swiftly circled her. They eyed each other, and their lips curled up into sneers before they rested their sights back on May.

The bearded man leered at May. A shadow cast over her, and the bearded man was knocked off his feet. Someone stood between her and her pursuers.

"Repent and God will have mercy upon you."

Her angel. No one could duplicate that voice.

"Die, Awakyn!" The bearded man crawled back to his feet and bulleted straight for her angel. Her angel sidestepped and swung his arm in a lateral arc. Something flashed through the bearded man's stomach. A bluish-black light erupted from the exposed wound. As fast as the light came, it disappeared, with his body crumbling into ashes.

The other three attacked simultaneously. Her angel pirouetted and created a halo with his blades. All three smoldered into bluish-black lights, and a burst of ashes snowed down around him.

He was real, but this moment felt more like a dream than a reality. How could he look the same as she remembered? His eyes confirmed that he was her angel.

"Malayah."

She watched his smooth lips pronounce her name. She wished to hear it again. All her worries disappeared.

"Are you okay?"

She shook her head from side to side. He squatted down next to her and gently touched her sprained ankle.

"Ouch."

"I'm sorry."

Sounds of movement in the bushes caught his attention. He looked back at May.

"We must get out of here."

May nodded. He lifted her up and supported her neck and knees with his arms. May circled her arms around his neck. She gave a short squeal as he took off running. She pressed her face into his muscular chest and embraced the comfort of his body. She breathed him in. He smelled of a sweet woody scent, almost nectar-like, but not quite.

He dodged and vaulted his way through the forest, holding her tighter with each obstacle. She reciprocated the closeness and enclosed her arms tighter around his neck. She was completely safe in his arms.

"I missed you so much," May proclaimed.

***

What did she mean she missed me? She couldn't have remembered him from back then. She had just been a child, who was falling in and out of consciousness when he pulled her out of her father's wrecked car.

Dao-Ren wanted to believe that she had missed him, yet he knew he had to remain impartial to his feelings. Her safety and protection were more important. He couldn't let his spirit get involved. His job was to ensure that she had a normal human life.

It would be hard—a battle within himself. The feelings he felt being this close to Malayah had been lost to him for over a thousand years. A feeling only two people had ever made him experience. He was free once again from his sorrows and pain. He wanted to run forever with her in his arms. They entered the parking lot, and he placed May down to open his car door.

"Unc's car is still here. Those things said they were going to take us to Jacques."

How did she know Jacques? He was a fool to leave her unsupervised for the last sixteen years.

"It's okay, Malayah. Your uncle is safe, but he's badly injured," Dao-Ren said. "I will heal him."

She gave him a skeptical look. He touched her hand.

"Trust me. I will heal him."

Malayah nodded. Dao-Ren assisted her into the back seat.

Dao-Ren went to retrieve Bernardo, who was still sitting in an upright position with his chin on his chest. He checked his pulse, it was weak before gathering Bernardo in his arms and returned to the car. He carefully lay Bernardo's head on Malayah's lap. She broke into tears and cradled her uncle's face with her hands.

Chapter 20

May watched her angel carry Unc into the motel room. She enclosed her hands together in prayer. He placed her Unc down next to her on the old bed. Unc's swollen and bruised face was caked with blood. May stroked her hand lightly over Unc's battered face.

Her angel returned from outside with a first-aid kit in his hand. May didn't know if she wanted to laugh or yell at him. What the hell was a first aid kit going to do for Unc? He needed a hospital, not a Band-Aid.

He straightened Unc's body and unclasped the first aid kit. He retrieved a pair of medical scissors and used them to cut through Unc's shirt and bulletproof vest. The clothes peeled away to reveal Unc's clobbered body. May covered her mouth with her hands. Three of his ribs were flat and concave. The area of the blow was crimson around the perimeter and a deep purple at the center.

May shifted her eyes to the side. Unc's left forearm was bent at an awkward angle. She bit her bottom lip. She wanted to be strong for Unc but she couldn't hold back the tears. They fell. A hand touched May's arm, and she peered up into her angel's eyes. He smiled and wiped the tears off her cheeks. She felt his strength, he was her rock. Her worries dissipated. She trusted him.

He turned his attention back to Unc. He placed both of his hands a few inches above Unc's upper body and closed his eyes. His mouth began to move. May wasn't sure if it was a song or a prayer. His hands hovered over Unc's damaged areas for several seconds, then he whispered something in Unc's ears. May strained to hear, but she couldn't make it out.

All of a sudden, her angel returned to chanting, and his body started to sway. May stared at him, then at Unc then back again. *What was he doing?* The skin of his hand burned with a reddish-brown hue. She felt the heat radiating from them. He lowered his hands on her uncle's shattered ribs. Unc's skin took on the same hue as her angel's hands. Unc's muscles and bones twitched underneath his skin. He kept his hands there for a couple of minutes, and then he removed them.

Oh, my God!

Unc's ribs were healed. She stared at her angel, unable to close her mouth.

He proceeded over to Unc's broken forearm and placed his hands over it. He moved his fingers as if he were massaging Unc's arm. The forearm straightened out like it had been before tonight.

Next, he concentrated on Unc's battered face. He stationed his hands over Unc's face and moved them in a slow circular motion. The swelling and damage receded back to normalcy. A soft groan rose out of Unc's mouth. Unc's body started to convulse uncontrollably. Her angel paused his chant and lifted the solid wastebasket from the side of the bed. Unc sat up, and his eyes popped open. They seem to stare into nothingness. Unc's mouth opened, and his head jerked forward. A black bile substance vomited out of his mouth. The stench of it was horrendous. May had to cover her mouth with the back of her hand and took a hard swallow. Unc's eyelids slowly closed, and her angel assisted him to lay back down.

"What was that?" May pointed to the wastebasket.

"Your uncle was bitten by a Judanite. It's the disease they leave behind in their victims."

"Judanites?"

"Yes, the same beings who tried to capture you tonight."

He carried the wastebasket into the bathroom. She had tons of questions to ask him. What the hell are Judanites? Where did they come from? By what she had witnessed tonight, they appeared and acted human, yet they didn't move or die like one.

Judanites were something completely different. What was her angel? He hadn't aged one bit in sixteen years. Could he really be an angel? One thing was clear: people held secrets, and the world had secrets too.

The toilet flushed and the faucet sounded. The water shut off and he came back out with a wet rag and a handful of clean towels. He wiped off the dried blood on Unc's body and face. This display of humanity touched her. She wanted to reach out and touch him.

He discarded the towel, reached behind his back, and drew out two long knives. Likely the weapons, he used to slay the Judanites. The reflection of the blades was exquisite—a golden rainbow. A type of metal she had never seen before. Pure artistry from another time, another world.

He took out a small aluminum bowl, a syringe, a needle, and a vial of some type of liquid from the first aid kit. He lined up his instruments in a row on the small table. He then picked up his knives, one upside down, and the other upright. He scraped the blade against the amber-colored gem embedded in the pommel of his second knife. A fine white powder flaked into the aluminum bowl.

"What is that stuff?" May said.

"It is called MaNa. You might have heard of it in Hebrew, manna."

"You mean manna, as in the Bible?"

"Yes."

May scooted closer to him. "So you're telling me the stuff you got right there fell out of the sky." Her face pinched in disbelief.

"No, what you've heard about manna is a story."

She tilted her head. "Where does it come from, then?"

Any of the transitional metals on the periodic table can form it, but gold is ideal.

"The stuff you have there is powder. It doesn't look metallic at all."

"The gold that was used to produce this MaNa is an ancient process that has been used for over seven thousand years. Only a select group of mystics knows how to produce MaNa. The knowledge is kept secret. But recently, though, modern scientists have developed working knowledge of this process, they call it m-state." He added a dab of liquid from the vial to the MaNa dust and started whisking it.

"How does it help, Unc?"

"It will help him recuperate faster."

May always knew there were mysteries that time had covered up, and now here she was rediscovering them. Her angel lined the syringe in the bowl and drew the MaNa liquid into it. He tied a rubber tourniquet to Unc's upper arm, and a vein popped out. He injected the MaNa into his system.

He repacked his tools. May noticed he moved with such fluidity, every gesture was measured, not a wasted movement. His demeanor portrayed a soulful manner. What had made him turn inward? She would find out.

She didn't know where they would go from here. It seemed foolish of her to love someone she didn't know anything about. It didn't matter, she believed her life was cut from the same source as his. All the episodes of her chasing his shadow seem justified. He was here with her now.

He stood over her. She wanted to kiss him.

"May I, Malayah?" He pointed to her ankle.

"Please call me, May. And, yes."

He knelt down, untied her shoe, and slipped it off. He gave her a reassuring look. His hands were attentive, and he carefully rolled down her sock. Her swollen ankle was the size of a softball.

"Believe May and your ankle will be healed." He cupped her ankle with his hands and mouthed a chant.

He didn't have to ask her to believe. She already believed he could do anything. Her ankle began to burn under his hands. It took on the same reddish-brown hue as earlier. The heat wasn't overwhelming or painful. It was like the warmth of a mother's embrace. She felt her energy converging toward her ankle. The throbbing ache went away, and the swelling regressed back to its normal size.

A wave of drowsiness crashed over her body, sleep invading her consciousness. She fought to stay awake. Her eyelids were too heavy. She grabbed his hands in hers.

"What's your name?"

"Dao-Ren."

Chapter 21

May startled awake and scanned the room for Dao-Ren. She knew she hadn't dreamed of the events from last night. She could still feel his caring touch on her ankle. She examined her past injury. She rotated it in a circular motion, clockwise and then counter-clockwise.

Where was he now? *Please, God not another sixteen years.* Her heart sank, and she took her hope with it. She yanked the shabby, threadbare blanket off her. She disliked these shanty motels. It stunk of sweat and stale cigarette smoke and probably showed nothing but porn on television.

May slipped on her tennis shoes. What type of car did he drive last night? All she could remember was that it was expensive. She glanced at the window. The day was still young by what she gathered through the bent metal blinds. It wasn't noon yet.

"Dao-Ren." At least knowing his name gave her a sense of comfort. She called out to him again and again, getting lost in the cadence.

"May, calm down!" Unc said, exiting out of the bathroom.

May focused on Unc's healed face. "Are you okay?"

"I feel great." Unc smiled. "No, I feel amazing."

The lock clicked and door knob jangled. Unc reached to his side for his gun. It wasn't there.

The door opened, and sunlight filled the room. The shadow of a man blocked the door. May held her breath.

*****

"What do we have, Pierre?" Jacques asked, standing behind the wide-eyed Judanite.

"One of the five looks promising," Pierre said, analyzing the graphs on the computer. He leaned to the side.

"What am I looking at?" Jacques questioned, staring at the colored zig-zag lines and dots on the monitor.

"It's probably easier to show you." Pierre rose from his chair. He motioned with his hand.

Jacques followed as he looked over the research lab. A lab technician wore a ventilation mask as he pipetted blood into glass vials and placed them into a centrifuge machine. Another technician put a tray of vials in the incubator. Multiple pieces of equipment covered the counters: a CRISPR electroporation, a high-performance microplate reader, a real-time PCR workstation, and other materials needed to manipulate the RNA of viruses.

"As you know, I have recombined different viruses to create a strain that has a high mortality rate and infection rate," Pierre said. "With the development of CRISP-cas13. I'm able to change the RNA of viruses to my liking." He pointed to a glass-covered container filled with vials of human blood. "We feed these vials to our fellow Judanites, hoping that one will mutate to our objective."

Jacques followed Pierre into a cavern hallway. Three steel doors lined both sides.

"We had our underlings feed on our human subjects until they became ill." Pierre paused by the first door. "When the human host gets sick, we put more human subjects in the confine area to observe if the virus becomes contagious." Pierre pointed to the door.

Jacques peered into the glass aperture. Three dirty humans crouched on the ground as one withered body lay on the cot.

"The one you're observing didn't become contagious or deadly," Pierre noted.

"How does this help our cause?" Jacques turned to Pierre.

Pierre smiled. "Until now." He moved to the last cell.

Two Judanites guarded the door.

"Get them out of there," ordered Pierre.

A guard opened the door to screams. Each went in and returned with a restrained human.

Pierre nodded. The two guards escorted the humans down the hallway.

Jacques walked in. Two desiccated humans were sprawled on the ground.

Pierre poked one of the dead bodies with his feet. "This one died this morning and the other last night."

Jacques crouched down and examined the bodies with his eyes.

"But patient zero is still alive," Pierre said. "She infected the others."

"What's the estimated mortality rate?" asked Jacques.

"My best guess is 40 to 50 percent."

"Does Caiaphas know of this development?" Jacques stood.

"Not yet."

"Let's keep it like that?" Jacques stepped over to the cot. "Feed on the other subjects and let them go."

"Yes sir."

Jacques sat on the cot and wiped the sweat off her forehead and brow.

"Her fever is already over 104 degrees. Her immune system is almost nonexistent to this point." Pierre looked down. "She'll be dead soon."

Jacques caressed her cheeks.

She blinked a few times before her sights settled on Jacques. She swallowed and smacked her dry mouth. "Ja-Jacques, help me."

Jacques grinned. "As you wish, Mademoiselle Kat." Jacques plunged his fangs into her neck.

Chapter 22

"What are you, Dao-Ren?" Bernardo asked.

Dao-Ren glanced at Bernardo, who was sitting at the table with a cup of coffee, and then at May. May's presence captivated him. She stared back at him from her standing position by her uncle. Her arms were down by her side, and her eyes were attentive.

"I'm an Awakyn," Dao-Ren said, "I had been resurrected from death by my spirit answering the call to re-enter my body. I'm no longer a human with a spirit. I'm a spirit with a body." He glanced at May, whose sight was locked on him.

"Are you immortal?" Bernardo leaned forward.

"Yes, but if I lose my body, my spirit returns to God." He heard May gasp.

Bernardo's brows furrowed. "Let me get this straight. If I die and I answer the call to resurrect, then I too will be an Awakyn."

Dao-Ren kept his arms by his side. "No, Bernardo. If you were resurrected from the dead, you would become an Elder. Elders can live anywhere from 300 to 800 years. They grow old until their physical bodies can no longer contain their spirits. Whereas an Awakyn is an Elder who has accepted the consecration of the Body and Blood of God revealed to us by Jesus."

Bernardo shook his head. "You're a Christian, then?"

"No. You don't have to be a Christian to become an Elder or Awakyn. You have to be someone with a pure heart and a sound mind."

"What religion did you follow before…?" Bernardo's eyes never blinked.

"My parents raised me Buddhist." Dao-Ren was surprised that Bernardo was taking the information well.

Bernardo took a sip of coffee. "What objective does the Body and Blood of God serve?"

"The Blood gives us immortality, and the Body gives us strength beyond mortal men."

Bernardo leaned his forehead against his fingers. "And what's the purpose of those gifts?"

"To keep balance on earth."

"From what?"

"Judanites."

Bernardo wiped his mouth with his hand and rested his chin on his hand.

"Judanites are those things from last night." Bernardo looked at him.

"Yes." Dao-Ren nodded.

"I thought they were vampires." Bernardo ran his hand through his hair.

"They're the myth behind vampires."

"They feed off human blood."

"Yes and no." Dao-Ren held Bernardo's stare. "Judanites siphon the spirit of their victims to remain functional. Blood only acts as a source of nutrients for their decaying bodies, like milk does for you."

"And the spirit does what for the Judanites?"

"It gives them immortality. Judanites spirit is contaminated with carnal energy. They need balance, so they must feed off other humans. If they don't, they would be in perpetual agony."

"And they kill their victims." Bernardo scooted to the edge of his chair.

"No. After they get their fill, the bite wound on the victim heals."

"That's why Unc didn't have a bite mark on him?" May asked.

"Correct." Dao-Ren met May's glance.

Bernardo's eyebrows rose. "I've been bitten."

Dao-Ren nodded.

"I don't feel like anything is wrong with me." Bernardo sat straighter in the chair, flexing his arms.

May touched Bernardo's shoulder. "Dao-Ren healed you last night, Unc. You don't want to know what was inside of you."

"What was inside of me?" He peered up at May and then back to Dao-Ren.

"A disease," Dao-Ren said.

"Why don't I remember any of this?"

Dao-Ren smiled at Bernardo. "You're perfectly fine. There's nothing wrong with you. Judanites have a special enzyme in their saliva that acts as a healing agent and anesthetic. During the siphoning of their victim's spirit, they give a part of themselves to the victim, like an exchange of life for death. It comes in the form of a disease or sickness."

"I have no spirit, then." Bernardo's arms shot upward.

"You still have a spirit. They can't kill a spirit. They can only leech off the spirit's life source."

"What's the purpose of this?" Bernardo's voice rose higher.

May patted Bernardo's back.

"To deceive. When a Judanite releases his victim, the enzyme in his mouth heals the bite wound in seconds and induces the victim into a deep sleep. When the victim wakes up, he has no idea he has been bitten."

Dao-Ren glanced at May to make sure she followed along.

"And when this person's affliction arises, he might blame God for this suffering. And if he remains in this contempt state, his spirit becomes contaminated with carnal emotions, and he would belong to Satan unless he repents."

Bernardo exhaled. "Satan, Judanites, spirits—for what?"

"Spirits give Satan greater power. And if he captures more spirits than God does, then Armageddon begins on earth. Satan is on a mission to destroy all of mankind because men are more powerful than him."

"How are we more powerful than Satan?" Bernardo shrugged.

"People have the ultimate power of free will. Satan can only be what he is."

Bernardo rotated his finger in a circular motion. "All this is about keeping balance between good and evil."

"Pretty much." Dao-Ren watched Bernardo get up and walk to the window.

"The diseases that Judanites leave behind in their victims must not be too difficult to treat. You healed me."

"You healed yourself, Bernardo."

Bernardo turned around.

"Laying of the hands is only assisting the flow of energy. My spirit guided your spirit to mend itself. You must have faith, though; if you don't, nothing will come of it."

Bernardo scratched the top of his head. "So basically, Awakyns battle Judanites."

"Most of us do."

"You're the good guys."

Dao-Ren allowed himself to chuckle. "Yes."

Bernardo exhaled and peered up to the ceiling. "It's so hard to believe. Nothing I had trained for at the bureau has prepared me for this. I just have so many more questions to ask you."

"I know you do, but it has to wait. Your ride is here." Right then, a knock echoed off the door.

Chapter 23

"The Exorcist Killer is a Judanite," Dao-Ren said.

Bernardo scrutinized Gasper and Otis before looking back at Dao-Ren.

"And how do you know this?" Bernardo asked.

"Those murders were a message calling me here. And I answered their summons on Olvera Street. I believe the Exorcist Killer murders should stop," stated Dao-Ren.

"Are you sure?" Bernardo said it with skepticism.

"Yes, unless there's a copycat."

Bernardo glanced at May, who sat on the bed with her hands folded in her lap. He didn't want her to go out there if the Exorcist Killer was still active. He needed to check on Kat's whereabouts as soon as possible.

"Okay." Bernardo let out a breath. "I need to get back to the office."

"Gasper and Otis will take you to your car." Dao-Ren motioned with this hand.

Bernardo faced the tall Spaniard with a thick-full beard and mustache and the light-skinned Black man. Gasper and Otis must be Awakyns, too. They held the same confidence and aura as Dao-Ren.

"I'm late for work. My partner is probably wondering where I'm at. I left in the middle of an investigation."

"You must be careful now, Bernardo. Judanites know who you are,"

Dao-Ren said. "Gasper, give me your gun and extra clips."

Gasper drew out a chrome gun from inside his leather jacket and handed it to Dao-Ren. Dao-Ren ejected the bullet out of the chamber and caught it. He held the bullet between his fingers.

"These bullets are made with a special mixture of metals called MaNa metal. They can stop and kill Judanites. One bullet won't do it, though. It doesn't produce enough energy to release them. You can release them by three ways with this ammo, two to the heart, three to the head, or five to the chest." Dao-Ren placed the bullet back into the chamber and closed it. "Regular bullets can't release them, no matter how many times you shoot them." Dao-Ren grabbed the barrel and held it out, handle first to Bernardo.

Bernardo accepted the gun and examined it. It was a Sig Sauer P320, a powerful handgun. He released the clip, sixteen bullets. The bullets were the same color as the shuriken he found at the crime scene. He popped the clip back in, shoved the barrel of the gun into the back of his trouser waistband, and covered it with the hem of the T-shirt Dao-Ren had bought him earlier. "Is there any other way to release them?"

"Yes, any mortal wound in daylight. The sun's energy will release them," Dao-Ren said. "Decapitation with any type of weapon should work. And any mortal wound delivered by a weapon forged in MaNa..."

"—I'll stick with the gun." Bernardo patted the gun. He studied May who stood next to him. "And about my niece?"

"She'll be under my protection until I believe it's safe," Dao-Ren said.

Bernardo hugged May. "I love you."

"I love you too, Unc."

He let May go and faced Dao-Ren. "I trust you. Just know that I love her very much."

Dao-Ren bowed his head. "I will protect her with my life."

***

Unc left with Gasper and Otis. May hated the idea of being separated from him. She was worried for Unc and for herself. The moment she stepped out of this room, her life would never be the same. May patted her pockets. She pressed her lips together. "Dao-Ren, may I use your phone?"

He studied her with his eyes before he handed her his phone. May dialed Kat's number and held it up to her ear. No answer. She hung up and started to pace the room.

"What's wrong?"

"It's my friend Kat. I haven't seen her since I left her at the club with Ricky."

Dao-Ren placed his hands on her shoulders and looked her squarely in the eyes. "We'll find her soon."

May ran her hand through her tangled hair. "I need to go home and get some stuff."

Dao-Ren thought a moment. He knew it wasn't wise to go, but he wanted to do something nice for May. "Judanites rarely move about during the day. Sunlight reveals their true nature. I think it should be safe to go."

***

"You stupid fool!" Jacqueline slapped Ricky across the face. Spit flew from his busted mouth. He remained on his knees.

"Why did you disobey me?"

"To prove myself to you." Ricky lowered his head.

"Don't tell me you're stupid, as you're attractive."

"I can kill him."

Jacqueline broke into a demented chuckle. "You're no match for Dao-Ren."

Ricky's face scrunched in anger.

"Why did you run then?" Jacqueline questioned.

"I thought the others…"

She seized Ricky's face with her fingers, her nails piercing into the flesh of his cheeks. "Look at the trouble you caused us."

Judanites were packing up the computer equipment around them.

"All I wanted you to do was capture Malayah, but you went after Dao-Ren… and now he has Malayah. You compromised us."

"It was never my intention…."

She pulled Ricky's head back by his hair. "I don't want to hear excuses. All I want is results. Go get me, Malayah."

Chapter 24

The shape of May's body diverted the sound of the steady stream of water from the shower nozzle. The distinctive notes that each splash made against her head, to the droplets on her shoulders that cascaded down her back, and then the rush off her legs were harmonious to Dao-Ren. He could breathe easy. She was safe.

He double-checked all the windows and entryways into her apartment. All were secured. Judanites hadn't broken into her apartment yet. They would soon enough. Most likely tonight.

By the looks of things, Kat never came home either. Her personal belongings had not moved since Dao-Ren viewed them last night. Her heart medication still sat atop the bathroom sink ledge. Dao-Ren didn't like that at all. Earlier, May had told him that she and Kat went to a nightclub the other night that she believed had Judanites there.

Oddly, Jacques didn't taste May's spirit. He detected nothing unusual when he healed her ankle. He needed to question her about that night, the sooner the better. There was definitely more to this than the obvious attempted kidnapping. *Cheng bai zai ci yi ju*—success or failure depends on his next move.

He opened the refrigerator and scanned the contents. He selected a bottle of Evian water. He uncapped the bottle and shaved some MaNa dust into it off the pommel of his knife. He capped the top and proceeded to shake the bottle as he walked into the living room.

The living room was styled with a collection of modern abstracts and classical flare. A thick, plush seventeenth-century couch in a rich, dark Victorian oak frame took up the center, which was placed on top of a posh Persian rug. The couch faced an intricately carved coffee table situated in front of a 52-inch flat-screen television with surround sound.

Two massive iron-cast bookcases with glass shelves lined the back wall of the living room. Dao-Ren paused to read some of the titles. She had an extensive collection of art books, ranging in topics from Roman sculptures to Asian porcelain making to Gothic paintings. She also had a fickle selection of different genre novels, from Jane Austen to Mark Twain to recent mass-market novelists.

The contents of the next bookcase snatched his undivided attention. A plethora of figurines and small statues covered the shelves. Not a single one was the same. Some were composed of jade or marble; others were carved out of wood; and a few were molded out of clay or plaster.

One specific statue stood out among all of them. It was etched from a deep-hued green jade stone. He traced his fingertips along the figure of a woman's slumped body, which was held up by an angel. Each dip and angle of her face was detailed the way he had remembered that night. May even captured the lifelessness of death on her mother's face.

The kneeling angel that cradled her mother was him. His head was thrown back, screaming up at heaven. She even added a pair of fiery angel wings that extended from his back. The flames were alive inside the jade. She carved a mirror image of that sorrowful night. How she recalled the intricate details of that night was beyond him.

"You like the statue?" May asked, walking out of the hallway. Her wet hair was tied back in a ponytail.

Dao-Ren faced her and hoped his expression could express it all. "I'm moved beyond words."

She stood next to him. "That's my favorite piece. It's the last moment I remember of my mom."

"I can't believe you remember that night."

"That night had burned into my memories."

"I'm sorry, May. I couldn't save her for you."

May touched his face. "Don't be sad. You tried. That's more than I could have ever asked for." She dropped her hand.

They both turned to the statue, lost in their own thoughts.

"You know, ever since that tragic night, I believed you were my guardian angel," May said.

"Your mother thought the same thing. That I was her guardian angel."

May grabbed his hand in both of hers. "You knew my mom."

"No, we had never met, but she sensed my presence. Some nights, when I watched over her in her childhood, she would talk to me about her day and thoughts. I would only listen."

"You watched over her for her whole life."

"No, I would check up on her now and then until she left for college."

"How were you there that night, then?"

"I was tracking a band of Judanites from Seattle. They left a trail of victims from Washington State to Oregon. I finally caught up with them in Eugene. They led me to downtown, and I ran across your mother. I was suspicious of the coincidence, so I diverted from tracking them and watched over your family." Dao-Ren held his eyes on hers. "Two days later, your father hit a patch of black ice and crashed into a power line. I pulled you out first from the wreck. You had a cracked skull and a broken arm. You healed yourself pretty quickly. I was proud of you." He squeezed her hand, and she held tighter to his.

"Your father was already dead. He had died on impact. And your mother was close to death. Her sternum was shattered, and two of her ribs had punctured one of her lungs. The ground reeked of gasoline."

"Stop, I know the rest." Tears swelled at the corners of her eyes. Dao-Ren wiped them away.

"Why did you leave?" May said.

"It has something to do with your family on your maternal side."

"What is it?"

"I wish I had the time to tell you right now, but we must leave here soon."

May nodded.

"Here, drink this." He handed her the bottle of water. "I mixed some MaNa into it. It will protect you from a Judanite bite for a couple of days."

May took the bottle and gulped down the water. Her expression relaxed on the last drop. "This stuff is better than coffee. My mind is totally clear, and I feel the energy surging through me."

"The MaNa acts like a superconductor in your body. They attach to your nerve endings, causing more impulses to shoot faster and quicker between synapses. It can heighten your cognitive ability and senses by up to fifty percent."

An object clanged against the floor, and the sound of footsteps commanded their attention. "May, we must leave now." Dao-Ren interlocked his hand with hers and guided her down the stairs. He stopped at the bottom of the staircase. He detected footsteps. He had to be extremely cautious with May by his side.

The air didn't have the foul scent of Judanites. This meant that the intruders were humans. Who were they? Maybe the police or the FBI? No. Bernardo would've warned them.

May squeezed closer to him.

He pulled a Beretta 92 from inside his jacket. He handed the pistol to May. "You know how to use this?"

"Yes." May studied the gun in her hand.

"If you feel you're in any kind of danger, shoot first."

"Two to the heart, five to the chest, or three to the head."

"No, May. These guys are humans."

"What?" She held him tight to his arm. "I can't shoot them."

"Don't worry. I'll handle these guys."

"How?" May's eyes grew wider.

"Awakyns can't kill humans. I'll knock them unconscious if they mean us harm." Dao-Ren crept to the end of the staircase and peeked around the edge. He viewed six hoodlums with their faces covered by a black ski mask and each armed with a SK. The hoodlums were spread out and headed towards their position. He turned to May and pointed up. Together, they ascended the stairs.

Dao-Ren directed his way toward the fire escape. His eyes reconnoitered on the go. A hoodlum with a gun was stepping through a window to his left. Dao-Ren punched him in the jaw. The hoodlum dropped to the ground. Another one came up from behind his fallen comrade with his rifle raised. Dao-Ren snatched the muzzle of the rifle and yanked him through the window. The gunman flew headfirst into the far wall.

Dao-Ren's senses flared up, and he detected the suppression of a trigger. He ducked down with May under him. Sniper shots erupted above them against the wall.

"Hide!" He pointed to the kitchen counter. May crawled around the corner, out of sight. When he was satisfied with May's relative safety, he stood straight up.

Multiple rounds hit Dao-Ren's upper chest.

He collapsed on the cold tiles.

Chapter 25

May looked in horror as Dao-Ren lay motionless on the hard floor. She wanted to go to him so she could help him. He remained still. She took a deep breath. He couldn't be killed that easily. He was immortal, right?

Gunmen quickly surrounded Dao-Ren's supine body, their assault rifles aimed at him. One of the intruders kicked Dao-Ren hard in the ribs. Dao-Ren didn't budge. Anger blazed inside May. She clenched the gun tighter in her hand.

"Is he dead?" one asked.

"I don't know. I thought he couldn't die from gunshot wounds," another said.

"He looks dead to me." The first one pressed the tip of his boot into Dao-Ren's head.

Dao-Ren kicked his legs to the side and spun on his back in a windmill swipe. He knocked down the gunmen around his vicinity with the spinning kick. He paused and flipped up to his feet before the other gunmen could regroup. He was on them. One strike, and each gunman succumbed to sleep. The last gunman got his assault rifle up and lit Dao-Ren up in the center of his torso. Dao-Ren scanned down at his chest, then back up at the gunman. The gunman's eyes got wide, and he took a step back. He discarded the rifle and scampered out the window.

Dao-Ren didn't go after him. He swiftly armed himself with his long knives and positioned his legs into a fighting stance, blades out front.

The smell hit May when the window imploded with hooded men with swords in their grasp. The same appalling stench as the substance Unc threw up last night. All the hooded men converged on Dao-Ren with their swords raised.

"Give me Malayah, and I'll let you live," Ricky said.

"Repent and God will have mercy."

"Kill him!"

A group of Judanites attacked Dao-Ren. Others began to search the apartment. May ducked back down behind the counter, both hands on the gun.

Steel clashed behind her. Dao-Ren couldn't possibly handle all those Judanites. She readjusted herself into a low squat. Bluish-black light reflected off the stainless-steel sink. She stared at the reflection, watching. Dao-Ren battled four Judanites. Despite their skills, none could get to Dao-Ren. He moved and attacked with a warrior's precision, commanding respect and fear from his opponents.

A Judanite suddenly eclipsed the reflection. May stared into the blackness of a hooded Judanite mirroring off the sink's shiny surface. The creature pounced onto the countertop as May spun around on her bottom, gun raised.

Sunlight filtered through the small kitchen window above the backsplash and washed the shadow away from underneath his hood. May took a sharp intake of air. His face was ashen and decomposed. His eyes were cloudy and dull. He sneered down at her, his mouth full of rotten teeth except for the long yellow canines glistening with saliva.

He inched closer. The gun shook in May's hands. He must have sensed her doubt. He smiled. May scooted back with her legs. He jumped toward her. She fired. Bluish-black light.

Covered in ashes, May didn't move. It took her a second to become aware of the Judanites around her. Malice lined their hideous faces. They wanted blood for their lost comrade.

A flash of MaNa metal whirled through them. May had to shut her eyes from the brightness of their simultaneous combustions. Gentle hands lifted her to her feet. She looked at Dao-Ren.

"Go down the fire escape. I'll be right behind you." He unburdened the pistol from May and turned his back to her.

May sprinted toward the fire escape. Gunshots fired behind her. She had to slow down—the shattered glass made the floor slippery. She stepped through the broken window onto the balcony. The ladder was already unlatched. She scurried down and dashed for Dao-Ren's car.

"Malayah, I need to talk to you."

May swiveled around to her name. Billy Jacobs strode toward her.

"What are you doing here, Billy?"

"It's about Kat," Billy said.

"Where is she?" May watched Billy with caution as she tried to keep a short distance from him.

"I'm going to take you to her." Billy lunged and grasped May's upper arm.

"Let go of me, Billy." May tried to pull away from his hold.

He held on tighter. "Shut up! You've already caused enough trouble."

"I said let go of me!" May twisted her hips and tugged her arm out of Billy's grasp. She reversed her motion and smashed her elbow into Billy's nose, feeling the cartilage snap.

"Ah! You bitch!"

May bolted for Dao-Ren's car.

***

The remaining Judanites encroached on Dao-Ren.

"I'm going to kill you and deliver your heart to Jacqueline," Ricky said, circling Dao-Ren.

Dao-Ren waited—he couldn't let them get behind him. Then he heard the soft purr of European engineering. The Judanites attacked. He dipped and evaded a killing thrust to his heart.

They reformed and attacked as one cohesive unit. Dao-Ren blocked a high sword blow with the gun and kicked another Judanite in the face. He took this opening and fired the pistol. The bullet struck the Judanite in the center of his forehead. Sunlight handled the rest. The others dove for cover.

Dao-Ren rushed towards the fire escape and jumped headfirst out of the shattered window. He enfolded himself into a tight double flip and landed in the alleyway. The Audi pulled up next to him, and the passenger door flew open. He slipped into the passenger seat as May stomped on the gas pedal and peeled out.

Chapter 26

"Why did the Judanites use humans to try to capture us?" May yanked the steering wheel sharply to the right into traffic.

"They use humans because Awakyns can't kill them or smell them like Judanites. Humans try to hold us down until Judanites can join the fight." Dao-Ren stared straight ahead with his hands on his knees.

"I could smell them, too." May wiggled her nose.

"The MaNa had made that possible. Humans can't detect their hideous scent. Unlike Awakyns, their bodies are decaying slowly."

"That's why they look like zombies." May looked out the corner of her eyes at Dao-Ren.

"Yes, sunlight exposes their true nature. Their corrupt spirit can't hide the truth from the light. Only in darkness do they appear whole and perfect."

May slowed the car down and pulled over to the shoulder. Dao-Ren faced her.

"I released a Judanite today," May confessed.

He placed his hands over hers. "You did right. He only meant you harm. The only mercy he deserved was being released."

"Why did you say, 'Repent and God will have mercy'?"

"It's their right to know that their corrupt spirit can be cleansed before they're released. If they full-heartily repent, their spirit will return to God. If not, they belong to Satan," Dao-Ren explained.

"Why couldn't you kill those human men who tried to kill us?"

"Judanites chose their fate when they became Judanites. No one can turn or force someone to become a Judanite. They chose freely and willingly, but humans have a divine right to be given a lifetime to seek forgiveness."

"You can't possibly mean that." May felt her body tense.

"Yes, I mean it. They're given this divine right. That's the gift of free will."

"So you're saying a person such as Stalin or Pol Pot will be shown mercy after they slaughtered millions of people?"

"Yes. If they genuinely seek forgiveness."

May narrowed her eyebrows and searched Dao-Ren's facial expression to find that he was joking. There was no denying it, Dao-Ren meant what he said. She had to fight against her own beliefs and values to understand his ideology. She was a strong believer in the phrase "you reap what you sow." His beliefs had no sense of fairness or justice, only mercy.

"Okay, let me put it like this. If you knew a certain Judanite would repent 10 years from now, would you let him live for the next 10 years?" May asked.

"No."

"That's the same with evil people like Joseph Stalin and Pol Pot. Kill one, save a thousand."

"Evil men are still people with a divine right and spirit, whereas Judanites are corrupt spirits living off of divine spirits. They're not the same."

"What would happen if an Awakyn killed a human?"

"That would never happen. Our spirits would not allow it."

May let his words filter through her mind, letting them marinate with her own thoughts. If Dao-Ren was dominated by his spirit, could he love her like she wanted and needed to be loved? Was it possible for him to feel her touch on his skin? He didn't even flinch when he got shot.

May met his eyes. His deep stare enamored her. He gave the impression that all was perfect in the world. He was close enough that she could smell his sweet scent. His penetrating gaze burned something in the center of her being. She let the moment gravitate her face toward his. Neither of them blinked. His exhalation touched her lips with anticipation. She parted her mouth.

A police siren blared behind them. "Do you need assistance?" the police officer said over his siren speaker. Dao-Ren pulled away, and May threw a sharp glare at the police officer. She faced forward and pulled back into traffic.

***

Dao-Ren used all of his willpower not to return his sight upon May. He was astounded at how quickly he had gotten lost in May's essence. He knew he had to deny her. As long as Jacques and Jacqueline walked the earth, his love was a curse.

"Head south down Highway 101 and exit off Grand Avenue," Dao-Ren instructed.

May cut her eyes at him, he could tell that she wanted him to look at her. He kept his head forward on the road. He had to be impartial. Humans do have a strong resilience to move on, and May had to move on without him, no matter how much it would hurt at first.

Chapter 27

M ay drove into an abandoned building.

"Keep going straight," Dao-Ren said, pointing straight ahead to a concrete wall. She hesitated and glanced at him for confirmation. He pointed with his chin. Anger rose inside her. She gripped the steering wheel tighter. Ever since their moment, he has retreated into some type of shell.

Five feet from the wall, the concrete floor descended into a ramp that opened up to an underground tunnel. May drove on. Overhead lights above the winding, paved road illuminated the tunnel. It was amazing how someone could have built this tunnel in the heart of downtown LA without the public becoming aware of it.

The tunnel was about a mile long and expanded into a massive cave at the end. May scanned the expanse. An enormous garage. There were hydraulic lifts, mechanic tools, and other equipment stationed throughout the place. A fleet of luxury vehicles were stationed in rows.

From the cache of exotic vehicles, May sighted her dark green Accord. She parked next to her car, got out, and retrieved her cell phone from the charger. She scrolled through her new messages.

"Dao-Ren, Kat hasn't..." She stopped short. Dao-Ren spoke with a tall regal woman. She couldn't hear their conversation, but the woman's brows narrowed as Dao-Ren talked. The woman shook her head.

Her dark eyes took May in. The woman gave her a friendly smile. Dao-Ren didn't even acknowledge May when he exited the garage.

"Peace be with you, May." Her voice was so sweet that it sang as she approached. "I'm Omarosa." She held out her hand.

May shook her hand.

"I'm sorry to hear about the difficulties you faced recently. It can be quite a shock to learn about Awakyns and Judanites without foreknowledge," Omarosa said.

May liked her immediately.

"You must be exhausted after your skirmish with the Judanites."

May leaned her head back. "How do you know about that?"

"We have high-tech equipment to detect Judanites' activities, especially when one is released. Their exposed spirit gives off immense heat."

The underground garage echoed with the high-pitched reverberation of a motorcycle. A street bike rode into view.

The rider was a mammoth of a man. He parked and erected himself to his full height of six feet and eight inches. He took off his oversize helmet, which revealed an angular, broad face with icy blue eyes.

"Hey, Willie," Omarosa said. "This is May. Dao-Ren brought her here."

With a raised brow, Willie looked at Omarosa.

Omarosa shrugged her shoulders.

"It's good to see you're safe, May. I just returned from investigating your apartment," Willie said.

May tilted her head as her eyes scrunched in confusion.

"I'm sorry." Willie smiled. "We investigate every single detection we receive from our tracking programs. We have to make sure no harm has been done to humans."

May nodded.

"Come, May. Let me show you around. I'll bet you have a ton of questions," Omarosa said.

***

Dao-Ren would apologize to Omarosa later. It was necessary to brush off her inquiry about May. It wasn't the time to reveal the truth about May's ancestry when the young woman herself didn't even know.

Dao-Ren felt the uncertainty stirring in Omarosa's spirit. He understood her worry.

In two days, he released sixteen Judanites, whereas the Los Angeles branch only released six Judanites in the metropolitan area in the prior eleven months and none in the last two.

Definitely, Judanites were staying under the radar. They had to be planning a major attack. Dao-Ren felt certain of this. He entered the command center. He focused his attention on the large computer screen. "Who-Dat, how many Awakyns are investigating the swine flu outbreak in Mexico?"

Who-Dat's fingers fluttered over the keyboard. The topography of central Mexico zoomed in on the screen. Red dots marked throughout central Mexico.

"We've got 23 Awakyns investigating the swine flu," Who-Dat said.

"Give me the updates from the last several hours," Dao-Ren asked, studying the topography.

"From the investigation, we're more than 90% certain that this influenza virus has been mutated by a Judanite. We were able to gather some samples from other Judanites before we released them. They've got the same type of protein and RNA from the original host. We're positive it came from a single source. These strains we found didn't mutate correctly to be spread to humans," Rita read off the screen on her desk.

"Did we locate the original human carrier?" Dao-Ren crossed his arms.

"When we found him, he was already dead. We ran some tests. They matched the strain we collected from the Judanites' samples. We haven't found the original Judanite as of yet." She focused her attention on Dao-Ren.

"I believe the original carrier is here," Dao-Ren stated.

"How do you know that?" Who-Dat swiveled in his chair to face Dao-Ren.

"Jacques and Jacqueline are staging something huge in LA." Dao-Ren let out a breath.

"Are you certain?" Rita asked.

"Without a doubt." He could see both of them from where he stood.

"I'm certain there was a large group of Judanites feasting in the nightclub called Les Tres on Thursday night. That means numerous people are walking around afflicted," Dao-Ren said. "Rita, I want you to screen the city's cameras on the Strip, where Les Tres is located. We must locate these partygoers and help the ones we can.

"Who-Dat, start calling back Awakyns from Mexico. I believe there's a massive contingent of Judanites under our very noses. They have been attacking me without concern for their losses. I fear a great battle is forthcoming."

Chapter 28

Ricky's screams echoed around the soundproof walls. The dreary room was dimly lit. A cool, moist film covered the stone walls. Chained, he hung naked by his arms as heat wafted off his fresh wounds.

A flash of a leather whip with a MaNa metal tip snapped against his back. He bellowed once more.

Jacqueline stepped from behind Ricky, dragging the whip onto the dirt floor.

"I'm disappointed in you, Ricky." She embraced the fury inside of her, her face tightened. "You're a fucking coward, unworthy to live amongst us." She flexed her arm. The whip lashed out and struck Ricky down his chest. His left pectoral split into two meaty slabs of flesh. His head slung back in a torrent of pain.

"In spite of your cowardice, I forgave you and sent you on another mission. Again, you failed me. You can't even do one simple thing I ask of you. What are you good for?"

"I'm sorry."

"Sorry!" Jacqueline twirled the whip over her head and popped the MaNa tip into the pit of his stomach. Ricky screamed in silence. The pain was too much to voice. His body revolted against the MaNa. Jacqueline tugged on the whip, which caused short stabs of pain to rack Ricky. His pain was the same as she felt about his disappointment.

"I had high hopes for you, and not only in my bed." She yanked the MaNa tip out of his stomach.

Quiet steps approached her, then arms encircled her waist.

"He's too young and weak to even throw blades with Dao-Ren," Jacques said into her ear. "But I do understand, my love. Ricky should have perished on the edge of Dao-Ren's knife to show his loyalty and commitment to you." He nuzzled his nose against her neck. "Ricky's too self-centered to die for you. That's what separates everyone else from me. I died for you already by drinking the blood of my Father." He kissed the nape of her neck. "My love, I have another mission for Ricky to redeem himself. If he fails us again, he'll suffer by thirst for a hundred years, and then we'll kill him."

Jacqueline shifted around in her husband's arms and peered up into his face.

"I devised a plan to get both Dao-Ren and Malayah into our hands. And then you can rip out Dao-Ren's heart again." He kissed her cheek. "And on that day, you'll love me the most in the world."

Jacqueline studied Jacques face. She noticed the slight twitch of anger under his dull eyes. The knowledge of Dao-Ren being a thorn in her heart had been poisoning Jacques' own heart. Whatever the feelings, she wasn't ashamed to use this infection in his heart for her own purpose.

She believed every word Jacques proclaimed. They had been together for over thirteen hundred years, and he had delivered on all his promises. All except the beating of Dao-Ren's heart on a silver platter. And one day he'll deliver that promise or die trying.

The thorn in her blackened heart had been festering with blistering hatred for Dao-Ren. The hate consumed her. That's all she knew, and she lived off it until Jacques entered her life. His commitment to her was beyond the outer limits of love. He denied his spirit and soul to be with his true passion, her.

Jacques stroked Jacqueline's smooth, pale skin. She concentrated on his dull eyes, eyes that were once filled with such passion that they blazed with inner brilliance. She felt a little tug on her heart, a tug that had been nonexistent since she turned into a Judanite. It was a nostalgic feeling of long-ago sympathy.

She slightly shifted in her memory of her role in manipulating Jacques. The Father had ordered her to seduce Jacques to join their cause. Sex was her most lethal weapon. She had used it in ways that made men and women kill for her. She had controlled some very powerful men throughout history for the Father. No one could resist her lure except Jacques.

Jacques Saint-Clair was a captain under his distant cousin, Charles Martel. He was the determining factor in the victory at the Battle of Poitiers. He had led a legion of knights and foot soldiers that flanked the army of Sultan Abd al-Rahman of Andalas. Jacques had changed history with his military brilliance.

Jacques was known among the troops as a man of God, a strict and devoted Christian. He didn't have any known vices. He didn't engage in sexual conquest, drink alcohol, or pursue wealth.

He preached to his men that they should be more devoted than any Muslim, for they followed and worshiped God in the flesh, Jesus Christ. He had demanded they pray ten times a day, twice as much as any Muslim. His men had cherished his spoken words. They secretly believed he was a descendant of Jesus because his bloodline was Merovingian.

Legends had spoken that the Merovingians were direct descendants of Mary Magdalene, who had mothered Jesus' only child. These legends were spun and spread by the Father. The truth about Mary Magdalene had been eroded and covered up by the sands of time. Only a select few humans had truly known the truth about whose child Mary had carried; and Jacqueline had been there to bring one of the lost sons back to his Father.

Charles Martel feared Jacques' influence over his army. He plotted to discredit Jacques. Therefore, he had sent his mistress, the Harlot, to seduce him. The Harlot's influence was deep, and many didn't even know when they were under it.

Not by any means would Jacques bite the apple of temptation that the Harlot had brought. He was immune to her advancements and ways. Yet the most unexpected thing happened. Jacques fell insanely in love with the Harlot, a love that went so far as to change his beliefs in God. He truly believed with undying faith that this love he felt was God's love manifested in the Harlot. This was not the Harlot's doing, but rather Jacques own heart and the fulfillment of his religious lust.

When the facts of his lineage were revealed to him, it shook him to the core of his faith. He tried to refute it, but the truth couldn't be denied when he met the Father, his progenitor, for the first time. Jacques saw his features reflect back to him when the Father stood before him. He was a seed of Judas Iscariot. He was sickened by this revelation and claimed the Judanites were evil incarnate. Nevertheless, his love of the Harlot was ubiquitous, he couldn't live or be without her. This self-inflicted love was the catalyst for his denial of his spirit and beliefs.

The Father siphoned Jacques spirit and blood, and Jacques drank the Father's spirit and blood to become what the Harlot was, a Judanite. Jacques struggled at first with the inner battles of what he considered right and wrong. The taking of the spirit of man to stay alive and functional had tormented him. First, he only took the spirits of evil men, the ones he thought should die a horrible death.

It took a century for the abhorrent ways of the Judanites to eat away at his conscience. His solace and alleviation for his deviant acts was the Harlot. He found refuge in her embrace. Yet the Harlot wasn't so forthcoming in reciprocating his spoken love and devotion. Her whole essence was filled with hate, she could love no one.

In time, she had come to cherish Jacques in ways that love could never define. Therefore, she honored him by taking the name Jacqueline, the first true name she had taken since she was human.

Now, Jacqueline felt pity when she gazed into Jacques' eyes. A person she couldn't fully love. She enfolded her arms around Jacques' neck.

"Make love to me, my husband."

Jacques slipped the straps of her chemise from her shoulders and yanked her close. He kissed her along the neck. Jacqueline saw Ricky watching Jacques with pure disdain. She winked at Ricky before she locked lips with Jacques.

Chapter 29

ay looked up at the ceiling. "You're telling me we're under the Cathedral of Our Lady of the Angels?"

"Yes, we donated funds to have it built," Omarosa said.

"So, Awakyns are part of the Catholic Church?"

"No, we're independent, but we do have secret sects in every major religion: Buddhism, Christianity, Islam, Hinduism, and some others. We've discreetly assisted in many religious constructions throughout the world, from orphanages to schools. The war between good and evil is fought on many fronts."

May nodded and followed Omarosa down to the end of the hall, which hived out into five different entranceways. Each door had a number and its own department name. Omarosa pressed a button by the door with the word "Training" written in white. The door slid open.

The training area was spacious and brightly lit. The very center of the room was open with a cushioned, plastic covered floor mat. The far wall was lined with rows of aluminum racks filled with weapons. There were racks of swords, from sabers to rapiers to samurais. Another section held axes and hatchets. There was even a whole row of spears. All were forged with MaNa metal.

The opposite wall had racks of modern weaponry. May saw bows and arrows, assault rifles, and pistols. Adjacent to this wall was a door labeled "Shooting Range."

"We mostly practice our swordsmanship," Omarosa said.

"Why MaNa metal?"

Omarosa smiled. "MaNa makes the metal of the weapon more conducive to our spirit. Our spirit flows through us into the weapon, causing a surge of white light. This invisible light releases the contaminated spirit of Judanites when you wound them mortally."

She selected a scimitar off the rack. May accepted the sword and examined the curve MaNa blade. Light shimmered off the blade like the sun reflecting off an ocean wave. She admired the artisanship. The handle was inlaid in gold in an intrinsic Islamic pattern that swirled into a three-blossom stemmed flower, the same symbol that she had viewed on Dao-Ren's knives.

"What does this symbol stand for?" May pointed to the flower.

"It's an almond blossom. You can say it's the unofficial symbol of Awakyns. We don't promote ourselves in any way or fashion. Yet the almond blossom share a history with us," Omarosa revealed.

May slid her fingers over the engraved symbol.

"The person who concocted the MaNa metal was a Hebrew. And in Hebrew, the word for almond is shakad. Shakad has the double meaning of vigilant or awakening. After he fashioned the first sword with MaNa metal, he stamped the almond blossom on it. The almond plays an important role in Hebrew history. The almond symbolized the dependability of God. And we've taken the name Awakyns, which means to be vigilant against the snares of evil. People depend on us to balance the powers of good and evil. We've awakened God's power within us."

May lifted the blade, and it sung through the air. *Almond-shakad-vigilant-Awakyns.*

***

Dao-Ren admired how Rita and Who-Dat typed on their keyboards. Such synergy between them.

"I found something," Who-Dat said.

Dao-Ren returned his view to the main screen.

"I cross-referenced the street cameras throughout the metro area against the database of the known leaders of the Judanites. There weren't any matches." Who-Dat peered up. "Until my genius wife incorporated the semi-reflection of people's profiles mirrored by the storefront windows. And we got one match six days ago from a storefront window on Melrose Avenue." Who-Dat tapped a few more keys. A blurry picture of a hooded figure appeared on Fred Segal's display window.

Immediately, Dao-Ren identified the face as Caiaphas. Their situation has gotten more serious than what he initially perceived with only Jacques and Jacqueline in the equation. Dao-Ren being called here with the murders didn't make sense. After he had thwarted Caiaphas' genocide missions multiple times. Caiaphas wouldn't have allowed Jacques and Jacqueline to call upon him personally. This meant Jacques and Jacqueline were acting on their own accord.

Regardless of their strenuous relationship, the three together were very dangerous. The last time these three were in bed together, they had induced a baby apocalypse, which the world knew as World War II.

Caiaphas directed Adolf Hitler's rise to power. He guided Hitler on how to exploit people's fears to form unity against other ethnicities and cultures. The same tactics Caiaphas had perfected during his time as the high priest. He rationalized Hitler's evilness and cruelty into the idea that Hitler should rule over Europe as the Supreme Leader of a Great Aryan Nation. Hitler blitzed through Europe and annexed countries before his god complex led to his death. As Hitler's ego grew, he became more convinced of his own infallibility. In the end, his own arrogance sealed his death.

Jacques had masterminded the climb of Benito Mussolini. He had advised Mussolini to imperialistically invade Ethiopia and Albania, and encouraged Mussolini to form an alliance with Hitler to strengthen their position in Europe and Africa. Soon, Mussolini's narcissism became his downfall. He disregarded Jacques advice and lost successive battles in Africa. Jacques had no patience for intolerance, he had Mussolini killed for his ineptitude.

Jacqueline had controlled and manipulated the Emperor of Japan, Hirohito. Through Hirohito, Jacqueline propagandized the mystical belief that Japan was a superior race. It was the catalyst for Japan's ambition to imperialize Asia. After they had gained a stronghold in the Pacific, Jacqueline had advocated for Emperor Hirohito to sign a pact with the Axis Powers of Germany and Italy. Japan's self-idealism caused their own destruction when they bombed Pearl Harbor.

It had been a struggle for Dao-Ren to sit back and let things play out when so many innocent lives were sacrificed by a few tyrannical, evil men. Still, Awakyns could not interfere in man's wars or conflicts, nor would they assist or aid certain armies to victory. Free will always prevailed in the midst of chaos, no matter how dire the consequences.

An Awakyn's mission was to balance out the evil acts of Judanites by battling and releasing those Judanites that fought alongside men. It was Awakyn's duty to weed out Judanites, keep the playing field of men even, and aid the downtrodden so they would not lose hope in humanity.

Dao-Ren heard the soft, padded footfalls of someone entering the command center. The ones he'd come to recognize as May's. He felt her piercing gaze on the back of his head. He didn't looked her way.

"I know that man," May exclaimed.

Everyone's attention locked on May. She pointed at the photo on the screen.

"He was in the club that night."

"Are you certain?" asked Omarosa.

"Do you have a clearer picture?"

Rita accessed Caiaphas' dossier. There he stood with his beady little eyes, a long face, and protruding ears. He was the Sadducee who hired Judas Iscariot to betray Jesus for thirty pieces of silver and orchestrated the conspiracy to kill Jesus. He became the first Judanite.

"That's him," May confirmed, shifting from foot to foot.

"Hello, May. I'm Rita, and the man over there is my husband, Who-Dat. When and where did you see Caiaphas?"

"At a nightclub called Les Tres on the Strip this Thursday night."

Who-Dat typed in the location. From street cameras, random shots of people flicked across the monitor.

"Can you find my friend, Kat?" May moved closer to the screen.

"Do you have a photo of her?" Rita asked.

May took out her cell phone and pulled up Kat's picture. Rita linked the phone to Thelma.

Photos flashed on the screen.

"Warning! Phone is being tracked." Thelma voice echoed off the speakers.

Who-Dat and Rita typed rigorously on their keyboards.

"We're reverse tracking now," Rita said, punctuating with a pound of the enter key.

On another wall monitor, computer codes flashed. "The phone is being tracked by." Rita did a few more keystrokes. "Trent Blake."

May gasped.

The flicker of pictures slowed to a single thumbnail. Who-Dat doubled-clicked on it. A video of a muscle-bound bouncer carried an unconscious Kat out of the club as a short guy walked next to them.

"That's Billy Jacobs," May blurted. "Oh, shit I forgot. Trent and Billy were lab partners in high school."

May's worried tone drew Dao-Ren's attention to her concerned expression. He felt his unease grow as things got more complicated.

"We have to go find her…" She grabbed his hand and yanked on his arm. "…before they kill her."

Chapter 30

The house on Olvera Street was sealed off with police tape, and the evidence had been packaged and delivered to the forensic lab. Bernardo came to further investigate if there was anything else he could learn about Awakyns or Judanites. He owed it to the victims' families to arrest the culprit. The killer being a Judanite was something he'd deal with when he located him.

Before yesterday, Bernardo believed he understood the world around him. They were good people and bad people, but they were still people. And now, his mind couldn't make sense of Awakyns and Judanites. Even after, he witnessed both of them.

Bernardo squatted and flipped over a fallen painting. It was a copy of the Mona Lisa. He surveyed the room and the other paintings along the walls. They were simple paintings depicting Jesus' last moments from his crucifixion to his resurrection—Stations of the Cross.

These paintings were the complete opposite of the Mona Lisa. He re-examined the Mona Lisa, there was an inscription at the bottom: *Truth is gold. You have to mine, drill, and dig to fully understand the nugget of knowledge that you obtain. Yet you have to be mindful to discern the truth, for it could lead you to a foolish end. Gold is not always gold.* He studied the Mona Lisa to see if anything would strike a connection with the inscription.

"Bernardo."

He shot up with his gun in hand and pointed at the doorway. Gasper stood there.

Bernardo exhaled and lowered his gun. He strapped the gun back inside his shoulder holster. His sights never wavered from Gasper's eyes.

"You're not here to stop me," Bernardo said.

"No." Gasper emphasized with a headshake.

Bernardo folded his hands in front of him and regarded Gasper. "Why?"

"Free will." Gasper wiped the dust off a table before he sat down. "And it is your job."

Bernardo grinned. "Then tell me how strong are Judanites."

"At least twice as strong as any man. The longer they live, the stronger they become."

Bernardo felt some hope. "Can a SWAT team handle one?"

"Yes, if they have MaNa bullets." He folded his arm across his chest.

How will he get the SWAT team to use MaNa bullets? He'll figure it out later. Bernardo touched his neck, where the creature had bitten him. There was something more pressing that he needed to know. "Will I turn into a Judanite?"

"No, there's only one person who can turn people into Judanites. The one they call Father. He must siphon some of your spirit and blood first, and then you must drink some of his spirit and blood to transform into a Judanite."

Bernardo's shoulders relaxed. "Who's the Father?"

"Judas Iscariot."

This whole situation got odder by the second. "So there's a Christian connection."

"Only because the writings were preserved in the Bible, it has nothing to do with Christianity as a whole."

"Why is there a portrait of the Mona Lisa here?" He directed his eyes to the painting on the ground. "It matches none of the other paintings."

Gasper followed with his eyes. "A long time ago, both Awakyns and Catholic priests lived in this house. The painting was a gift to this branch by a devoted friend to Awakyns."

Bernardo didn't want to know who the friend was.

"What's the meaning of the painting?" He asked instead.

"It represents balance."

Bernardo's eyebrows gathered, and his head cocked slightly back, not understanding Gasper's words.

"You have to search for the answer," Gasper said.

"And where do I begin?"

A glimmer flashed in Gasper's eyes like an old memory resurfacing. "Mona Lisa is an anagram, and the key is prime."

He considered Gasper to see if he was joking. Prime, that helps a lot. "Anyways, I need to know something. Were they after May last night?"

"I believe so."

"Why?"

A noise thumped from the upstairs dormitory. Bernardo peered up and drew his gun. When he looked back, Gasper was gone.

***

It didn't make any sense. How could Trent be involved with Judanites? May paced the floor. The only person who could have put the tracking app on her phone was Trent. But how? He was an NFL quarterback. When did he learn to become a hacker? May patted her head with her hands, hoping to shift everything into perspective.

The door opened into the entertainment room. May looked, hoping that Dao-Ren would walk through. Disappointment hit when she saw it was Omarosa.

"Did you find Kat?" May asked anxiously.

"I'm sorry. We're still searching," Omarosa said.

May closed her eyes to get her thoughts and emotions under control. When she was ready, she opened her eyes. Omarosa greeted her with a warm smile, as if they were old friends. The genuine warmth in her eyes put her at ease.

"I know you must be overwhelmed by everything that has occurred. You're more than welcome to share your concerns with me," Omarosa offered. "Please, have a seat."

May sat down, noticing for the first time that Omarosa had a tea set on a tray in her hand. As she settled into her seat, May couldn't help but admire the delicate porcelain cups and the aromatic steam rising from the teapot. Intrigued, she observed Omarosa's graceful movements as she skillfully poured hot water over the tea leaves, creating a soothing atmosphere in the room.

"How close are we to finding Kat?" May accepted the cup.

"I think we're close. We discovered Billy Jacob is a major producer in the porn industry." Omarosa looked directly at her. "One of the main sources of income for Judanites is the porn business. They use it as a means to fund their operations and maintain their secrecy."

The connection between Judanites and the porn industry piqued May's curiosity. "Why the porn industry?

Omarosa watched her momentarily, as if she wanted to reveal the information. "The porn industry serves two purposes for Judanites. One is money, but the second is their main purpose."

May leaned forward, her eyes narrowing with intrigue.

"They use it as a weapon against humanity by manipulating and controlling individuals through the exploitation of their desires and vulnerabilities," Omarosa explained. "By infiltrating the porn industry, they use lust as a tactic to tempt people away from God and lead them down a path of moral decay."

May nodded, her curiosity growing. "So, you're saying that the Judanites see the porn industry as a means to corrupt society and steer people away from their spiritual beliefs?" she asked, trying to grasp the extent of their manipulation tactics.

"Yes, it's a strategic method to weaken society and create chaos, ultimately hindering spiritual growth and unity among people," Omarosa further explained.

May leaned back. "What's the point in this for Judanites?"

Omarosa held May's gaze. "To corrupt spirits for Satan and usher in Armageddon."

May's eyes widened in disbelief, not fully understanding what she just heard. "Let me get this straight. Do Judanites believe that by corrupting society through the porn industry, they can bring about the end of the world?" she asked, her voice filled with doubt.

"Yes, they see it as one of the ways to fulfill their apocalyptic beliefs and pave the way for Satan's ultimate reign," Omarosa said.

May couldn't help but feel a chill run down her spine. It was disturbing to know that Judanites devised a method to manipulate spirits toward Satan. And with the aid of instant communication, how close were they to their goal? This was a lot to take in. May took a sip of tea, spotting that Omarosa hadn't made herself a cup. May spit out the remaining liquid in her mouth and put the cup down.

Omarosa detected her unease. "I'm sorry, May. You're probably wondering why I didn't make myself a cup."

May's mind was racing with questions about Omarosa's intentions. She needed to talk with Dao-Ren. She couldn't help but wonder if there was a hidden motive behind Omarosa's actions. The unease in the room grew thicker as May anxiously awaited Omarosa's explanation.

"Awakyns don't need to eat or drink," Omarosa revealed.

"What?" May exclaimed, her confusion deepening. She couldn't fathom how they could survive without sustenance. The revelation only heightened her curiosity about Awakyns and their mysterious abilities.

"Our bodies no longer need food or sleep to survive. Our spirits nourish our body and protects it."

May somewhat understood. "I saw Dao-Ren get shot multiple times and he didn't even flinch. Does this mean Awakyns can't feel?" May said, tilting her head forward waiting for an answer.

A coy smile appeared on Omarosa's face, as if she understood the real purpose of her question. "No, we can't feel mortal pain. Our spirit can't comprehend it. Our brain tells us we've been hurt, but it's inconsequential. On the other hand, we're not immune to emotions or feelings. Our spirit feels the power of love and even the sadness of loss. We feel everything that a human feels inside."

"You can love as we love?" This was her real question.

"Yes, we can feel love in all its aspects. Our spirit is the essence of love, the source of life, God's breath."

"You love everyone the same?" May leaned in even further.

"Of course not. There are many shades of love. A mother's love for her children is different from her love for her husband. Let me put it this way, if you touch my hand with love, I'll feel the emotion behind it because your spirit touches mine. We only experience the feelings of the spirit."

"Can you hate?"

"Not possible." Omarosa shook her head.

"How can you suffer if the spirit is pure love?"

"Compassion is a shade of love. When someone suffers, the spirit suffers as well. Sufferance is a measurement of love."

This was the reason for Dao-Ren's sorrowful expression. How much had he loved to endure so much?

The door opened, and Dao-Ren entered the space. He gave May the briefest smile, which was more of a twist of his lips. She looked into the depths of his eyes and saw the concern and worry. May's heart dropped in the pit of her stomach, and the tips of her nerves tingled with dread. She inhaled to steady her nerves and pushed herself up, ready to face whatever challenges lay ahead, standing on her own two feet.

Chapter 31

"Lock in your tranquilizer guns," Dao-Ren said against his throat sensor without speaking the words. The throat microphone detected the vibration from Dao-Ren's vocal cords, relaying the message to the rest of his team. He loaded his own rifle a dart.

Rita pulled out her laptop from a green satchel. A detailed satellite image of Billy Jacob's estate appeared on the screen. Red infrared figures marked all humans that were on the property.

"Two men are coming around the corner," Rita said.

Dao-Ren and Who-Dat sighted their rifles and took aim from the tree line at the back of the property. They fired their darts, and both found their targets. The guards passed out before they could report in.

"Let's move." Dao-Ren and Who-Dat gunned it straight across the bluegrass lawn to the gray stone mansion. They leaned against the wall by the front door.

"Rita, how do we look?" Dao-Ren asked.

"The infrared is picking up four bodies upstairs in the master bedroom, and there are five moving targets on the first floor. I'm sending their movements and layout to all your phones," Rita relayed.

Dao-Ren peered down at the phone screen strapped to his forearm. It displayed the layout of the mansion and the moving targets.

"Otis and Gasper, handle the three targets in your area. Willie, take the one on your end. Who-Dat will handle the one on this end. I'm going upstairs."

Everyone affirmed his or her assignments.

Who-Dat pulled out a set of metal lockpicks. He inserted two picks into the keyhole and twisted the lock counterclockwise. The heavy metal pin clicked. Who-Dat turned the knob, and they both swept into the foyer. Dao-Ren darted upstairs, and Who-Dat took off to the left.

Dao-Ren reached the double oak doors to the master suite. Loud giggles and hard moans could be heard. He viewed his phone for one last confirmation of where everyone was located. He freed his tranquilizer handgun from his hip holster. He adjusted his body and landed a front kick at the center of the door. The doors smashed inward.

Shrieks punctuated the silence. He aimed the gun at the bed. Three young ladies were naked, with sexual paraphernalia littered all over the king-sized bed. Two of the girls covered their exposed chests with their rail-thin arms. The third lay supine on the blanket, eyes wide open and glazed in a drug-induced haze.

Dao-Ren arched his gun to the left. Billy Jacobs was reclined in a high-back chair wearing a bathrobe. He lifted his face from a platter of white powder. He had a protective brace over his nose. His eyes were bruised and bloodshot. He gave Dao-Ren a dead man's grin, raised a bottle of bourbon to his mouth, and gulped a swig.

"Where's Catherine?" Dao-Ren questioned.

"I don't know. If you want some pussy, you can have one of them whores." Billy waved the bottle at the bed.

"I don't have time for your games."

"Or what! You're going to kill me?" Billy laughed. "I'm human."

Dao-Ren sensed the presence of his brothers entering the room. He approached Billy.

The drunken pig drew a pistol from his waistband and pointed it at Dao-Ren's chest. "You think you can take me on, huh?" he slurred.

Dao-Ren twisted the gun from Billy's grasp before he could shoot. He tossed the gun to Willie.

"Gasper, please escort these ladies out."

Gasper motioned for the young ladies to follow him.

Billy spat on Dao-Ren. He snatched Billy from under his neck and elevated him from the chair.

Dao-Ren's voice grew cold. "I might not be able to kill you, but you forget that I can break every bone in your body. One for every young, innocent woman you enticed with money and drugs."

"Fuck you." Billy squirmed in Dao-Ren's grip, his face turning red with anger and defiance.

Dao-Ren tightened his grip, causing Billy to gasp for air—his gaze widened with fear. Dao-Ren shot Billy in the stomach with a tranquilizer dart. The stench of excrement filled the air. He tossed him onto the bed.

"Rita, what's the intel on the basement?" Dao-Ren inquired.

"The walls are too thick. I can't get a read," she said.

"Send me the diagram of the secret basement then get the Hummer ready," Dao-Ren requested.

"Done."

Dao-Ren faced his brothers. "We're going in there blind."

Everyone nodded.

"Willie, stay out here and protect our backs."

Dao-Ren studied the diagram on his phone as he walked over to the built-in bookshelf stocked with pornographic DVDs. He dislodged two DVDs in the center. The bookcase slid over and revealed an elevator shaft. Dao-Ren unsheathed his two knives, with the others arming themselves with their MaNa weapons. They filed into the elevator.

The elevator descended three levels to a cavernous, man-made basement. A very faint smell of decay lingered in the cool, stale air. Judanites had been here recently, but they were all gone now. Dao-Ren crept into the basement. The basement was cleared out in a hurry. The only things left were two desktop computers and paper trash. He didn't detect any usual noise either. No one was here. Jacques and Jacqueline knew they were coming.

Dao-Ren motioned his hand toward the hallway at the back. Gasper and Otis broke off to investigate. Who-Dat sat down and started to hack into the computers.

Dao-Ren sheathed his knives and paced the room. He traced his sights along the edge of the ceiling. A shimmer caught his attention. It was a camera lens. He stared at it. A red light blinked—someone was watching them.

"Dao-Ren, come check this out." Who-Dat waved.

He obliged, peering over Who-Dat's shoulder. Circles marked certain areas on a map of Los Angeles that was displayed on the computer monitor.

"Download everything," Dao-Ren said.

Who-Dat took out a thumb drive and inserted it into the USB port. Dao-Ren picked up movements coming his way.

Gasper appeared with a body wrapped in a bed sheet. "She's close to death."

"Any others?"

"There's two more dead," Otis said, returning from the hallway.

Dao-Ren sighed. "Head back to the base."

Gasper and Otis disappeared into the elevator.

"I got it," Who-Dat stated.

"Let's go." Dao-Ren gave one last glance back at the camera. He knew Jacqueline was watching him. He turned his back and got into the elevator.

Chapter 32

Jacqueline stared at Dao-Ren on the monitor that sat on a table, her body tensed with rage. Dao-Ren gazed into the camera, his lips were pressed together, his eyes unblinking. She sprung at the monitor. She wanted to rip his face off. Jacques hooked his arm around her waist before she could murder the equipment. She twisted her whole body and freed herself from Jacques' hold.

She struck out with an open hand and clawed her fingernails across Jacques' face, strips of skin dangled off the four deep wounds. She positioned herself in a low stance, ready for an attack. Saliva dripped from her elongated canines.

Jacques lowered his hands, and his shoulders hunched in. He exhaled. "I love you," he said, walking past her out of the room.

Jacqueline kept her sight on him, her hands balled up into fists. The door closed behind him. She reverted her sights back to the monitor. Dao-Ren still stared into the camera's lens. His eyes narrowed into a scrutinizing gaze. She remembered that expression. He knew she was watching him.

Jacqueline returned his hard stare. The color of his eyes was no longer the same shade as she had remembered them. Sorrow and suffering had given his once light brown eyes a darker hue. She wanted to comfort him. She snatched her hand back when she caught herself reaching out to Dao-Ren. The rage was there to remind her of his abandonment.

There had been a time when Dao-Ren's presence was all that she needed. She had dreamed of a simple life together. The memory of their childhood was never too far from her consciousness. Memories came flooding back, obtrusive and unwanted. Why couldn't she forget them, or free them from the emotions of the past? Nothing was ever simple. Dao-Ren had helped shape who she was and who she was to become. They would always have a tragic history. She was a princess, and he was the third son of the Master Builder.

She and Dao-Ren had spent a great deal of their childhood together outside the palace walls in the vastness of the wilderness of her father's sacred kingdom. The landscape of their hometown was enchanted, littered with multiple crystalline lakes connected by bubbling streams and majestic waterfalls. A legend spoke of a goddess named Wonosmo dropping a mystical mirror given to her by her lover, the sky god, Dag. The glass shards created the clear lakes and waterfalls that dotted all over their kingdom.

Dao-Ren would imitate Dag, and she would be the goddess Wonosmo. It amused her how Dao-Ren could create a new version of the legend. He had created the best stories when he wasn't brooding or sullen. It was difficult for him to be the third son, ignored by his family and forgotten by his people, yet he had stayed loyal to his family.

Nevertheless, life was fragile. The lesson from this truth was harsh. Dao-Ren and she should have run away when they became lovers. Loyalty to his family was too strong to break away. Civil war came to the Middle Kingdom enflamed by greedy men with power. Everyone with an army wanted to be Emperor, and Dao-Ren marched off to war with his family for her father's ambition. Before he left, she gave him one-half of the broken turquoise stone, a symbolized piece of Wonosmo's fabled mirror, she had found in Mirror Lake. She expressed that he was the only one who could ever make her whole, and she would keep the other half of the stone until they reunited, making them whole again.

If she knew fate would be so cruel, she would have never let him leave. It would be ten years before she ever saw him again. During that span of time, she had been sold into slavery by her father; raped by her captor; betrayed by her people; and used by her enemy. Nothing had been left inside her except death.

Dao-Ren somehow made his way to her, and they were able to finally run away together. Could it be true that they would have another chance at life? He had changed as much as she had, but their love endured. She believed the nightmare was over and a dream was about to unfold. She was dead wrong.

The same army that Dao-Ren led to victory chased after them. The general wanted her. There was no escaping them. They were just too many. Dao-Ren decided to fight the soldiers to give her enough time to escape. She wanted to stay and fight by his side, but the last several years of survival overrode her desire. She ran fast without looking back.

Judas apprehended her as she attempted to flee. She knew who he was and what he stood for. He controlled the warlord who had her imprisoned. Judas was there from the very beginning, watching her through all her hardships. Judas made his proposal, and he knew her answer before she gave it. He must have detected the promise of hate in her to be a powerful Judanite. She was tired of her life being so precarious due to the whims of people in power. She could fight back now and win. Selling her spirit was nothing compared to being with Dao-Ren. God wasn't here anyways. It was an easy choice.

Dao-Ren had been captured and was jailed to be tried. She located the dungeon where Dao-Ren was being held. She killed all that stood in her way. No one could stop her. The power she possessed was unimaginable. She freed him from his chains and damnation.

When they reached a safe place, she had offered him what Judas had given her. She explained how the two of them could be together. The curse of a Judanite wasn't anything compared to the life they could share. They could finally be together, forever.

Dao-Ren couldn't bring himself to accept the offer of immortality. He had fought and battled Judanites and witnessed their pernicious nature. They had to find another way. She argued and pleaded with him, using their love as leverage. In the end, he refused and suggested she repent, so they could die together. The last of her hope faded, and darkness settled over her. Xin-Ji had perished.

She viewed Dao-Ren in a new light. He was the same as those who used her. He didn't want to share the burdens of life with her. So be it, her hand ripped into his chest, to his beating heart. He didn't even fight back. The only thing he managed to say was, "I love you."

She laughed in his face, not believing that he would think that she would grant him some mercy. She wrenched out his beating heart, and he died before he hit the ground. She fed his heart to a hungry mongrel dog. She gave Dao-Ren one last look of disgust and tossed the broken turquoise stone onto his exposed wound.

Days later, when she had been torturing her father, Dao-Ren, now an Awakyn, had come to rescue him. He was a warrior for God. The same God who let the world beat them down and steal their happiness and joy. *A God who sits idle and does nothing in the name of free will, a sworn enemy of hers.* In that moment, she had avowed to herself that she would kill Dao-Ren no matter what.

Now, Jacqueline glared down at her lifetime enemy. Damn him. A tornado of emotions wreaked havoc on her body. The hatred pulsed from her limbs. She snatched the monitor off the table and slammed it against the head of the dead woman that lay on the ground.

Chapter 33

"How long have you known Dao-Ren, Omarosa?"

"Around 800 years."

May studied her. She noticed the unique bond Dao-Ren and she shared, and the trust they had for each other. A platonic relationship?

"How old are you?" May asked.

"I'm 1023 years old. I was born in 996."

May's eyes widened in astonishment. The realization that Dao-Ren had been a part of Omarosa's life for the majority of Omarosa's existence left her in awe. That's why their connection ran deep. Still, Omarosa didn't look a day older than twenty-five.

"Awakyns must not age, then."

Omarosa shifted to another station in the command center. "Yes and no. If you were a child or a teenager when you accepted the call to become an Awakyn, you would age until you were about 28. And if you were older than 28, you would regress back to 28."

"Why's that?"

"That's what the spirit looks like. Our bodies' mold to the shape of our spirit," Omarosa explained.

"So your appearance is that of your spirit?"

"No, I'll say more of a projection of our spirit," Omarosa said. "Our physical appearance reflects the essence of our spirit, capturing its true nature and energy."

Curiosity got the best of May. "Did you change much from your former self?"

"I pretty much look the same." Omarosa wore a Chanel outfit tailored just for her. The off-white silk shirt and tan slacks complemented her dark, flawless skin.

May leaned back in her chair and reflected on what she just heard. Everything an Awakyn was and was about, dealt with the spirit. What about Judanites? Weren't they once humans with a spirit? If they had a spirit that was pure love, then how could they do the things they do?

"Omarosa, do Judanites still have a spirit?"

"Yes and no." She typed a few more codes into Thelma and turned to May. "You know that Judanites were once humans, and like all humans, they have three aspects that make them human: a spirit, a soul, and a body. The body is the flesh and bones of your carnal self. The spirit is energy with a single purpose of love. No human can live without a spirit, the source of all life. With that said, what do you think the soul is?"

May paused for a moment, contemplating Omarosa's question. She hadn't thought much about what a soul was. "I believe the soul is the essence of who we are as individuals," she finally responded. "It encompasses our thoughts, emotions, and consciousness, and it's what makes each person unique."

"You're not too far off. The soul is the connection between your spirit and your body. Some people like to call their mind. What you fill it with is what you become. There's a constant battle and struggle against your spirit and body. The source of free will," Omarosa said. "The soul is also the ultimate gift to mankind from God. The soul is the power of free will. To choose to do as you please is to be god-like."

May stared off and bit her bottom lip. Could it be? She looked back at Omarosa. "So you're saying the struggle between your spirit and body is the source of free will at work, to do as you wish."

"That's about right." Omarosa nodded in agreement. "The struggle between our spirit and body is what allows us to exercise our free will. It is through this battle that we are able to make choices and decisions according to our own desires and beliefs." She paused for a moment before continuing, "If we only had a body, we wouldn't have free will because we'd do whatever the body wanted. However, with a spirit, people have choices about right and wrong."

It made sense what Dao-Ren told her. May looked directly at Omarosa. "That's why Awakyns don't interfere with people's lives because all people have the power to change—the power of free will. By honoring and nurturing free will, we allow each person to shape their own destiny and take responsibility for their actions."

Omarosa smiled and nodded. "And your spirit talks to you through your conscience. That's the reason why people have an innate sense of right and wrong. Your body uses carnal emotions such as hate, envy, and so on to control you in this world. And this struggle between your spirit and body wages on until death. When death comes and a person is filled more with the fruits of the spirit, they'll return to God. But if they're consumed more with the bondage of the body, then they'll remain on earth."

"What do you mean on earth?" May asked.

"Our spirit is pure energy, the source of God's love. Nevertheless, there's also carnal energy. Emotions that hold people down, like anxiety, fear, and lust. These carnal emotions can weigh the spirit down and convert its energy. The same way solar energy can be converted into electrical energy. The corrupt carnal energy coalesces with the greater source of the spirit. The spirit will be in a constant flux of emotions. They will no longer be a spirit but a ball of carnal emotions. And when that person dies, their energy will remain on earth."

May was lost. "How does this pertain to Judanites?"

"Judanites had chosen the energy source of carnality. When they turn into a Judanite, their spirit is polluted with the emotions of the carnal world. It cannot sustain life like a spirit should." Omarosa paused for a moment. "How quick does anger fade when you're upset?"

"Within several minutes."

"Do you feel drained and tired afterwards?"

"Definitely."

"That's what carnal energy does to Judanites. They'll be in constant agony and pain, and if they cannot balance it with the spirit. They'll…"

"They are returning," Thelma announced.

May and Omarosa leapt out of their seats. May followed Omarosa out of the command center. They ran to the transportation area. The black Hummer's tires squealed to a stop. The doors flew open, and Gasper hopped out with a body in his arms.

May noticed the pink highlights in her blond hair. They found Kat. May started to breathe heavily. Kat's limp body didn't look right.

Gasper headed straight into the hallway. May couldn't decipher Gasper's expression. Was Kat dead? May remained there by herself as everyone else trailed after Gasper. She folded her arms over her chest, scared to face the truth of Kat's situation.

Another car pulled to a stop. Dao-Ren and Who-Dat got out. "Check out the communication links," Dao-Ren said.

"Got you."

Who-Dat paused and touched May's arm. "She's going to be okay. Have faith."

May nodded, and Who-Dat rushed off. She met Dao-Ren's eyes, and he offered his hand. Kat needed her. She inhaled and accepted his hand.

Dao-Ren led her to the infirmary. Everyone surrounded a single bed. Kat lay there her face was pale and dry. It looked as if life were saying goodbye to her. Gasper had his hands over Kat's midsection, and his lips moved in prayer.

Rita pulled out a needle from Kat's arm. She held a tube of Kat's blood in her hand and left with it. May released Dao-Ren's hand and slid over to the bed. She leaned over and tucked loose strands of Kat's hair behind her ear. She brushed Kat's cold cheek and bent close to her ear.

"Hey, you, guess what? I found my angel. He's even more handsome than I remembered." May stroked her face. "He's perfect. And, yes, he smells good." She laughed softly. May grabbed Kat's hand and kissed it. "You were right. All those self-healing classes you attended were true. You can heal yourself. You've got to believe." May shook Kat's limp hand. "You can't go. I need you."

Tears fell from May's eyes onto their intertwined hands. A breath later, May felt a glowing warmth stirring in the center of her being. Instead of pulling away from it, she embraced it.

The warmth raced through her body and exploded. A bright light imploded in her mind. It felt like a dream. She experienced herself leaving her body into Kat's.

May streamed up Kat's body. Everything inside of her was black and decaying. Little starfish bugs devoured Kat's internal organs. She pressed past Kat's heart, which barely pumped with life. She plunged deeper into the darkness, towards the slither of light in the far distance. She didn't know what to do next. She just journeyed onward to the light source.

The light ran away from her. She knew it was Kat.

"Kat, stop!" May shouted in her mind. "Kat!" The light stopped. May crashed into Kat's spirit, she felt how weak Kat was.

"Kat. It's me, May. I'm here for you." She experienced Kat letting her in. She circled herself all over Kat's spirit.

What was she supposed to do now? All she could think of was to backtrack. May spearheaded back into the darkness. The darkness ran from them. Kat's presence grew more powerful with each space they reconquered. Kat's heart pumped stronger and black starfish bugs imploded into a liquid waste.

Gravity pulled at May. She couldn't hold onto Kat. Her heart raced, and her eyes snapped open. It was bright and unfocused. Soon, it cleared. Kat laid there unmoving and still as death. Did she do enough?

All of a sudden, Kat's body jerked up. Otis had a bowl under Kat's mouth, and she vomited up a black substance. Someone touched her shoulder. She peered up into Dao-Ren's proud eyes.

"She will live," Dao-Ren proclaimed.

Chapter 34

Ricky could still hear Jacqueline's moans when Jacques took her in front of him. The image of their copulating burned in his memories. His own mind turned on him. Those flashbacks tormented him worse than the whipping Jacqueline had unleashed on him. The stabs of jealousy from their lovemaking had infected Ricky both mentally and physically. Nothing could bandage those wounds except Jacques' death.

Those agonizing memories tended to pop up when all was quiet. He had to control himself. He began to tap his finger on the cherry wood armrest. He was in Jacques' spacious study room, which was decorated with a few pieces of classical French furniture. The dim chandelier lights hung above him while he sat still in a cherry wood, satin-covered armchair in front of Jacques.

Ricky wanted to reach across the desk and rip Jacques' throat out. He despised that Jacques had saved him from Jacqueline's punishment. His intercession highlighted Ricky's failures for all to see, with the true torment of Jacqueline's mercy being that she did it for Jacques. She had no sense of mercy. The act showed Jacqueline's affection for Jacques.

Jacqueline strolled into the room in a tight dress. She ignored Ricky when she past by. Jacques rose to greet his wife with a light kiss. Ricky's fingers clutched the armrest, cracking the century old wood.

Jacqueline did this to punish him even more. She really didn't care for Jacques. She told him this much. She had always reminded him that he had a face she had once loved. She would attack him without warning, and he would welcome the abuse, for afterwards they would make love.

Jacques sat back down behind his enormous, detailed cherry wood desk. Jacqueline positioned herself by Jacques side, her arm draped over his shoulder. Jacqueline acknowledged Ricky with a disdainful smirk. She knew his weakness, and she exploited it.

"If you fail this time, Jacqueline will have her way with you," Jacques said.

Hatred blazed inside Ricky.

"Capture Bernardo Vega and bring him to us."

"Your order is my duty."

Ricky held Jacques' stare. Jacques' time would come. He took his time getting up. He hoped Jacqueline would say something to him.

The massive double doors burst open, and Caiaphas barged into the room with his retinue chasing after him. Caiaphas positioned himself in front of the desk and glared down at Jacques.

"What's this I hear about Billy's residence having been breached by damn Awakyns?" Caiaphas slammed both of his hands on top of the desktop.

"They were searching for Catherine," Jacques said, not bothering to stand up.

"I don't believe they chanced up and found her. They knew where to look." Caiaphas sneered, exposing his elongated canines.

Jacques held up a finger and looked at Ricky. "You may go."

***

"Have a seat, Caiaphas." Jacques motioned with his hand.

Caiaphas studied Jacques with narrow eyes before tugging on his blazer and sitting in the armchair. Ricky left unoccupied. He flicked his long, thin hand. His retinue shuffled out and shut the door behind them.

"Don't worry about the host. We have enough samples to give to our men to spread the virus. Catherine should be dead by now. Awakyns have nothing," Jacques said.

Caiaphas twisted his goatee with his finger. "That's not my worry. It's Dao-Ren. How the hell is he here? The last report I received three days ago was that he was in Eastern Europe. And this Exorcist Killer looks very much like Jacqueline's pet, Ricky." Caiaphas threw Jacqueline an accusing glare.

"I believe Dao-Ren is protecting the last of Father's lineage. I haven't confirmed it yet, but I believe I know who this person is."

Jacques noticed that Caiaphas didn't seem surprised. He knew about Malayah. There was a traitor in his house.

Caiaphas frown turned into a snicker. "It wouldn't happen to be a girl named Malayah Vega?"

"It would." Jacques kept his composure and saw the disappointment in Caiaphas' expression.

"I believe she is, too. She's the spitting image of Mary Magdalene," Caiaphas said.

"The mission is still on track with no real complications. And I've set a plan in motion to capture Malayah."

"The Father would be pleased with the development of Malayah." Caiaphas uncrossed his legs and leaned forward. "But I tell the both of you this. If the two of you have a hidden agenda or hamper this mission, I promise you, Jacques, that you'll be back on guard duty and your wife will become the Harlot again. And you know I keep my promises."

Jacques stood up and leaned forward with his hands on the desk. "Watch who you threaten, because I'll bring death upon you. What you rightfully deserved so long ago?" He spoke through his teeth.

"If all goes to plan, we've got nothing to worry about." Caiaphas got up from the chair and departed.

***

Caiaphas trod down the bare hallway with his retinue trailing behind him. A lone figure stepped out from the shadows. Caiaphas' two bodyguards stepped in front of him.

"Will you assist me in killing Jacques?" Ricky asked.

Caiaphas studied Ricky's face.

"What's in it for me?"

"Malayah Vega's capture and Jacques' wealth."

"And for you?"

"Jacqueline."

Caiaphas calculated his options. Capturing Malayah would please the Father. He will be generous. Plus, killing Jacques would strengthen his position, and if Ricky didn't succeed, Caiaphas could kill Ricky and cover up the plot.

"Let's talk."

***

May pressed her hand against Kat's forehead. The heart monitor beeped, and Kat's chest rose and fell. This simple movement of breathing was magnificent. Kat was going to make it through. Her pinkish tone had returned to her complexion. She looked peaceful.

May drank more of her protein shake to revitalize her body. The laying of the hands took a lot out of her. She was still stunned by what she had done. She wouldn't know what to do if she had to do it again.

Dao-Ren adjusted the IV line on Kat's arm. Their gazes met, and he blessed her with a lopsided smile. She loved the way the outer corners of his eyes squinted together with his toothy grin. It was a fresh joy squeezed straight from the fruit of his spirit.

"I'm proud of you," Dao-Ren said.

May felt her cheeks blush. "I didn't do anything except love Kat."

"You saved her life. That's something."

"Nothing you wouldn't have done." She looked into Dao-Ren's eyes, wishing she could take the sorrow away for him. "I was filled with the Holy Spirit," May joked.

Dao-Ren chuckled. "You can say that. The key to laying of the hands is love alone. All you did was evoke your spirit to guide Kat's spirit to heal herself."

"So it's like those miraculous healings I read in the bible when I was younger." She stepped closer to Dao-Ren.

"You're correct, but the laying of the hands had been going on for several millennia." All holy religions based on love mentions the power of laying of the hands in one way or another."

Dao-Ren sat down on the edge of the bed, one leg hung down the side with the other foot stationed on the floor.

"How did you learn about the laying of the hands?" May leaned against the bed.

Dao-Ren looked at May with a thoughtful expression on his face. "I met an old man in my youth named Thomas. He performed the laying of the hands on my childhood best friend when she injured herself."

May threw him a look. Who in China would be named Thomas? "Don't tell me you're talking about Doubting Thomas."

"I wouldn't say 'doubting.' He was an Elder and he preached that all religions are a part of the whole of God."

May shook her head from side to side. "How can that be when each religion teaches that their way is the only way to God?"

"Who do you believe God is?"

May pondered this question. What had she learned in Sunday school about God? She didn't want to say anything blasphemous.

"God is the Lord of Hosts, the omnipresent being who watches over us. The One who created the earth in seven days, the Punisher who punishes the sinners, and the Blessed who blesses the good."

"Very good, May. Your views of God are based mainly on the Western idea of God. Your views aren't right or wrong. God is not defined by any religion," Dao-Ren said. "We Awakyns know God. We all witnessed God when we died. We know the Truth. And I'm willing to share my understanding with you if you wish to know."

"Yes, I would love to hear it." May held onto Kat's hand.

"Very well. For us Awakyns, God is the perfect state of contentment, the pure source of love. There's no imbalance in God's conscious being. When you're reunited with God, you'll see and understand everything God knows. You'll view the world as God does because you're a part of God now."

May cocked her head, thinking about what Dao-Ren had just said. She found the idea of reuniting with God and acquiring a divine viewpoint on the world to be intriguing. She wondered how this understanding would shape her own perceptions and experiences.

"I wish God would have made the world perfect then we wouldn't have Judanites or the adversity of this world." May glanced at Kat.

"It was perfect," Dao-Ren said.

May's jaw dropped, and her head jerked back. "Nothing is perfect in this world."

Amused, Dao-Ren grinned before continuing. "People changed it. It all comes back to the concept of free will. If God were to interfere, free will would no longer exist. God's relationship with people would be as a Lord and servant instead of a parent and a child."

"So our lives aren't predestined or written?" May challenged.

"That's right. Each person's life is a blank page. God doesn't even know which way a person's life will turn out because of free will. He's all-knowing, because he can read a hundred moves ahead. He knows the outcomes of a choice."

Soft groans from Kat caught May's attention. Kat's eyes creased open, then they blinked a few times. She bolted upright.

"It's okay." May touched her shoulder. Kat pushed herself further back toward the headboard.

"You're safe now, Kat," May said.

Kat focused on May. Tears fell from Kat's eyes. "Oh, May, they did awful things to me." Kat threw her arms around May. "They injected me with a virus and told me I had birthed a plague that would kill everyone it touched."

Chapter 35

That peevish, spineless dog wouldn't know the difference between his mouth and his ass because both were full of crap. It infuriated Bernardo that Graham was trying to distance himself from the Exorcist Killer's case. He had referred all questions about the case to Bernardo's desk.

The priority of the Exorcist Killer jumped to the top of every law enforcement agency in the state. Even the governor's office called every hour on the dot for any new developments. The trail was growing cold. Time was of the essence, and Graham knew it. He assigned Bernardo to escort and show the evidence to the special forensic team from Quantico. Graham was setting up Bernardo to fail. Graham didn't know who he was messing with. He wouldn't let Graham get that satisfaction.

The Exorcist case had hit a roadblock. They weren't able to track down the person who sold the SWAT uniforms or the assault rifles found at the "House of Angels." The swords were authentic, and it added more mystery to the case than fact. They were trying to investigate if any of the swords were unique enough to have come from a certain buyer or auction house. There are no leads on that inquiry yet.

Tonight was the first night Bernardo had a chance to step away from the case. He and Tessa had a late dinner. Lying to Tessa complicated things. He couldn't bring himself to tell her about Awakyns and Judanites when he didn't even know what he was dealing with himself. The hardest part was he could tell Tessa knew he was lying to her.

He had witnessed some of Tessa's qualities that assisted in her speedy rise to detective. She discerned the small details that most people missed. She noted how he no longer walked with a slight limp, and that his body movements were more fluid than before. Her probing and her misdirected questions had him on edge, which led them into a huge argument that transmitted into their first night together.

Tessa snuggled tighter in the crook of his arm. Bernardo smiled down at her. He hadn't been this robust in bed since his twenties. After their lovemaking, Tessa had told him something was definitely up and that she would get to the bottom of it sooner rather than later. However, she was going to take her time if every night was going to be vigorous like tonight. They had made love again.

A cool breeze from the open window waved through Tessa's hair. Bernardo sat up. Neither he nor Tessa opened a window. He slid his hand underneath his pillow. His fingertips grazed the gun handle before he was yanked by the neck. He reached up and tried to pry the fingers loose from his throat. The blood pounded in his head. Tessa screamed. It sounded like a mile away.

Bernardo was thrown across the room. He crushed hard against the wall, which made him bite his tongue. Two men grabbed him and pinned him against the wall by his armpits. By their strength, he knew they weren't humans. His vision cleared. The Exorcist Killer scowled.

Bernardo looked past him. Two Judanites held Tessa down with their hands. She struggled against their grip. A primal rage tore through Bernardo's body. He thrashed against his captor's hold. The Exorcist Killer punched him in the gut, folding him up. He then used his hand to force Bernardo's head up by lifting Bernardo's chin.

"This is what I'm going to do to your niece when I catch her," the

Exorcist Killer said. He went over to the bed. His two henchmen let go of Tessa. She scooted all the way back to the headboard. He snatched Tessa by her ankle. She kicked out with her free leg and connected solid blows to his face and chest. He didn't even seem to feel them.

"You had better not touch her, you sick bastard."

The Exorcist Killer leered up at him before he yanked his arm, and Tessa swept under him. Tessa screamed and fought hard, her fists and legs striking her attacker.

"I'm going to kill you." Bernardo struggled against his captors.

The Exorcist Killer howled and played with Tessa. He slapped her hands to the side. His henchmen cheered him on. Tessa jerked her knee up into his groin. He shrank back, the pain registered on his face. He recovered and backhanded Tessa on the face, knocking her out cold. He ripped off her panties and bra and began to undo his pants.

Bernardo's heart raced as he desperately searched for any sign of a weapon or tool that could aid him in freeing Tessa. A surge of ferocious determination to defend Tessa at all costs caused his muscles to strain against the tight grip of his captors. There had to be a way. The bitterness rose inside him.

Only refusing to observe was all he could think of. He turned away, feeling less than a man. How will he face Tessa again after this? The damage and suffering she was about to suffer weighed heavily on Bernardo's conscience. He couldn't bear the thought of her enduring such pain because of him. A seed of vengeance took root in his heart. He would kill this motherfucker.

"Repent and God will have mercy!" A shimmer of MaNa blade streaked across Bernardo's vision. A bluish-black light burst next to him. The other Judanite let him go, and he crashed to the carpet. Bernardo scrambled to his feet and dashed to the bed. The Exorcist Killer had fled, and Tessa was unconscious. He grabbed the gun from under the pillow.

The commotion of metal clanged all over the room. Otis dueled with a Judanite, and a giant man battled two Judanites at the same time. Bernardo swept past them to the other side of the room. A lone figure was crouched on the windowsill. The Exorcist Killer gave him the middle finger.

"Bastard!" Bernardo ran straight at him, firing his gun. The Exorcist Killer leapt out the window. Bernardo reached the window and peered out. The bastard was nowhere in sight.

Bernardo turned back to the ongoing skirmish. Otis slashed the Judanite across his chest, bluish-black light. The giant beheaded another one, bluish-black light. The last one took off towards the window. Otis came out of the shadow and mowed him down, bluish-black light.

Bernardo lowered his gun and rushed over to the bed. He wrapped Tessa in his arms. Otis placed his hands over her for a few seconds.

"She'll be okay," Otis said.

"What's that son of a bitch's name?"

"Ricky."

"He's all mine."

***

Columns of zeros and ones scrolled down Thelma's vast screen.

"Thelma is deciphering the information we've retrieved from Billy's," Who-Dat said.

The ease of obtaining this information didn't sit well with Dao-Ren. He sensed that Jacques let him collect this data. "Who-Dat, is Thelma scanning for any type of virus or worm?

"You insult me. Thelma scans all foreign programs before she boots the data into her mainframe. All the downloaded material has been clean so far."

Why the camera? The computers would be the first thing they took. All this was too easy, and nothing about Jacques and Jacqueline was easy. His cell phone rang in his pocket.

"Hello." Dao-Ren listened.

"Judanites tried to capture Bernardo tonight," Willie said. "We got to him and Tessa before any real harm was committed."

Dao-Ren's body tensed. "They were probably trying to capture Bernardo to get to May."

"I believe so."

Dao-Ren's mind raced as he processed the information. The thought of May being in danger heightened all his senses. He needed to act quickly to ensure her safety. "We need to increase our security measures immediately. We can't afford to take any chances."

"Okay. But Bernardo wants to speak to May?"

"That's fine. I'll go get her." He hung up.

"Who-Dat, call me when you have any new developments," Dao-Ren said, walking out of the command center.

Dao-Ren paced down the hallway. Soft laughter and chatter came from the infirmary. He knocked before he entered. May was reclined on the bed with Kat, sharing a gallon of ice cream. Their conversation trailed off.

"May, your uncle wants to talk to you." He selected a number and handed her the phone.

"Hello," May answered. "What's going on, Unc?" She listened as her fingertips turned white around the cell phone. "You haven't been hurt... Okay, I love you." She ended the call and handed the phone back to Dao-Ren.

"I'm sorry. Judanites will try to murder, rape, and torture your family and friends to get to you. You've got to make a choice now.

You can learn how to fight or stay out of sight."

May's eyes blazed with anger, and her lip twitched. "Fight."

Chapter 36

Dao-Ren swung the steering wheel hard to the right, and the tail end of the car whipped from side to side as he turned onto a dirt road that led to the Santa Ynez Mountain Range. He shifted up and gassed the acceleration straight for the mountain base. The mountain came nearer, and May saw no visible turnoffs. She gave a quick glance at Dao-Ren. Both of his hands were firmly on the steering wheel, and his head pointed straight ahead. She looked back at the coming mountain. Her hand clutched tighter against the door handle. She shut her eyes and yelped right at the moment the car appeared to crash into the rocky surface. They punctured the mountainside, where a hologram camouflaged a cave entrance.

Rows of gas lamps illuminated the path into the cave. The narrow tunnel soon opened into a dirt courtyard lined with old wooden stables. Dao-Ren maneuvered the car into a one-eighty spin, so the car pointed towards the exit.

They emerged into the cool, damp air that carried a strong scent of ocean salt and pine. An old, thin man dressed in a flowing dark brown robe with a beaded rosary attached to a hemp rope belt came around the corner of the nearest stable.

"Peace be with you, Padre Serra," Dao-Ren said.

"And peace with you, Dao-Ren."

They embraced.

"Padre, this is May Vega."

Padre turned his attention to May. "An honor to meet you, May." He bowed his head.

Dao-Ren's phone pinged. The text was from Who-Dat. He read the message: Rita finished the analysis of Kat's blood.

"Excuse me, I must attend to this."

***

Dao-Ren headed in the opposite direction from May and Padre Serra. The packed dirt turned into a bluestone tile walkway. The cracked and chipped tiles revealed the age of this place. The edgy walls of the cave had smoothed out from the soft erosion of time and air. It had been a very long time since Dao-Ren had been here. Not since the Judanites released a terrible plague amongst the indigenous native population two hundred years ago.

That plague had spread quickly. The epidemic killed the natives mercilessly up and down the coast. Dead bodies of the old, young, and healthy were lined up in rows and stacked five high from village to village. The smell over the land was just as bad as Judanites. Awakyns were hapless to curtail the spread of the plague. The native people were suspicious of them. They didn't trust the foreigners, believing Awakyns had brought the plague with them. Not until Who-Dat had become an Awakyn did the natives believe in the Awakyns' ability of laying of the hands. It was too late by then to curb the destruction of the plague. The native population in California dwindled to a couple thousand. It was still far better than what happened to the Mayans.

Dao-Ren stepped into the old command center. The equipment was up-to-date. He positioned himself in front of the main screen and pressed a button. The center whirled to life with an electric hum. The screen came on with a live feed of Who-Dat.

"What have you learned?"

"Rita had finished the analysis of Kat's blood sample, and the initial report isn't too good. The Judanites incubated another flu virus." Who-Dat frowned. "And it's not a regular flu virus either. It's something new. Hold on. Rita will explain everything to you."

Rita appeared on the screen in light green scrubs. "The virus we found in Kat's blood has a very similar DNA to the influenza virus. As you know, influenza viruses are classified into A, B, and C groupings based on the antigens in their protein coats. This classification is due to the frequency of changes that occur in the antigen of its protein coat.

"The antigenic variation can be small or large. It occurs yearly in the A-class, less frequently in the B-class, and it has never occurred in the C-class until now."

"Why does it sound like a vaccine can't be concocted in the short term?" Dao-Ren said.

"Because this virus is only one-half of the influenza virus. The other classification for this virus would fit the bill of a retrovirus. Especially the way it reproduces and attacks the immune system, just like the Human Immunodeficiency Virus—HIV," Rita explained. "This new strain is also enveloped with a cylindrical core inside its capsid. The core contains two copies of its single-stranded RNA genome and the enzyme reverse transcriptase, which can synthesize a DNA copy of the viral RNA. The virus infects and kills T-helper cells by making the immune system unable to combat the virus."

Dao-Ren crossed his arms. "You're saying that this virus strain is a recombination of the HIV and influenza virus."

Rita nodded. "Precisely."

"How does it spread?" Dao-Ren asked, his eyebrows furrowing in concern.

"Through the respiratory tract."

"The mortality rate?"

"My preliminary calculation is around 40 to 50 percent."

Dao-Ren took a moment. "Rita, have your original analysis and sample of the virus ready for pickup. I'm going to give it to Agent Vega to forward to the CDC."

She bowed. "I started my own testing and development of an antiviral drug to combat this virus. I'll enclose those files too."

"That's good. Time is of the essence." Dao-Ren drew Rita's attention. "Death is right around the corner."

***

May followed Padre Serra through the maze of tunnels. At first, she thought the cave and its chambers were man-made. She was wrong. The cavernous system was indeed as natural as the mountain itself. The sedimentary layers of gray stone and granite were not cut but eroded. Years of use had compacted the dirt ground.

Most of the walls were undecorated and barren. What artwork she did view were simple paintings done on some kind of animal hide. The place was ascetic, a setting a monk would have preferred.

"Padre Serra, who used to live here?" May asked, taking in the scene.

Padre faced her. He had bright brown eyes that projected kindness. The wrinkles around his eyes portrayed a look of wisdom, like he had seen and learned what only a few would ever be privileged enough to know and understand.

"A secret sect within the warrior priests of the Franciscan order," Padre Serra replied, his voice filled with reverence.

"Were you part of this sect?" May inquired, her curiosity piqued by the mysterious nature of the sect.

"No my dear. I was a warrior priest, but I wasn't privy to this secret sect." Sadness clouded Padre's expression. "This secret sect was in accordance with Awakyns, and they were true men of God."

"Then how did you come to be here?"

"When I came to the New World from Spain, the Catholic Church commissioned me to establish mission towns. I began my conquest and built missions down the coast of Alta California by the force of my blade. The monks under my command forcibly subjugated the native people to peon slavery and forced them to convert to Christianity. It was a dark period in my life, and I deeply regret the pain I caused those indigenous communities."

May could tell his demeanor revealed his anguish.

"It was just that I was determined to leave God's footprints on this virgin land."

May watched as tears trickled down his dry face. He didn't wipe them away, his mind far gone back into distant memory.

"I didn't understand my cruelty and error until my deathbed. My dear friend, Brother Garcia, came to hear my last confession. He told me my good deeds would override my mistakes. Still, the pain of the lives I had taken was heavy on my heart. And out of compassion, Brother Garcia had initiated the call to rise from the dead when I died, and I answered that call in 1784."

"You don't look like an Awakyn."

"I'm an Elder. I haven't sanctified myself with the blood and body of God. I promised God and myself that I would never yield another sword or weapon against anyone or anything, not even a Judanite. I have enough blood on my hands," Padre Serra said, then gave a slight smile. "Enough about me. Let me show you the main chamber."

He offered May his arm, and she hooked her arm through his. It was a short walk before they reached the main chamber, the heart of the cavernous system. The chamber was dome-shaped and huge. The ceiling had a mural depicting heaven. The constellation converged into scenes of winged angels and humans.

The rich, vibrant colors of the mural seemed to come alive in the dimly lit chamber. May couldn't help but be in awe of the artistry and attention to detail. As she studied the celestial masterpiece, she felt a sense of tranquility wash over her, as if she had been transported to another world entirely.

The floor was blue marble inlaid with gold trimmings that formed into an almond blossom. The only furniture in the chamber was the dark-stained wooden benches that encircled the chamber in multiple circular rows. The benches were intricately carved with celestial motifs, mirroring the theme of the mural above. The soft glow of candlelight flickered across the room, casting dancing shadows that added an ethereal touch to the already mesmerizing atmosphere.

"This was the place where Awakyns and the monks used to congregate," Padre Serra said.

"It's more than splendid. It's a glimpse of heaven. Do you know who painted and designed it?"

Padre Serra's eyes filled with admiration as he peered up to the ceiling. "You'll meet Ariel soon. She's been Dao-Ren's companion for about the last millennium."

Chapter 37

"You've got to be kidding me!" Bernardo stated as he threw his hands in the air.

"No, sir, this is a hospital procedure," the nurse said, and she wrote something on a clipboard.

"Domestic violence. That's absurd! I'm the one that brought her here."

"Still, sir, her injuries are consistent with battery." The nurse scowled.

"We were in bed when a burglar hit her over the jaw."

The nurse cut her eyes. "Hmmpp."

"Okay." Bernardo motioned with his hands in front of him. "Let's slow this down. I'm just as upset as you are about what happened to her."

"I bet you are."

"I'm an FBI agent, and she's a LAPD homicide detective. There's no domestic violence, so I'm going in there to talk with her."

"I can't let you go in there." The nurse blocked the entrance with her body.

"Call the police." He squeezed past her.

"You can't go in there!" she shouted behind him.

Bernardo stopped his entry when he saw the deep bruise on Tessa's jawline. The nurse got between them.

"It's okay, I want him here with me," Tessa said.

The nurse's face pinched in, and she stomped out of the room.

"Come and hold my hand." Tessa said.

Bernardo approached Tessa cautiously, his heart heavy with concern. He gently took her hand in his, providing a comforting presence amidst the chaos. "I'm so sorry. I never thought this would happen. I told the hospital administration that a burglar hit you over the face as he escaped."

"That's fine, but you owe me an explanation. I want the truth." Tessa stared straight at him.

Bernardo just stood there for a moment, unsure of how to respond. He knew he couldn't hide the truth any longer, not from someone he cared about very deeply. Still, he couldn't find the word.

Tessa's voice quivered with a mix of fear and determination. "Who were they?"

Bernardo knew it wasn't right but he still couldn't express what he wanted so badly to say.

"They tried to rape me, and you're not going to say anything." Tessa's eyes began to moisten.

Bernardo loosened his grasp on her hand. "I'm sorry."

"That doesn't answer my question."

"It's hard to explain."

"Start from the beginning."

Bernardo's cell phone sounded. It was Dao-Ren. He read the text: I need to see you. ASAP.

"I have to go," he said.

She gave him an accusing glare, then turned her attention out the window. There was nothing to see, only night.

Bernardo stood there for a moment. He saw the tears streaming down her pale cheeks to the deep blue and black bruise. He could make out the palm shape of Ricky's hand. He reached out his hand towards her. Who was he kidding? He pulled back his arm and lowered his head. What could he do? He walked out the door, never looking back.

***

Bernardo discarded his half-eaten chow-mien in the trash bin. He jumped back, going for his gun when Dao-Ren appeared next to him.

"Damn, Dao-Ren."

"I'm sorry. I didn't mean to startle you." He bowed his head.

Bernardo took a much-needed deep breath that he wished was infused with nicotine and asked, "What's going on?"

Dao-Ren removed a legal envelope from inside his mid-length trench coat and passed it to Bernardo.

He thumbed through the contents. "What's this?"

"It's an analysis of a new virus the Judanites had created. It's a recombination of the influenza virus and the HIV virus, which we named the X-virus. We believe they're planning to expose it into the population real soon."

"How soon?" Bernardo looked at Dao-Ren with his head covered in a baseball cap.

"We're not sure yet."

"Why would they want to do this?" Bernardo questioned.

"To cause disharmony among the population and steal spirits for Satan."

Bernardo shook his head. "Okay. I don't know about the spiritual part. Just tell me if the virus is deadly."

"Yes, from our preliminary analysis, it has the potential to have a high mortality rate of around 40 to 50 percent."

"That's incredibly high." He sucked his teeth. "Let's walk."

They started down the deserted street.

"You're telling me the Judanites are going to use a biological weapon on the United States?" Bernardo asked, his voice filled with disbelief.

"In a way, yes."

"I'll get on this ASAP."

"No, I need you to surreptitiously deliver the analysis and this to the CDC headquarters in Atlanta." Dao-Ren produced a small sample of a vial of blood from his pocket and handed it to him.

He examined the vial in his hand.

"They'll begin their research and start to develop a vaccine."

"I can't sit around and not do anything when those damn demons are trying to smuggle weapons into the United States."

"The virus is already here, Bernardo. The Judanites carry it within them. They'll affect the population as they feed, leaving the consequences of the virus in their wake."

"How did they engineer this new virus?" Bernardo furrowed his brow.

"You already know that Judanites infect victims with a disease after they leach off their spirit. Judanites' bodies are a host for diseases to mutate. This time, they genetically recombined the influenza virus with HIV. Judanites' bodies deviate from normal human function. Diseases and viruses can't harm or kill them, nor could they spread them through the air or bodily contact except through a bite," Dao-Ren said. "The question to all this is how the virus will react within a population. The virus might be isolated from the victims and might not mutate to the point where it becomes contagious. This scenario is the most likely to occur. But the Judanites will coordinate a stealth mission to infect the most people they can to increase the possibility that the X-virus will mutate and become contagious or airborne."

"The more people they infect, the higher the probability that the X-virus will mutate into a killer virus," Bernardo said. "But it might not." He looked off to the side in thought.

"That's the gist of it. And after the Judanites inject themselves with the X-virus, it has a half-life of three to four days before it mutates in their bodies. That—"

Bernardo felt Dao-Ren grab his shoulders and swung him to the ground as a bullet struck the wall above his head.

Chapter 38

May's temper raged inside her heart. Blood pounded in her head. She glared at Dao-Ren, who stood before her. She hated him at the moment because she felt betrayed for no apparent reason. Dao-Ren didn't owe her anything. He could be with anyone he wished to be with. May prided herself on being independent of her emotions. She learned to be alone. Now, seeing Dao-Ren in front of her, made her feel like an emotional wreck. She wanted to yell at him to make the confusion go away. Her chest rose and fell.

The concern on Dao-Ren's expression begun to defuse her hostile manner. He held her with his stare. It was just as sweet as a hug. He was too handsome and considerate not to attract other women. Why would he want someone like her? She was merely a human. The possibility of his love was wishful, like a birthday candle flame.

"Are you alright, May? Padre Serra had told me you collapsed earlier."

"I'm fine." She couldn't look at him.

"If you're up for it, I'll like to cook you dinner tonight. I'll make you my specialty: roasted lamb chops sautéed in my secret honey-nut sauce with steamed rice and stir-fried vegetables," he said with amusement, accentuating the lines around his smile.

He was hurting her, and he didn't even know it. He crouched down until he was eye level with her. He covered his hands over hers. Why did his touch said so much?

"I'm sorry. I know the past few days have been difficult for you. I will do my very best to make your life the way it was before all this happened." Dao-Ren patted her hand.

She welcomed his affection. It felt like he would bear the whole world on his shoulders for her. The same way, he had to touch Ariel. She pulled her hands away.

His lips dropped as sadness shaded his countenance. He got up and headed to the door. "If you decide to come to dinner, I'll be waiting for you at the main chamber."

***

The sadness in May's demeanor had replayed in Dao-Ren's mind for the last few hours. The excitement and shock of the last several days must've taken a toll on her psyche and body. He never meant for her to face any of these ordeals. He couldn't bring himself to inform her about her uncle getting shot at. Otis and Gasper investigated and came to the conclusion that it was a ploy to see how many Awakyns were guarding Bernardo. Judanites were getting bolder.

The light clicks of stilettos bounced off the enclosed space. He looked up and lost his breath. Heaven Gate's opened up and a real angel approached him. May had her lustrous brown hair pinned up with two strands of her bangs hanging loosely to the side. She wore a silk cocktail dress. The light green color complemented her natural olive complexion and the open-toe stilettos added three inches to her height.

Dao-Ren's spirit stirred.

***

May watched Dao-Ren poured the red wine into the glass. "I borrowed this wine from Padre Serra's hidden stash," Dao-Ren said with a smirk.

May grabbed the glass and took a sip to wash down the lamb chop. Dao-Ren grabbed his fork and steak knife. He cut a piece of lamb and ate the meat.

"I thought Awakyns didn't eat," she said in surprise.

"No, we don't have to eat, but I enjoy a good meal here and there." Dao-Ren took another bite of lamb.

"Can you taste the meal like a human?"

He grinned. "Yes."

They stared at each other momentarily. She smiled, and he returned her gesture with his own.

"How long are we planning to stay here?" she asked.

"Until we stop Jacques and Jacqueline."

"Why do the Judanites want me so bad? I'm not anyone special."

"It has to do with your family lineage." He locked eyes with her. "I was planning to discuss it tonight, but I didn't want to overwhelm you. You've been through a lot these past few days, and I just wanted you to have a relaxing night." He paused before continuing. "Nevertheless, if you wish to know about your family history, I'll tell you."

May could tell by the tightness in Dao-Ren's face that he didn't want to discuss her family history tonight. Still, his offer had piqued her interest. She wanted to know.

"I appreciate your concern, but I would like to know about my family."

"Very well." Dao-Ren set his knife and fork aside.

May scooted to the edge of her seat.

"Be open-minded to what I'm about to disclose to you. It might sound a bit outlandish, yet it is still what I came to learn to be the truth."

May shook her head in earnest anticipation.

"It begins with the time of Jesus' birth. The Star of Bethlehem wasn't really a star. It was the wisdom of God manifested in the soul of Jesus. Jesus' soul burned bright with God's knowledge and understanding." Dao-Ren raised three fingers. "Three wise men journeyed to Jesus so he would be prepared if certain events came to pass. Jesus would be ready to equalize evil with good.

"The Three Wise Men were all Elders. They had taught Jesus until his physical mind was in accordance with the wisdom of God in his soul. The oldest wise man was Lao-Tzu, the founder of Taoism. He had brought the gift of frankincense. Another was Siddhartha Gautama, the founder of Buddhism, who carried the gift of gold. And the third was Hillel, a Hebrew teacher who preached peace and service to the poor. He had delivered the gift of myrrh. Each of these gifts was important to the resurrection of the dead."

May motioned with her head for him to continue.

"Jesus grew up in Alexandria, Egypt. His childhood best friend was Lazarus. These two had been inseparable and closer than brothers. When both families decided to return to Israel, Lazarus' family settled in Bethany, whereas Jesus' family returned to his parents' hometown of Nazareth. Both families had kept in touch and had married into each other's families. Lazarus had married Jesus' first cousin Salome, and Jesus' younger brother James had married Martha."

May didn't know which way this was heading, but could she really be part of this intertwined family history? As May pondered her connection to this ancient bond, she couldn't help but wonder if there were more surprises waiting to be unveiled.

"Jesus started his ministry at Mary's wedding by changing the water to wine. This was the sign of his ordination of God's word. Mary was a free spirit who always sought the truth in the world around her. She made her own way and did things from her heart. She had even refused the tradition of arranged marriages and chosen who she would marry—Judas Iscariot."

May gasped in astonishment at Mary's unconventional choices. It was intriguing to think that Mary had defied societal norms and followed her own path, even in matters of love. This gave her hope for her own desires for Dao-Ren.

"It was Mary's nature to seek the truth, and the truth flowed from Jesus' mouth. Together, Judas and Mary had become followers of Jesus when he began to preach the Good News of God. They believed that Jesus knew the way to eternal life and became one of Jesus first disciples. As the years went by, Jesus and Mary formed a strong personal relationship in spirituality.

"Judas had taken notice of this relationship, and instead of sharing in this intimacy, a seed of jealousy was planted in his heart. It was watered by his hatred of what Jesus could give his wife that he could not, eternal life. This had caused Judas to start questioning Jesus' teaching and authority."

May listened but questioned how all this tied in with her. She wanted to ask but held her tongue until Dao-Ren finished.

"It all came to a head when Lazarus died. He welcomed death, for Salome had died six months prior. She was stabbed in the heart during a riot. Jesus would have let it be, yet he was moved by Martha and Mary's grief and pleas. Jesus went to Lazarus' burial tomb and prayed the incantation of resurrection taught to him by the Three Wise Men for the first time.

"Lazarus rose from the dead. Martha and Mary were so joyful that their brother had returned to them. Mary became more devoted to Jesus and caused the treachery to fester inside Judas' heart, which had bred into a murderous intent for Jesus' blood.

"Tension brewed between Mary and Judas. They would often argue about Jesus. She would plead with Judas to rededicate himself to Jesus' teachings. Judas no longer desired to have anything to do with Jesus' ministry.

"The opportunity to give Mary what she wanted presented itself to Judas. Satan had tempted Judas with a kingdom as far as he could see and the ultimate power to bestow eternal life to his followers. Judas had quickly accepted. He now had the power to give his beloved Mary, eternal life. She wouldn't need Jesus anymore."

May shook her head. How could Judas be so easily swayed by Satan's temptations? She couldn't understand how he could turn his back on Jesus and betray him after witnessing all the miracles and teachings—even for love. Or better yet, love for whom?

"Lazarus was tormented. The time had arrived for him to become an Awakyn. Even though he had risen from death, an Elder couldn't escape death. And death was his only ride back to Salome. Even so, Lazarus knew the whole of humanity was more important than being with Salome at this time. He had sealed his fate at the Last Supper, when he had eaten and drunk the body and blood of God. He became the first Awakyn."

May thought about how Lazarus's transformation into an Awakyn marked the start of a new era for humanity.

"Later that night, Judas betrayed Jesus to Caiaphas. Armed guards detained and arrested Jesus. Judas swiftly sought out Mary, who was praying in the Garden of Gethsemane. Judas had broken down to his knees and confessed to Mary his covenant with Satan and his betrayal of Jesus.

"The deceit of Judas beat Mary down in sorrow and grief. He had tried to console her and reason with her that his agreement with Satan was for her, so he could give her eternal life. Mary would have none of it. She had disowned him and claimed her husband, whom she loved with all her being, had died a long time ago. And the person she looked at now was a blasphemy of his former self."

May couldn't comprehend the pain that Mary must have felt as she told Judas that he was dead to her. *How brave she must have been?*

"Mary's words pounded with the hammer of truth, and they shattered Judas' reality. All that he had strived for was an illusion. He was filled with despair and ran away from Mary. Two days later, Judas brought a rope and hung himself, and he had died. Satan's essence filled Judas' body, and he rose from the dead to do Satan's will on earth."

May sat back and folded her arms as she took a breath. She couldn't help but feel a mix of sadness and shock at the tragic end to Mary and Judas' story.

Dao-Ren paused before continuing. "It was discovered that Mary was pregnant with Judas' child. And when Judas received word of Mary's pregnancy, he wanted his child. He had grand visions of establishing empires throughout the world with his own lineage. Mary wouldn't let the devil get his hands on her child, so she went into hiding in a land called Gaul, which is modern-day France. In Gaul, she gave birth to a son, whom she named Samuel.

"Judas' minions had grown in number and began to call themselves Judanites. They had hunted for Mary and Samuel to please Judas. Lazarus had come to protect his sister and nephew from Judanites. Samuel stayed safe and he grew up, and had children. Judanites then went after Mary's grandchildren and almost kidnapped them. Lazarus had asked his fellow Awakyns if some would like to become Watchers over Mary's lineage to protect them from Judanites. Some had accepted the task and taken Mary's grandchildren into hiding.

"Judas was relentless and determined to have his grandchildren. Through the centuries, Judas had found some of his grandchildren.

Some joined him and became Judanites, others denied him, and he killed them. The rest never knew the truth and lived a normal life with Awakyns secretly guarding them."

May bit her bottom lip. *Could she be part of this legacy? There was no way.*

"In the nineteenth century, one of your ancestors chronologically listed his lineage several centuries back, the Judah family. Judas had gotten his hands on this journal. There were five descendants left. All of them were captured except a little boy named Benjamin Ben Judah.

My Awakyn brother Jairus hid Benjamin, and he asked me to watch over him. I hid the boy in America. And this boy was your great-great grandfather on your maternal side."

"Bobby Wilkerson is my great-great grandfather's name," May said, puzzled by the revelation. Her hands dropped to the table.

Dao-Ren reached across and placed his hand on top of hers. "A Christian family adopted him, and he had grown to have two sons, Jared and Steven."

She studied Dao-Ren's face for a moment, trying to process the information. "So, you brought my great-great grandfather to America," May repeated, her voice filled with curiosity.

"Yes. His oldest son Jared had been killed in World War II on the beaches of Normandy. And Steven had gotten married and had two children, Jay and Jackie. Jay was childless, and Jackie had your mother, Erin."

"And my mother had me. The last of the living descendants of Mary and Judas," May finished. Her mind raced as she contemplated the weight of her family history. She couldn't help but feel a deep sense of responsibility as the last living descendant of Mary, not so much of Judas.

"That's right."

"And this is why Jacques is trying to kidnap me for Judas?" May questioned, connecting all the dots.

"Correct."

May raised her head. "Am I related to him?"

"He's your cousin."

She inhaled. "How many children had Judas taken into his circle?"

"Six," Dao-Ren stated.

"How many Awakyns?"

"One."

"Are you serious? Only one?" May exclaimed.

"Yes." Dao-Ren's eyes never wavered. "Her name is Ariel."

Chapter 39

After last night's diner, May had twisted and turned in bed, her body in a constant flux of emotion. Nightmares replayed vividly in her delirious imagination. There was Dao-Ren kissing Ariel, holding her close to him. Ariel was breathing in his intoxicating scent. May couldn't stop these images from popping into her head. Their bodies meshed in the heat of passion. She cringed at the thought. Was this jealousy she felt? It couldn't be, she was a grown woman, not a heartbroken teenager. She needed some fresh air. She swung her feet out of bed and onto the floor.

"May," Dao-Ren said from outside her door.

She didn't want to see him right now.

"I'm coming in."

Damn it. There's nowhere to go.

Dao-Ren entered her room, his lips pressed together. "Padre Serra has mentioned to me that you haven't eaten breakfast or lunch. He swept his eyes over the untouched breakfast and lunch plates on the table. "Are you okay?"

May folded her arms and shifted on her feet. "I'm not hungry. I'm bored to death. I need to do something active."

"Very well, but you need to eat something. Your training begins in an hour."

***

Gas torches illuminated the capacious training cave, which had the look of something ancient where arcane fighting styles were taught. May took in the selection of different types of handheld weapons that were hung on the walls by hooks. Dao-Ren sat in a lotus position at the center of a large feather-stuffed mat, where he appeared to be meditating.

May approached Dao-Ren. He opened his eyes, and he got up from the mat. He wore a charcoal-gray compression cold gear that outlined the tone of his body through the synthetic material. Her cheeks warmed, and she looked away.

"Ready?"

"More than you know," May whispered.

"Let's see how well you shoot first."

Dao-Ren made his way into a smaller cave off to the side. Sound-proof walls enclosed the area. Inside were five alley booths with a retractable shooting target at the end. Dao-Ren chose a middle booth and picked up the black handgun from the tabletop.

"This is a Glock-40," Dao-Ren said, loading a full clip of ammo into the gun. He then slid the chamber back and offered the pistol to May, handle first. She grabbed the gun and faced the target. She widened her stance, shoulder-length apart. Before he could give her instructions, May held the pistol straight out in a two-handed grip and sighted down the barrel. She squeezed the trigger and exhaled her breath, emptying the whole clip in rapid succession.

Dao-Ren stared wide-eyed at May. He re-tracked her target. It showed a tight pack of shots in the upper body area of a human outline. He whistled in admiration.

May shrugged. "Unc made sure I knew how to fire a gun properly.

He said you weren't fully independent until you knew how to protect yourself."

"I guess you're fully independent then. And this target is your declaration." He teased her with a smirk. "Okay, you don't need any more target practice. Let's move onto handheld weapons training."

May motioned with her arms. "Lead the way, Master Dao-Ren."

They returned to the main room.

"Have you ever trained with hand-held weapons before?" Dao-Ren asked.

"I was good with the bo and sai in martial arts class."

Dao-Ren moved down the rack and kicked the bottom of the two bos into the air. He snatched one in each hand. "Here." He tossed May one.

She caught it in midair with both hands. The bo was heavy, each end had a six-inch MaNa tip. May twirled the staff in her hands. Dao-Ren strolled toward the center of the mat. May stalked after him. The instant they reached the middle of the mat, he spun in a pivot and struck the bo at her. Without thinking, May lined up her shoulders and blocked the strike.

The half-smile was wiped off her face when he attacked with a combination of blows and strikes. May tried to block his offensive assault. He lightly tapped and poked her whenever she left herself open, which was most of the time.

May controlled her breathing and concentrated on his body, especially his shoulders and hips.

"Don't square up so much." He poked her in the ribs with the end of the bo. "You make yourself a larger target."

May adjusted her feet, north to south. He threw some blows. Her confidence grew with each block. She began to relax more and trust in her past training. She saw the strikes before he cast them. Patience was the key.

"Most Judanites lack proper combat training. They rely on their strength and speed. They usually leave their frontal area unguarded. That's where you direct your attack."

Dao-Ren crouched low in a nimble stance, and his movements became more feline. He was less graceful and more aggressive. He squared himself, exposing his upper body. He leapt into the air and cocked the bo in a two-handed grip. He slammed the bo down at May. She raised her bo horizontally and blocked his chop. She used this opening to throw a sidekick into his sternum. He shuffled backward and regained his balance.

He pounced forward and swung the bo like a baseball bat with no trace of technique. He was a madman. May bobbed under the wild swing and struck Dao-Ren on the shoulder. He absorbed the blow and reversed his swing at her head. She ducked under it at the last instant. The bo made contact with the tip of her ponytail.

She reset her feet and waited for his assault. He rushed her, bringing the bo over his head. May sidestepped and bashed him in the gut with the length of the bo. She swiveled the bo over her head and clobbered it down onto the back of his head. He collapsed on all four.

She placed the bo underneath him and flipped him over onto his back. She jumped on him, slamming the bo down across his throat. She exhaled a hot breath of exertion. Their eyes met.

"Congratulations! You defeated your first Judanite." His face endeared her with a lopsided grin.

May laughed. "I was good, huh?" His proximity suddenly occurred to her—unnerved her. She felt his hips between her inner thighs. Her head gravitated toward his mouth. She witnessed his life, his spirit, and his love.

Their noses touched ever so softly.

"Pardon me."

Both of them turned to Padre Serra, who beamed from ear to ear as his eyes crinkled in enjoyment.

"Dao-Ren, Who-Dat has broken the encrypted files."

Chapter 40

"What have you learned?" Dao-Ren asked.

An enormous monitor on the wall displayed Who-Dat's face via video call. He peered up from his computer. "Thelma broke the encryption. It contained coordinates, numbers of Judanites, and dates. I believe it's where the Judanites are going to attack. A battalion of 200 Judanites is coming through Mission Bay, 400 at Lindbergh Field, and another 350 at San Diego Bay. The invasion date is December 25, three days from now."

Realizing the urgency of the situation, Dao-Ren needed to alert his Awakyn brothers and sisters to mobilize a defense force to intercept the impending Judanite attack. "Dispatch the scouts to the location."

Who-Dat typed away on his computer. "Done."

"Send Al-Auhaymin Ar-Rashid, Yosef Agnon, and me a copy of the decoded encrypted files." Dao-Ren caught Who-Dat's gaze. "It's time for battle."

***

Jacques leaned over the green-haired Judanite's shoulder as he typed on the keyboard.

"It's done. The computer virus has been activated," Quin said.

Jacques patted him on the back. "Great job."

His eyes fixed on the screen displaying the progress of the computer virus. The anticipation grew as they awaited for the results. He beamed at his good fortune. He didn't think it would have worked. The data Dao-Ren had retrieved from Billy's mansion included a unique tracking virus that could only be triggered if all of the files had been decoded.

The virus tracked wherever it was sent, and where Dao-Ren was, Malayah would be too.

***

"So, you're telling me those men who attacked me on Monday night at my apartment were Judanites?" Tessa said. "And Judanites are something like vampires?"

"Yes," Bernardo said.

"And the people who saved us are Awakyns, and they're guardian angels?"

"Pretty much."

Tessa rolled her eyes to the ceiling and let out a deep breath. She walked away from Bernardo and faced the pictures on the mantel above the stone fireplace. "You're serious about all this? You're not fucking with me?"

"Dead serious. I could call Willie or Otis for you." Bernardo reached for his phone.

"No. I don't think I can handle it right now." She touched a photo of Bernardo standing next to May, both smiling. "How does this help me, Bernardo?"

"It's the truth." Bernardo sighed, not fully understanding her question.

"No, to cope with what happened to us." She looked down at the photo again, tears welling up in her eyes. "I need something more than just the truth, Bernardo. I need support, guidance, and healing."

Bernardo looked away from her.

"I wear my independence like a medal of honor." Tessa stepped up to Bernardo and made him look at her. "I know we have only known each other for a short while, yet when I think of someone who can help me deal with what I went through, it's you."

"I'm here for you." Bernardo moved closer to her.

"No, you haven't been. It feels like I've done something to you, and you're pulling away from me."

Bernardo wanted to say it wasn't her, that the problem was him. He wanted to share with her how he felt like a total failure for not being able to protect her from Judanites. Her vulnerability tugged at him. He wanted to say so much, but he couldn't find the courage to open up. He let this moment passed in silence. This was about her and not him.

"I know that night has affected you, too," Tessa said, her arms twitching at her sides.

Bernardo should pull her into an embrace and tell her all would be okay, but he couldn't find the strength to do it. His ego wouldn't let him. He cast his eyes downward.

"You're not the only one hurting!" Tessa said. Her mouth trembled, and tears rained off her face.

Bernardo wouldn't let her down again. He would protect her from him. He turned his back to her and went out the door.

***

Stars appeared above the horizon. May felt the cool air refresh her and calm her mind as she stood at the cliff's edge and gazed out towards the San Buenaventura Mission. She concentrated on the towering brick steeple, miles away, with the massive bronze cross on the apex. The cross appeared to burn like a vigil candle off the streetlights. She had no idea what the flame was burning for. Maybe they waited for Jesus to return.

May heard the familiar movements of Dao-Ren making his way to her. He stopped short. She continued to focus on the bronze cross.

"I'm sorry, May. I couldn't get back to you yesterday. There was some information I had to review, and it looks to be good news for you."

May didn't turn around to reply.

"We figured out the Judanites' plan. You'll be able to return to your life very soon."

"What's soon?"

"The Judanites' planned to execute their mission on Christmas night. So, your life should return to normal several days after that."

"What about Jacques and Jacqueline?"

"If they aren't released, they'll run straight out of LA. Awakyns will be everywhere."

Streams of headlights in the distance cut through the darkness. Vehicles approached.

"What's Ariel to you, Dao-Ren?" May turned to confront him, holding her breath. It took him a second to find his words.

"I guess, you can pretty much say that Ariel has been my companion for about the last nine hundred years. A bright spot in my life, she's the closest individual I have on this earth."

May's heart shattered into a million pieces. She had to force herself to remain upright. Dao-Ren held her up close to him. "What's wrong?"

"Just tell me, you'll always watch over me." Her voice trembled with a mix of vulnerability and hope, as she searched for reassurance in his eyes.

"I'll never leave you as long as you're alive."

She heard the sincerity in his voice.

"You're not alone in this journey. I promise to be by your side, protecting and supporting you through every step of the way."

May smiled. "Thank you." She still had a chance to win him over. "Let's go inside, Dao-Ren. Your brothers and sisters are here."

***

Hundreds of Awakyns occupied the chamber. Dao-Ren held May's hand as they strolled into the gathering. All the commotion faded into silence, for everyone's attention was on them.

May felt herself blush.

"Dao-Ren." An angelic voice sounded from the back of the chamber.

May steeled herself for the encounter with Ariel. The throng split as Ariel rushed to Dao-Ren. Her dark auburn hair streamed in the air, quiet as a winter ocean. Her joyful expression highlighted her smooth, unblemished features. May felt his hand go slack in hers, the anchor to her poise. Her insecurities tossed her around in a storm of self-doubt.

Ariel's facial features got clearer and more defined. She had a slim, oval face with a small, pointy nose and a delicate mouth and chin. Her eyes were large and golden, rising above her high, rosy cheekbones. She moved gracefully, highlighting her contours. May wanted to throw up.

Ariel jumped into Dao-Ren's open arms. He embraced her tightly and spun her in circles. Her melodious laughter teased May's ears. How could she have ever believed she could compete with that? The moment Dao-Ren stopped spinning, Ariel planted kisses all over his face. Anger pounded in the center of May's being. She balled her hands. Dao-Ren whispered something into Ariel's ear. Her gaze found May.

Ariel made her way to her. Her brows were narrow, yet her mouth and shoulders seemed relaxed. Was she brooding, or was it sadness? May turned to Dao-Ren for support, his face was expressionless. May wanted to hate Ariel. She couldn't be friends with Dao-Ren's companion. Ariel opened her arms wide for an embrace. Confusion took control of May.

But there was one thing she could do. She turned and bolted.

Chapter 41

May refused to acknowledge Ariel, who had stood outside her room. She was determined to maintain her distance, even though Ariel's presence tugged at her curiosity.

"I'm coming in, May," Ariel announced, entering the room and positioning herself next to May.

Despite her best effort to hold onto the anger, May felt drawn to Ariel's presence like a kindred spirit. Still, she forced herself not to notice her.

"Dao-Ren had shared with me how much you've been through," Ariel said. "I'm so sorry that you faced these ordeals."

May remained silent, her eyes fixed on a spot on the wall.

"If there's anything I can do to help you, let me know."

May could feel Ariel's genuine concern, which made her even madder.

"But I am happy that you're safe. Dao-Ren will protect you with his life."

May finally turned her gaze toward Ariel. "I appreciate your concern," she said. "But I've learned to rely on myself. I don't need anyone else to protect me, especially not him."

"I can feel how strong and resilient your spirit is, May. And I know Dao-Ren can be off-putting sometimes, but he means well."

"What do you mean, he's off-putting?" May arched one of her brows, offended that Ariel had possibly slighted Dao-Ren. She crossed her arms.

Ariel sighed. "I'm sorry, May. I feel like I'm starting off on the wrong foot." Ariel swayed. "May I sit?"

May soften her stance with Ariel's discomfort. She acquiesced with a nod.

Ariel sat beside May. "I haven't seen Dao-Ren this happy since I was a kid," Ariel related.

May couldn't keep quiet about her curiosity. "So you knew him for a long time."

Ariel smiled. "The funny thing was, I was never supposed to know Dao-Ren. By pure accident, he and Soraya came into our lives."

"Our lives?" May responded with confusion. "Soraya?"

"Dao-Ren's Spiritmate. She was my family's Watcher."

"I thought we weren't supposed to know that we were being watched," May stated.

Ariel chuckled. "Fate has a way of bringing unexpected connections into our lives." Her smile fade. "Bandits ambushed my elder brother Malachi's caravan. They had murdered everyone except for my brother and another worker. Nobody thought Malachi would live. His stomach had been slashed from hip to hip. The odor that came off him smelled like death crawling out of him." Ariel looked to be lost in her thoughts, her eyes remote as she spoke. "Dao-Ren appeared at my family's estate, and he laid his hands on Malachi and healed him."

"He did the same for my uncle," May shared.

Ariel smiled and patted the top of May's knee before continuing, "My father, Jonah Ben Joseph, had been so thankful that he offered Dao-Ren land and money. Dao-Ren declined. My father wasn't so easily deterred, and somehow he persuaded Dao-Ren to live with us. I suppose he could really sell a Christian a Koran and a Muslim a Bible." Ariel laughed at the memory.

May uncrossed her arms and smiled with her.

"Dao-Ren and his lovely wife had moved in with us."

"Dao-Ren had a wife?" May dropped her jaw in surprise.

"Yes, her name was Soraya. The bond between them was like one person in two bodies. They were what all people dreamed about—living love." Ariel took a breath. "Jerusalem at this time was a place of peace. Jews and Arabs coexisted. Christians worked next to Muslims. It was a haven of tranquility for all people."

May detected the weight in Ariel's voice.

"This peace ended when the first wave of Frankish Norman Crusaders had invaded on July 15, 1099. They had come to slaughter all non-European men, women, and children from the Holy Land. Rivers of blood spilled down the streets, with levees of bodies stacked high."

May turned her head to the side. Ariel's eyes were misty, peering back into another time and place.

"My father was worried about vandalism and theft of his merchandise. He believed the Crusades would be a brief moment in history. Many armies had invaded Jerusalem before, and all had retreated with their tails tucked between their legs. Therefore, he had taken three of my brothers, Dao-Ren, and ten armed men to protect his warehouses. My father left fifteen armed guards with my mother and me.

"The next night, the Crusaders smashed down our door. The fifteen armed guards were no match for the Frankish Crusaders. I was frightened beyond words as blood and body parts splashed on our once white stone walls. I had assumed Soraya was only a housemaid until she yielded a scimitar against some of the Crusaders. Those Crusaders she defeated burst into bluish-black flashes. My mother held me tight against her bosom and shielded me from the most sickening parts."

May took hold of Ariel's hand and squeezed.

"For a moment, I thought I would survive. Then a loud howl sounded in the gruesome night. It made my bones rattle with fear. A minute later, I felt a terrible burning sensation in my stomach, like it was on fire." Ariel's voice quickened. "My mother went rigid and collapsed on top of me. A crusader pulled my mother off me. I saw panic in his face before a sword cut him in half. A man with wavy brown locks stood over me. It was Jacques."

May gasped.

"A crusader had plunged his sword into my mother's back. It went all the way through her and pierced into my stomach. Blood pulsed out of my gut. The last vision I remembered was a small woman holding Soraya's decapitated head by her hair." Ariel glimpsed down as she was looking away from the horrible memory. "The next thing I remember was Dao-Ren's calling me forth. The pain and sorrow in his voice awakened my spirit. I rose from the dead on July 18, 1099. I was eleven years old."

May sat up straighter. She felt the heaviness of the moment.

"After years of pleading with him, I finally got him to tell me what had happened to my father and brothers. He told me that after they had barricaded the warehouse doors, my father asked him to go check up on us. When he had arrived at our house, it was on fire, and the smell of death was strong. He searched the house and came upon my lifeless body first, and then Soraya's corpse in the vestibule.

"He collected our remains and carried them back to my father's warehouse. When he got there, the Crusaders were chopping up the bodies of the rest of my family. You couldn't discern whose body parts belonged to whom. It was a massacre.

"So that night I lost my whole family. My father was a descendant of Judas and Mary. My father, brothers, and I had been targeted by Judanites; more specifically by Jacques and Jacqueline." Ariel's words trailed off.

May threw her arms around her and pulled her into a hug. "I'm so sorry. I know the pain of losing family."

Ariel hugged her back. "I learned to deal with my loss and sorrows." Ariel wiped her eyes. "Dao-Ren, on the other hand, is a whole different story. He was never the same after that. The light in his eyes grew dimmer until sorrow was its shade."

Ariel held May's hand in hers. "Now, the light has reignited in Dao-Ren's eyes. The same way he used to look at Soraya. You've rekindled the love in his being, his true spirit. For that I thank you with all my heart."

"You think Dao-Ren loves me?" May whispered, afraid the possibility would disappear if she said it too loud.

"Yes, he loves you more than the world can hold."

A sprout of joy bloomed inside May, and she broke into laughter. "I thought you and Dao-Ren were together."

Ariel shook her head. "Oh, no. Dao-Ren is like my father, my brother, and nothing more." Her face took on a bright red glow.

"He loves me!" May jumped to her feet. "I have to go see him."

"There's…"

May rushed out of the room into the tunnel system. She went left, then right. The labyrinth of tunnels wasn't so confusing a day earlier. This journey of love was far and beyond, and now it was just a step away.

She turned the corner and saw the candlelight that emanated from Dao-Ren's room. She burst into his room, not bothering to knock. She was tired of banging on his heart and not getting an answer. And as if hitting a force field, she slammed to a complete stop. This wasn't what she was expecting. Her eyes fell upon his shirtless torso, and she didn't know what to do—cry or cradle him.

***

Bernardo punched the sketch of the Exorcist Killer on the bulletin board. Rage consumed him. He could practically feel his hands on Ricky's neck.

"Bernardo, I brought you some coffee," Otis said.

The interruption brought Bernardo back to reality. He took a deep breath and tried to compose himself before responding, "Thanks, Otis."

Otis had two Styrofoam cups of coffee in each hand. "I understand your feelings, Bernardo. I used to be filled with anger and hate." He put one down on Bernardo's desk.

"It was difficult for a Black man in the 1950s. I thought I had to use violence to be respected and earn my rights as a man. And I battled hard for it, but the more I fought, the more I struggled, and the hate devoured me. I felt so useless, which caused me to fight even harder." Otis sat down in the chair in front of the desk. "It wasn't until I found myself in prison."

Bernardo sat up and leaned forward. "Prison?" he asked, intrigued by Otis' revelation.

Otis nodded solemnly. "Yes, prison. Everything was stripped from me, from my family to my ideals. All I was left with was my anger. And that left me soon enough too. All that I fought for was for nothing." Otis sighed, his voice sounded with regret. "I had to rebuild myself from the ground up." Otis crossed his legs. "I'm telling you this because you'll lose everything if you let your pride rule your thoughts. You're going to hurt the ones you're trying to protect if you let this anger unbalance you. Keep in mind, revenge always strikes first at those you hold dearest."

Bernardo tapped his finger on the desk. He heard Otis, but his anger still filled his body. The Mona Lisa stared up at him with that smirk of hers from atop his desk. He snatched the print, ready to rip it to pieces, but his mind detected a pattern with the letters and numbers he had written down a day ago.

He had assigned numerical values to the letters of the Mona Lisa based on their order in the English alphabet.

$$[M = 13] \ [O = 15] \ [N = 14] \ [A = 1]$$
$$[L = 12] \ [I = 9] \ [S = 19] \ [A = 1]$$

When Gasper told him, the key was prime, did he mean prime numbers? A number greater than one that can only be divided by one and itself. There were two prime numbers in the anagram: M = 13, S = 19.

If he simplified it and added the extra letter to the number:

$$1(A) \ x \ 13(M) =$$
$$1(A) \ x \ 19(S) =$$

Then, if you multiply the prime letters, you get A x M = AM and A x S = AS

Bernardo grabbed a pen and rearranged the letters. He smiled. He had figured it out. He understood why it represented balance. The anagram MONA LISA with the primes AM and AS, reads—As I Am Also Man. He marveled at the hidden message within the anagram. He welcomed the sense of clarity. His rage subsided.

"The truth behind the Mona Lisa is that for one to reach their prime, they must be balanced as male and female, yin and yang, the perfect union of God," Otis explained.

"I'll be damned." Bernardo pulled out his cell phone and searched for Tessa's name. It didn't matter. He received an incoming text from Tessa.

He grinned and read the text.

I hate you. I hope you die and go to hell!

***

May walked up to Dao-Ren's backside. His back was symmetrical, where his traps started from his shoulders to his lats, that spread out into wings of muscles. Though they did nothing to camouflage the thick, jagged scars that crisscrossed and slashed in complete disorder on his back. These scars weren't clean, precision cuts, but rugged hacking scars induced by a blunt blade designed to inflict the most pain. Each scar on his back protruded out like dark, stormy clouds that deluged a hurricane of agony.

He didn't move from his spot. She stood there engrossed by his scars, brushing them with her fingertips. The scars were hard and rough.

He shifted and faced her. May gasped. He bore the same marks on his chest and arms. How much had he endured? Each cluster of tissue healed with its own sorrow. How could a mortal man bear this much blistering pain and not have succumbed to death? Who could he have loved to sustain all this?

Both of her hands brushed over his body as if she were reading Braille. This was another story and time. Her spirit yearned out to him. She kissed one of the scars that zigzagged through his chest. Dao-Ren guided May's head upward by lifting her chin with his fingers. He then cupped her face with his hands. She stared into his torrential, sorrowful eyes. If he shed a tear, he would cry a river.

Before May knew it, his soft lips touched hers. The hunger of want gnawed through her. She pushed up against him. She was soaring high, and as fast as it began, her wings were clipped.

He pulled away. "I'm sorry."

May grabbed his hand. "What are you sorry about?"

He shook his head. His expression was a mask of disbelief. "We can't do this."

"What do you mean? I don't understand," May pleaded, her voice filled with confusion. She couldn't comprehend why he would suddenly back away. Their connection felt undeniable, and she couldn't bear the thought of losing him now.

"My love is a curse." He broke free from her grasp and grabbed his shirt off the bed.

"Stop!" May cried out, tears welling up in her eyes.

He paused by the door.

"I've waited for this moment for a very long time. Please, don't reject me. Don't let your sorrow be my grief."

The silence grew, and he walked out with his head hung low. His footsteps faded, leaving her heartbroken and full of unanswered questions. She collapsed on the dirt floor. Arms wrapped around her.

"I'm sorry, May," Ariel said.

"Why is he doing this to us? I know he loves me." May choked on her sobs.

"It's not you, May. It's him. He's troubled by the thought of harm befalling you because he loves you the way he does."

"Why does he deny us then?" Tears fell from May's cheeks.

Ariel forced May to look at her. She wiped the dirt and mud from May's face. "I was trying to tell you that Dao-Ren's spirit is in constant sorrow. He had lost everything he truly loved. He couldn't protect them or save them. And he blames himself for that. His love had transmuted into perpetual sorrow."

"Who was it that he couldn't save?"

"Soraya and Xin-Ji."

May raised her eyes to Ariel.

"Xin-Ji was Dao-Ren's wife when he was human. She had become a Judanite to rescue him. And when he refused to become a Judanite, she ripped out his heart."

May felt a shiver run down her body as she tried to comprehend the depth of Xin-Ji's betrayal.

An Elder named Thomas performed the resurrection. And Dao-Ren returned as an Awakyn to save Xin-Ji from eternal damnation." Ariel stroked May's hair away from her face. "He never saved Xin-Ji. And Xin-Ji had changed her name to Jacqueline."

May raised her hand to her mouth. "No."

"And Jacqueline killed Soraya."

The reasons to the shadows of Dao-Ren's sorrowful eyes.

"If Jacqueline finds out Dao-Ren loves you. She'll go to the ends of the world to kill you."

"So Dao-Ren is pushing me away to protect me?"

Ariel nodded her head.

"I must help him to carry some of his burdens." May grabbed Ariel's hands in both of hers. "Will you help me?"

Ariel sighed. "I might know of a way."

Chapter 42

It took all of Dao-Ren's willpower to force himself away from May. He had to put distance between them. He couldn't be selfish and put her life in more jeopardy than he already had.

He paced into the command center. Al-Muhaymin Ar-Rashid and Nina Maria Velazquez examined the topographical layout of San Diego County. The three targeted areas of Mission Bay, Lindbergh Field, and San Diego Bay were highlighted on the screen. Ar-Rashid used a laser pointer to indicate the points of emphasis.

"I'll lead 72 Awakyns with me to Lindbergh Field," Ar-Rashid said. "Nina you'll take 36 Awakyns to Mission Bay."

Nina nodded her head in acknowledgment.

"And Dao-Ren, you'll command 45 Awakyns to San Diego Bay."

"That's fine. What's the latest on the scouting intelligence?"

"Our scouts saw a few Judanites at each location. We assume the majority are hiding. The air was strong with their scent."

"Very well. Let's go brief the others on our plan," Dao-Ren said.

They all walked out. Dao-Ren peered over to his brother Al-Muhaymin Ar-Rashid, who strode along with a straight back that made him seem taller than five feet and eight inches in height. He still wore his mustache long with pointed tips, as he had in 1557.

Dao-Ren focused next on Nina Maria and her thick black hair braided down the center of her back. He empathized with Nina

Maria's history. She had taken a vow of silence since 1221 in penance for not speaking her heart to the man she had loved. The same man who ignited the Inquisition because of the hurt that festered into hate. She could have prevented so many innocent deaths.

They entered the main chamber. Hundred and sixty-two Awakyns settled around the wooden benches. Ar-Rashid's booming voice gave out the instructions and orders. Dao-Ren searched the chamber in the hopes of catching a glimpse of May. She wasn't there.

"Unit leaders, do you have questions or concerns?" Ar-Rashid said, looking over the commanders who stood in front of the congregation.

"I have something to say." May's voice was magnified inside the dome ceiling.

Dao-Ren caught a glimpse of May and Ariel hand-in-hand, heading towards the altar. He couldn't read the expression on May's face or Ariel's. Ariel stopped, and May continued until she was directly in front of him.

"As God as my witness, I, Malayah Vega, give Dao-Ren Chan my spirit to cherish and love until death do us apart."

Dao-Ren stepped back, stunned by May's drastic measure. He couldn't speak. The hush deepened as the seconds passed. What was she thinking? This wasn't the time for this.

Nina Maria grabbed his hand and leaned into his ear.

"Denying your heart is denying God."

He gaped at Nina Maria. He had never heard her voice before. The resolve in her countenance solidified his decision.

He focused his full attention on May. "Yes, May I accept your spirit."

Tears fell from her eyes as she cupped her mouth in shock.

"With God as my witness, I, Dao-Ren Chan, give May Vega my spirit to cherish and love until death do us part."

"Yes."

The whole chamber thundered and shook with applause.

***

May's lips moved with Dao-Ren's. Nothing could have tasted sweeter than his mouth. He broke away and May nestled her head on his chest. His woody scent whetted her appetite for what was to come.

He carried her into his cavernous room and tossed her on top of the plush feather-down blanket. If love was a scene, it was displayed in the depths of his brown eyes. His fingertips combed through her hair, and her breathing increased. She enclosed her arms around his neck and pulled him into a kiss.

He moved his mouth back and traced his tongue over the contours of her wet lips. The coolness of his tongue trailed down her throat, sending pure intense heat to every inch of her body.

"Make love to me."

Chapter 43

"Make the call," Bernardo said through clenched teeth. He had both hands on the counter, and he leaned forward toward the front desk sergeant.

The desk sergeant glared back. "I already told you, it's against policy."

"Something isn't right. I can't locate Detective Richards. She hasn't been home for the last two nights, and she won't pick up her phone."

"All I know is that Detective Richards is on paid leave until she meets with the departmental psychiatrist about her recent assault."

"God damn! I know that." Bernardo felt the blood rise in his face. "I'm telling you she's missing."

"It's not my problem. And you better control your temper. I'll arrest you for threatening a police officer, FBI agent or not."

Bernardo thrust his finger at him. "You piece of—"

The desk sergeant placed his hand on his gun.

Bernardo gave him one last disgusted look and stormed out of the building. He stood on the street and took a deep inhale. He ran his fingers through his hair. Where was she?

Bernardo glanced down at both sides of the street, hoping Tessa would materialize. There had to be a perfectly good reason why she hadn't returned any of his messages. He had messed up, but she wouldn't have ignored him like this. He had every intention to ask Otis to watch over her, but the thought of vengeance made him forget.

Now, his instincts told him something was terribly wrong.

The cell phone in Bernardo's pocket rang. He retrieved it and saw Tessa's number on the screen. He sighed relief and accepted the call.

"I'm so sorry, Tessa."

Only silence met him on the other end.

"Hello?"

A muffled cry came through the speaker. Fear punched him in the gut.

"Cat got your tongue, Bernardo?" Ricky's demonic laugh seared through the speaker.

"If you do anything—"

"Stop with the nonsense. Just hope that I don't kill her." Ricky's voice dripped with sadistic satisfaction.

Bernardo squeezed the phone tight in his hand, his heart pounding in his chest. "What do you want?"

"I want you to lose your Awakyn bodyguards and meet me somewhere."

"Where?"

"Hold on, Bernardo. You're going to explode before you get the deed done. You're not going to lose your Awakyns tonight. You'll have to figure out a way to lose them. I'll text you tomorrow night on our meeting spot. If I see any Awakyns or even feel that I do, I'm going to kill your slut very slowly. But rest assure, she'll live through tonight. She might even enjoy what I have in store for us."

***

Dao-Ren stroked May's arms as she ran her fingertip along the edge of his tattered scars. She felt the weight of his past struggles. These scars told the journey of the strength that he possesses. She wondered how much he already endured. With each gentle caress, she vowed to mend not only his mental wounds but also the pain that lingered within him.

"We have to get ready to go," Dao-Ren said.

"So soon? You just came back from preparing your team."

"I should've never left. I snuck back here to be with my wife." He smiled.

May pushed up, kissed his lips, and rested her chin on his chest. She bathed in the tingle, the remnant of the sensation that ravaged her body moments earlier. Being this intimate with him made her feel so complete.

"Do you have to go to battle tonight?"

"You know that I do."

She looked away and bit her bottom lip. "Can Awakyns be killed easily?"

Dao-Ren wrapped his arm around her tighter. "Judanites must puncture our hearts first, which exposes our spirit from our bodies. Then they must behead us to kill the body. It has to be done in that order."

"Have you ever been close to death?"

He guided May's face to meet his gaze. "I've been weakened before, but never close to death."

"What do you mean weakened?"

"As we strike with light, Judanites slash with hate. The mortal wounds won't affect us, but the malicious energy troubles our spirit. We're more susceptible to death as our spirit combats those energies."

May saw all that could go wrong in her mind. The thought sent a shiver down her spine, reminding her of the immense danger they were facing.

"Don't worry, my love. I won't let a Judanite separate us, that I can promise you."

"Ariel told me about Soraya and Xin-Ji," May said. She rubbed her index finger in circles on his chest. "Do you still love Xin-Ji?"

"Yes, but she had been dead for a very long time. Jacqueline isn't even a shadow of her former self. Still, I don't hate Jacqueline. I want to save her. I don't believe I could release her if she didn't repent." Dao-Ren kissed May's brow. "Remember this, though, if she means you any harm, I won't hesitate to release her. Forgiven or not."

Chapter 44

"God, you're holy indeed, the fountain of all holiness. Let your spirit come upon these gifts to give us the strength and wisdom to do your will," intoned Cedric, a tall, dark Awakyn. He lifted up a round, flat bread in one hand and a golden chalice in the other. Twelve other Awakyns beside him had followed his lead and raised either a loaf of bread or a chalice into the air.

The surrounding temperature stirred with a pleasant heat, as if it were gathering energy from the air itself. May could feel the pulse of the living air that moved about her. She smelled the flowery incense of frankincense that wafted out of the chamber bowls stationed around the alter. She glanced at her husband, who had his eyes closed, and inhaled the power within these walls.

Cedric and his assistants strolled to the center of the main chamber and formed a circle in pairs. Each pair held one loaf and one chalice of wine between them. The attendees got up in an orderly manner and descended to one of the pairs to accept the gift of God. Dao-Ren intertwined his hand with May's and led her into a line. They proceeded to the front. She paid attention as Dao-Ren received a piece of bread and drank a sip of wine from the chalice, so she could mimic him when she received the gifts.

May stood before Cedric. Amazed that the bread was still whole. He broke a piece of bread and placed it on her tongue. It dissolved in her mouth, and warmth flushed through her. She felt revitalized. MaNa times ten. She stepped over to a gorgeous, slim Awakyn, and she served her a sip of wine from the chalice. The wine was sweet as nectar. A radiant heat grew in the center of her being. Her spirit was filled with a peaceful resolve, and her faith grew in bounds. The protection of God was over her. Dao-Ren waited for her on the side. She joined him and hooked her arms through his. They made it back to their seats as the last Awakyn accepted the gifts.

Cedric returned to the altar with nothing in his hands. The bread and chalice were gone. He faced his audience. "Brothers and sisters, go in the safety and protection of God, for His strength and will are manifested through us. His will be done."

*****

Jacques admired Jacqueline's sleeping form. He lived for this small, devilishly beautiful woman. She lay naked under the sheets. Desire stirred in his groin. He loved this woman so much that he loved enough for the both of them. Yet, he still held onto the hope that Jacqueline could love him like she had once loved Dao-Ren.

The large bedroom with a high ceiling and thick walls amplified the loud ringing of a cell phone. He reached over to the nightstand and answered the call before the next ring woke up his sleeping beauty, who shifted in the bed.

"What is it?" he asked.

"We've got a location from the tracking virus," Quin said.

"Very well, let me know if anything changes."

He pulled open a drawer on a nightstand. He grabbed a long velvet-covered jewelry case from inside the stand and plucked a black rose from the vase. He moved closer to Jacqueline and leaned over to kiss her on her chilled lips. She kissed him back fervently for a few seconds. They stared at each other.

"Happy Anniversary, my Queen." Jacques gave her the jewelry case and a flower.

Jacqueline sniffed the perfect black rose, her eyes twinkled in the nostalgic act. She placed the rose on the bed and opened the jewelry case. It contained a platinum scalpel with rubies embedded down the handle. She gave Jacques a bewildered look. He placed his hands over hers and kissed her fingers.

"Tonight, you'll cut the thorn from your heart."

***

Bernardo nursed his third mug of beer. He couldn't drink much more and not be impaired. He needed all his senses and wits, coupled with a bunch of luck, in order to have a fighting chance against Ricky.

He glanced over his shoulder and spotted a group of roughnecks getting pretty inebriated. The drunker they got, the louder and more obnoxious they became. His cell phone vibrated in his hand. He scanned the screen—Harbor Scenic Highway. He dropped a twenty on the bar and took a quick glance around the barroom. He didn't see any sign of Otis or Willie.

He got up and staggered every few steps towards the group he had eyed earlier. Four burly, young guys dressed in blue jeans and flannel shirts gulped down mugs of beer. Two ladies dressed in tight clothes sat between them. The hot pink mascara on their faces looked more clownish than sexy. When Bernardo got close enough, he heard their conversation about fat women and penis size. Perfect.

Bernardo swayed, bumped into the biggest roughneck, and knocked over his beer into his lap. The largest one shot up to his feet, veins popping from his neck.

"Watch where you're fucking going, Gramps!"

Bernardo carefully pronounced his words. "No, *you* watch where you're fucking sitting."

"You better go on before I break your brittle bones." Spit flew out of the edge of the young man's mouth.

"Fuck you and your ugly friends. I'll beat the snot out of all your young asses. Then I'll go fuck your mothers."

"What?" He got in Bernardo's face. "What did you say about my mom?" All of his buddies stood up from the table.

"I said I'm going to…"

Otis suddenly stepped in front of Bernardo. "Excuse my friend here. He's pretty wasted right now."

Willie stood close by with his arms crossed and his chest out.

"Let me buy you and your friends a couple of rounds." Otis produced a hundred-dollar bill from his pocket.

The guy eyed the hundred and snatched it. He pointed his finger at Bernardo's face. "Next time I see you here, I'm not going to be so nice."

Otis and Willie escorted Bernardo back to the bar. Bernardo shook off their hands. "I have to piss. You two wait for me at the bar." Bernardo headed to the restroom. He glanced back. Otis and Willie looked the other way, talking. He hurried his pace to the restroom hallway and went straight out the door marked exit.

Chapter 45

"Is it true about Mary and Judas?" May asked.

"To my knowledge, yes," Padre Serra said.

"But why hasn't it ever been written about?"

"To protect you and all your relatives that came before you, and to keep it silent, was the best way to do so. Think about it. If the first century Christians knew of this knowledge, they would've tracked down all of Judas' bloodline and murdered them because of Judas' role in Jesus' crucifixion. Revenge would have ended that line pretty quickly."

May scanned the vast library, where redwood bookshelves lined the entire room. Over a hundred thousand books, texts, scrolls, and manuscripts occupied every shelf space. "If that were the case, why are there other gospels not in the Bible that proclaim the union of Mary and Jesus?"

"First of all, you must understand that all of the gospels were written by humans, so all the gospels were tainted to some degree by the writer's point of view. Nothing was ever divinely written," Padre Serra said, moving closer to May as if he were about to tell her a secret. "Yet truth lies in the midst of everything. You've to search for it with an open mind and heart.

"Yes, there are books and gospels mentioning the union of Jesus and Mary that would seem plausible. If you didn't know any better, you would come to believe it. Each gospel or story gives you bits and pieces, but not the whole cake." Padre Serra pointed up with his index finger. "One story is a single candle flame trying to view the whole vault of Truth. Just as world religions do."

May tilted her head. "What do you mean?"

"Religion only gives you one candle flame to illuminate the darkness of the whole world and their point of view to explain it."

"What you just said doesn't make much sense to me. Each person has his own personal view of the world around them?"

"Yes, each person may translate written words through their own expression and previous knowledge. But their cultures and traditions taint their understanding. For example, if you get ten people from different cultures and let them read about teen pregnancy. They'll be small or large discrepancies in each person's response, but those with similar cultures and races will tend to view it in the same direction. The same concept holds true for religions. Christian values are the bedrock of most European countries. This commonality in Christianity gives a certain viewpoint to all Western countries to some degree or another. The more you have in common, the greater your chances of looking at the world in the same way. With one candlelight." Padre Serra pointed to a candle at the center of the table.

May drew her head back, her eyes narrowing.

"Let me put it like this." Padre Serra got up and walked down the aisle. "The 52 texts discovered at Nag Hammadi in 1945 rocked the traditional foundation of Christianity."

He dislodged an old text from a shelf.

"When the gospels were read by Western theologians, they viewed the words in the light of their own education and knowledge using one or two candle flames. This is an English translated copy of the Gospel of Phillip, one of the texts found in Nag Hammadi." Padre Serra set the old manuscript on the table and began to flip the pages.

May knew that this library contained many texts, books, and scrolls lost to the outside world. This could be the greatest treasure ever buried in the California mountains.

"Here we go." Padre Serra slid the book across to May and sat back down. "Read Phillip, 63:32 to 64:5"

"The companion of the Savior is Mary Magdalene. Christ loved her more than all the other disciples. He used to kiss her often, often on her mouth. The rest of the disciples were offended. They said to him, 'Why do you love her more than all of us?' The savior answered and said to them. 'Why do I not love you as I love her.'"

May returned her focus to Padre Serra.

"Many Western theologians would agree that this passage gives evidence of Jesus and Mary's true relationship as husband and wife. Their candlelight illuminates a certain way or degree. Companionship and kissing on the mouth would be interpreted as a physical act."

May recalled how she had assumed Dao-Ren and Ariel were lovers when Padre Serra mentioned Ariel being Dao-Ren's companion.

"But if you saw this passage from an Eastern theologian's perspective, you would come away with a different interpretation. A companion would be seen as a close friend or a disciple. And kissing on the mouth would have been taken figuratively, as in passing on a secret knowledge. And I believe that the Eastern candlelight is the right one."

"Why would you think that, Padre? Isn't Greek history and philosophy apart of the western culture?"

"Yes, so let me show you the power of hidden words." He tapped the text. This gospel is considered a gnostic gospel. Gnostic comes from the Greek word 'gnosis' which translates to knowledge. The Greek language uses gnosis differently when used in speaking of scientific knowledge and reflective knowledge. The Gospel of Phillip uses the reflective knowledge of the word gnosis. Therefore, in this light, the word gnosis means insight, the intuitive process of knowing oneself. You must read ancient texts with the right candlelight and always remain open-minded and hearted, for Truth is hidden but also clearly seen."

"Why wouldn't it be scientific knowledge?" May inquired, wondering if there were specific reasons why the Gospel of Phillip chose to use the reflective knowledge aspect of gnosis instead.

"The Gospel of Phillip is based on mysticism and inner-reflection. When you have the chance to read it for yourself, you'll see what candlelight is illuminated."

"You sound heretical for a Franciscan monk," May teased in a lighthearted way.

The lines around his eyes crinkled. "I do, but I hold firm in my beliefs about Jesus. Christianity is where I found Truth and it is my main source of light. Like I claimed before, Truth is everywhere. You have to go search for it. That's why there isn't any wrong way when righteous is exalted. Buddhism, Hinduism, Islam, Judaism, and other religions all hold truth about God. Each religion of Truth is a patch on the quilt of God's knowledge. Everything leads to the next. There are many ways to God, and free will is the compass."

May thought for a moment. His words made sense. "I think I understand your teachings, but why enlighten me on this when it sheds no light on my question about Mary and Judas?"

"But it does. I just have to light your way. And remember that just because it wasn't written down doesn't mean it's not true. Truth lies within us, and you'll know it within yourself. Truth is whatever people believe. It is the foundation of faith. With that said, let's make a connection between Mary Magdalene and Mary of Bethany." Padre

Serra wrote down the two names on a piece of paper and handed it to her. "What similarities can you make?"

May considered the two names. "They're both named Mary, which is a female name, so you can pretty much infer that they're both females."

"…And?"

"Both are probably Jewish because their last names are towns in ancient Israel."

"And what town are they from?"

One is from Bethany, and the other is from wherever Magdalene means."

"Magdala."

May simply nodded, looking over the paper.

"Now, do you see any distinctions?"

May concentrated on the names. What did he see that she didn't? She grinned to herself. It was in the names. "It's written Mary of Bethany and Mary Magdalene, and not Mary of Magdala or Mary Bethanene."

"Very perceptive, May." Padre Serra grinned. "That's the key. One says the place of where Mary is from, Bethany. And the other is a person from the place of Magdala or Magdalene. Why do you think they wrote it like that?"

"To distinguish the person."

Padre Serra patted May's hand. "You're correct. Characters in the Bible distinguish themselves in two ways, hometown or nickname. Such as Jesus of Nazareth, Judas of Galilee, Mary of Bethany, and nicknames such as Jesus Christ, Peter the Rock, or Mary Magdalene."

"What does Magdalene mean?"

"Magdalene does mean a person from Magdala. And the word *migdal* is the root word for Magdala. Migdal connotes two different meanings. One means great, and when you combine it with the suffix -lene, which means person."

"Mary the Great!" May felt the excitement.

Padre approved with a nod of the head. "Yes, Mary the Great, the greatest disciple of Jesus," Padre Serra said. "But, there's even more. Another meaning for migdal means tower. A tower is great because you can watch and guard against your enemy. Magdalene also means someone you watch."

"For this reason, Awakyns who watch over Mary's grandchildren are known as Watchers." May spotted an additional link. "And Mary is Lazarus' sister, which implies Mary of Bethany is also Mary Magdalene."

"They're one and the same." Padre nodded in approval.

"I still don't see any connection between Judas and Mary."

"So let's make the connection. Judas was a popular name around the time of Jesus. And to distinguish Judas from the others, he's known as Judas Iscariot."

"What does Iscariot mean?"

"It has multiple meanings, all pointing to his deeds. First, literally, Iscariot means a man of Kerioth. Kerioth is a Hebrew word that translates into cities. Cities of Judanites, the covenant Satan made with Judas. A second meaning is a dagger bearer, a euphemism for a betrayer." Padre Serra waited until May met his eyes. "And the final interpretation is a Man of the Lie which means Father of Judanites or Son of Satan."

"Are Judas' nicknames widely known?"

"Yes, they can be found in any Christian concordance, minus the reference to Judanites."

May shrugged, lifting both hands out. "And how does this connect Mary and Judas?"

"These nicknames of Mary Magdalene and Judas Iscariot are the only two Judeans named like this in the Four Gospels. It is their connection. In order to protect Mary's children, you had to protect

Judas."

May grinned. "Now, I understand the reason why Judas was jealous of Jesus because his wife was Jesus' greatest disciple and confidante."

Padre Serra carried on. "And there was a great friction between Jesus, Mary, and Judas that became the decisive factor that moved Judas to betray Jesus. And all is written in the Gospels."

May threw her head back. She never remembered reading about that.

Padre Serra flipped opens a worn Bible and turned it around to May. His finger pointed at Matthew 26. "Read verses 14-16."

She obliged:

"[14]Then one of the Twelve- the man called Judas Iscariot- went to the chief priest [15]and said, 'What are you willing to give me if I hand Him over to you?' So they weighed out 30 pieces of silver for him. [16]And from that time he started looking for a good opportunity to betray Him."

"What do you think pushed Judas?" asked Padre Serra.

May scanned the verses. "It doesn't say."

"If you read the previous verses 6 to 11 you'll discover why."

May used her finger to locate the passage.

"[6]When Jesus was in Bethany at the house of Simmon, a man who had a serious skin disease, [7]a woman approached Him with an alabaster jar of very expensive fragrant oil. She poured it on His head as He was reclining at the table. [8]When the disciples saw it, they were indignant. 'Why this waste?' they asked. [9]'This might have been sold for a great deal and given to the poor.' [10]But Jesus, aware of this, said to them 'Why are you bothering

this woman? She has done a noble thing for Me. [11]You always have the poor with you, but you do not always have Me."

"It doesn't say who the woman is or the disciple that questioned Jesus," May said.

"Turn to the Gospel of John, chapter 12, and read verses 3 to 5."

May flipped through the pages and found the scriptures.

"[3]Then Mary took a pound of fragrant oil- pure and expensive nard- anointed Jesus' feet, and wiped His feet with her hair. So the house was filled with the fragrance of the oil. [4]Then one of His disciples, Judas Iscariot, said, [5]'Why wasn't this fragrant oil sold for 300 denarii and given to the poor?'"

Padre Serra's tone grew more animated. "The characters are named. Mary had poured the anointing oil, and the concerned disciple was Judas. Judas had confronted Jesus about Mary's deeds. You must keep in mind the Jewish laws during Jesus' time that a wife was subordinate to her husband. Mary had disregarded this and brought shame to Judas.

"First, Mary's hair is unveiled, and she used it to dry Jesus' feet. Her modesty is in question, for all to see. And the second, Jesus' comments to Judas undermined his lawful authority, as a husband in front of others."

May leaned back while contemplating what she just heard. The truth was between the lines of the passages. It had nothing to do with the perfume. It was the brewing drama between Mary and Judas. It made perfect sense. She now believed Mary and Judas were married. Yet there was still a nagging question that ate at her. She sat up straight, placing both hands on the table.

"Did Mary and Jesus have an affair?"

***

"We're closing in on the Dragon Lady," Omarosa said.

In the shadow of night, Dao-Ren peered out at the ocean but saw nothing. Their cruisers trudged through the black pearl waves of the Pacific Ocean. In the cool, salty air, a faint scent of Judanites lingered. This wasn't the reek of three-hundred and fifty Judanites. They had been misled, or Who-Dat's decryption program was incorrect.

"Omarosa, any new updates on the other teams?" Dao-Ren folded his arms across his chest.

"Ar-Rashid is reporting now. They encountered a force of about a hundred and fifty-three Judanites. Nowhere close to the four hundred listed," Omarosa replied.

Dao-Ren's confusion deepened. He glanced over at Omarosa, whose expression mirrored his own bewilderment. Something was definitely not adding up.

"Dao-Ren, Nina-Maria is reporting in. She battled ninety-six Judanites, not two hundred," Omarosa communicated, her voice filled with disbelief.

Dao-Ren furrowed his brow, his mind racing to make sense of the discrepancy. Why would the files have inflated numbers? If this was a ruse, then there wouldn't be any Judanites at the location.

"What are you thinking, Omarosa?"

"Maybe not all the Judanites have arrived yet."

"Perhaps, but we know Jacques and Caiaphas are here, so their battalions will be nearby," Dao-Ren replied, contemplating the situation.

Omarosa shook her head. "These reported numbers seem like only one battalion and not two."

"You're right, Omarosa. It doesn't add up. If these numbers are accurate, then where is the second battalion? And why would they report false information?" His voice trailed off as he saw the outline of the Dragon Lady in the distance.

He stepped around Omarosa's backside toward the monitor. Four red dots made a square perimeter around the Dragon Lady.

"The others are in position," Omarosa said, her voice steady and commanding. "It's a go."

Through a pair of night vision binoculars, Dao-Ren could see the Dragon Lady glowing green. He observed Judanites with RPGs on the upper deck aimed at them. The hiss of air cannons firing projectiles could be heard in the distance from their cruisers. He observed Awakyns shimmying up ropes against the yacht's hull. He signaled Omarosa with a hand motion.

"Repent and God will have mercy upon you!" Omarosa spoke through a microphone.

All four cruisers flipped on their floodlights, illuminating the Dragon Lady from all sides. Dao-Ren discarded his night vision binoculars. The first wave of Awakyns engaged the Judanites. From the deck of the Dragon Lady, the sounds of grenade rockets could be heard overhead, followed by explosions nearby.

Omarosa triggered the hydraulic compressed air cannons, shooting grappling projectiles onto the Dragon Lady's upper deck. Taking hold of the rope, Dao-Ren shimmied up its length onto the deck. He slung himself into a flip, landing in a crouch with his knives exposed. Judanites attacked him. He parried and slashed through them. These Judanites were careless and young. As he moved through the crowd of attackers, his senses heightened, allowing him to anticipate their every move. He blocked their blades with ease and countered with ending slices. Bluish-black light danced in the darkness, casting an eerie glow on the deck.

Omarosa came onboard. "We've started the search for any trace of the X-virus."

Grey ashes covered the deck, but nowhere close to three hundred and fifty Judanites. Something just didn't feel right to Dao-Ren. This whole mission was too easy. Warnings of impending danger swept over him.

"Everyone off the ship, now!" Dao-Ren scanned the immediate area for any threats as Awakyns withdrew to their cruisers. A powerful need to return to May overwhelmed him. The scars on his body burned like fresh cuts. *She was in jeopardy.*

A tremor resonated from underneath the deck, he sprinted in the direction of the railing. He dove into the air, feeling the immense heat of the explosion engulf him.

***

The king-sized bed swarmed with nubile bodies. Jacques bit into a creamy thigh of a red-haired woman as Jacqueline wrapped her hands over the woman's breast.

The phone rang. Jacques broke away.

"Hello?" Jacques kept his sights on the intertwined bodies. Little drops of blood trickled down Jacqueline's mouth as she suckled on a breast.

"Congratulations," Pierre exclaimed. "Awakyns have just decimated Caiaphas' battalion."

"Are Awakyns still in San Diego Bay?" Jacques asked, his voice filled with excitement.

"Yes, they're having a blast of a time." Pierre broke out in a sinister laugh.

Jacques chuckled. "Get everybody ready, it's time to party."

The news of the Awakyns' victory filled Jacques with a sense of triumph. This was the moment he had been waiting for—the fulfillment of his meticulously planned takeover of Caiaphas. As he turned his gaze back to the scene before him, Jacqueline locked eyes with him. He couldn't help but feel a surge of satisfaction. Finally, their long-awaited revenge on Dao-Ren was also within reach.

Chapter 46

"No, Jesus and Mary Magdalene didn't have an affair."

May shifted in her chair. "But, they knew each other before she married Judas."

"Remember the place and time. The Pharisees, the Sadducees, and the other Jewish leaders wanted to bring Jesus down because his ministry threatened the foundation of their power base, especially with the Romans. Any salacious relationship would've been all they needed to end Jesus' ministry."

"There has to be some truth to the gnostic gospels that indicates Jesus and Mary's union."

Padre laughed. "May, my dear, you have stumbled upon the greatest propaganda the world will ever know. It started two millennia ago, and it's still counting."

May's brows furrowed as she cast a curious glance at Padre.

Padre Serra folded his hand in front of him. "Judas spread Jesus and Mary's union rumors to discredit Jesus' life and teachings and to locate Mary's children."

"Why would he do that?" May questioned.

"So people would lose faith in Jesus if they heard or read these rumors? To believe in one thing all of their lives, then find out it was a lie. Believers would grow resentful. This was Judas' main purpose for spreading Jesus and Mary myth. It was a win-win situation for him." Padre Serra tilted closer. "Even today, there's a battle with many Christians hearts about the personal life of Jesus Christ. What people choose to believe, whether it is a lie or the truth, is the deciding factor on how they see the world."

May felt the truth in Padre Serra's words and nodded him on.

"Judas knows the truth and didn't care what people thought of Mary. He knew believers would search for Mary's descendants to find out the truth."

May was part of this truth, and it frightened her that apart of her wanted to meet Judas, but her family's history also included Awakyns.

"Aren't Awakyns part of my family story?"

Padre Serra's eyes twinkled. "They are, indeed. The Gospel of John contains a precise description of the first Awakyn to your family."

May reached across the table and grabbed the Bible. She realized that without her maternal lineage, she might never have been born. The thought sent shivers down her body, and she couldn't help but feel a deep sense of gratitude for the intricate web of connections that had led to her existence.

"Go to John 11 verses 2, 3, and 5."

May flipped through the pages to the verse and read:

"²Mary was the one who anointed the Lord with fragrant oil and wiped His feet with her hair, and it was her brother Lazarus who was sick. ³So the sister sent a message to Jesus. 'Lord,' they told him, 'the one you love is sick'... ⁵And Jesus loved Martha and her sister and Lazarus."

She remembered Dao-Ren telling her that the original Awakyn was Lazarus.

"These three people are the only ones in the Gospel whose names are mentioned that Jesus loved them. Even the people knew Jesus' love for Lazarus. Read verses 34 to 36."

"34Where have you laid him? he asked. 'Come and see, Lord,' they replied. 35Jesus sobbed. 36Then the Jews said, 'See how much he loved him.'"

"It's clearly written that Jesus loved Lazarus, and Lazarus is only mentioned in this fashion in John's Gospel. It's easy to infer that Lazarus was a disciple."

May shook her head in agreement. She felt a fondness for her first great-uncle.

"When Lazarus rose from the dead, the other disciples began to call him 'the disciple Jesus loved'. Note that the verb love is in the past tense. Lazarus had evolved from a human to something more, and the phrase "the disciple Jesus loved" was used to refer to him after his resurrection. Let's look at John 13 verses 23 to 27."

May located the passage.

"23The disciple Jesus loved was next to him at the table. 24Simon Peter motioned to that disciple. He said, 'Ask Jesus which one he means.' 25The disciple was leaning back against Jesus. He asked him, 'Lord who is it?' 26Jesus answered, 'It's he to whom I shall give this piece of bread, and He gave it to Judas Iscariot, the son of Simon. 27Now after the piece of bread, Satan entered him..."

"These verses are occurring at the Last Supper. Events had passed that set into motion the creation of Awakyns and Judanites. If Judas hadn't accepted Satan's offer, Awakyns and Judanites wouldn't have come into existence. When Judas took the bread, the covenant was sealed. Judas would betray Jesus," Padre Serra said. "Later that night, Lazarus had accepted his fate and consumed the body and blood of God, turning himself into the first Awakyn."

Sacrifice was the greatest act of love one could perform for another. May was aware of how much Lazarus had given up.

"In chapter 20, verse 4, tells of Lazarus' new ability."

May found the right page.

"⁴So they both ran together and the disciple Jesus loved outran Peter, and came to the tomb first."

"Awakyns are four times faster than any man," May said.

Padre nodded in agreement. "Finally, Jesus gave Peter and Lazarus their commission in the final chapter." He further elaborated. "The disciple Jesus loved saw Jesus first, as it is written in John 21 verse 7. Lazarus is coming into his heighten senses. Then Jesus enlightens the rest of his disciples about the powers of the Holy Spirit and how to use their spirit to assist others in healing themselves."

May finished the chapter on her own.

"²⁰Peter turned around and viewed the disciple Jesus loved. Peter had questioned Jesus, "Lord, what will happen to him?" Jesus answered, "Suppose I want him to remain alive until I return" What does that matter to you? You must follow me." Then this saying went out among the brethren that the disciple Jesus loved would not die. Yet Jesus did not say to him that he would not die, but, "If I will that he remain till I come, what is that to you."

May knew Awakyns could not die by natural death. It amazed May how Padre Serra had added another candlelight to something she had read countless times. The wool had been lifted from her eyes, and she had learned something only a few would ever get to know or understand.

A sharp knock on the glass door startled May. She quickly turned her head and looked in that direction. The two Awakyns, who manned the control center, barged in. The tall one with winter gray eyes and pale skin named Ragnar spoke in a soft voice. "We have intruders. Don't worry. We have measures in place to protect the two of you."

The word 'intruder' triggered alarms in May's mind. Who could infiltrate this compound if it were concealed from the rest of the world? The first wave of panic crashed on the beach of her mind.

"Who are they?" Padre Serra asked.

"Jacques and his minions," Ragnar said.

Jacques came to capture May. Sweat beads formed on her brow. Her heart raced as she tried to comprehend the danger she was in. She glanced at Padre Serra, hoping for a plan to escape Jacques and his minions.

"How many are there?" Padre Serra inquired.

"About a hundred. We've got two of our brothers and a sister in position to hold them until the others can get here. They've been notified and will be here shortly," Ragnar explained in a reassuring tone.

Dao-Ren was on his way. May upbraided herself for letting the fear take over. She should've had more faith in her husband.

Ragnar locked the glass doors and reinforced them with tables and bookshelves. Marthese, the tan-skinned Awakyn, joined her brother and quickened their pace to complete the makeshift barricade. May had an uneasy feeling. The air was thick with tension. Both Awakyns locked and loaded their machine guns.

Marthese smiled at May, which eased the anxiety she felt.

"We'll risk our lives to keep the two of you safe. Still, I need the two of you to take cover," Ragnar suggested, gesturing towards the back.

"Thank you," Padre responded, directing May to the rear of the library, where she disappeared from view by squatting low behind a shelf.

May's nerves were on edge due to the eerie stillness. She needed a weapon. "I'll be right back," she whispered to Padre Serra. As she stood, Padre Serra snatched her hand and gave a definitive headshake. Gunshots could be heard in the background. Padre yanked her back down and covered her with his slim body.

"Repent and God will have mercy on you!" Ragnar and Marthese cried in unison. The air in the library was sucked out before the glass doors imploded. Dark smoke plumed into the cave. Thundering shots rattled out from the Awakyns' machine guns into the smoke. A torrent of yells emanated inside the smoke as bluish-black light erupted all around.

Ragnar and Marthese were on the same wavelength. They never broke stride in their shooting, even when they reloaded their guns. A grenade rolled to a stop between them. They both flipped into the air before the grenade went off. Wooden bookshelves and tables combusted, with fiery paper fluttering around them.

Out of the haze, a tidal wave of Judanites charged with swords drawn. Ragnar and Marthese put their backs together and spun in a synchronized pattern as they shot their guns. They twirled and dipped through the Judanites, leaving a path of bluish-black light.

A shimmer of hope sparked inside May. Maybe they could hold the Judanites off until reinforcements could arrive.

A blur of a human form missiled out of the cloud of smoke and chopped off the barrel of the Marthese's gun. Before the chopped barrel hit the floor, Marthese unsheathed her MaNa broad sword, parrying Jacques' sword thrust to her heart. Marthese attacked with the same speed as Jacques. Their movements became so fast that their swords disappeared. Ragnar kept shooting at the mass of Judanites to protect his sister's blindside. He tossed his gun when he fired his last round, and armed himself with a double-blade axe.

May knew it wouldn't last much longer. Their numbers were overwhelming. *Hurry up, my husband.*

Jacques laughed as he jigged and juked with Marthese. He landed a gashing slash across her face and chest, a wound that would have killed any mortal person. The wound didn't bleed much or healed quickly.

Another Judanite snuck behind her and plunged his sword through Marthese's back and into her heart. Without wasting a second, Jacques sliced through the Marthese's neck with one horizontal swing. May squealed. Jacques' eyes gravitated towards the noise. Marthese's body crumbled to the ground, and her head thumped to a stop.

Ragnar kept on fighting as Jacques sauntered in May's direction. He kicked aside the debris that impeded his path. A sense of pride swelled inside May. She wouldn't give Jacques the satisfaction of finding her cowered away.

Padre Serra must have felt the same, for they both got up to their feet. He offered May his hand, and they walked together. Jacques chuckled at their approach. He stretched his arms out wide and shook his head. "Now, don't we have two brave people?"

They halted a few yards from Jacques. Padre Serra placed a hand on May's forearm and shielded her with his body. *No, no, he can't die for me.*

"Padre, don't be a fool. There's no escape, and the other Awakyns won't arrive in time to save you," Jacques said.

May peeked over Padre Serra's narrow shoulder. Four Judanites managed to restrain Ragnar. Multiple slash wounds marked his body.

The rest of the Judanites swarmed around the single exit. Ragnar forced his head up to meet his fate. A Judanite thrust a spear into his heart. Ragnar's face contorted in pain, yet he didn't voice it. Another Judanite swung his battle-axe and severed Ragnar's head. His eyes were still open as it spiraled downward. Before the head could strike the ground, a Judanite kicked it into the air.

Others joined in, and bounced and kicked Ragnar's head around like a soccer ball. Their laughter inflamed May's hatred. She never thought she could consume this much enmity. One last Judanite kicked the head up high and bicycle kicked the head between two shelves.

"Goal!" he shouted. The head rolled to a stop.

"You've got a lot of promise, Malayah, if you can hate like that," Jacques said, his gaze fixed on her.

Jacques' words were a dagger to May's psyche. The hatred she harbored was for what she despised the most: a Judanite. Remorse for Ragnar and Marthese dissipated the malice she felt.

"Come, Malayah." Jacques put his hand out.

"No!" Padre Serra said.

Nothing could prevent Jacques from capturing her. She had to strike a deal to keep Padre Serra safe, because if he died, she wouldn't be able to forgive herself if she could have prevented his death. After placing a hand on his shoulder, she moved past him. She fixed her gaze directly into Jacques' lifeless eyes. "I'll come with you if you promise not to hurt Padre Serra."

Her desperate attempt at negotiation clearly amused Jacques, who grinned. "Oh, how noble of you, Malayah." He sneered. "But rest assured, I have no intention of killing that old fool. In fact, he might just be useful to me."

May felt a mix of relief and suspicion at Jacques' response. She wondered what ulterior motives he had for sparing Padre Serra's life. Despite her doubts, she had no choice but to trust him, knowing it was the only way she could safeguard Padre Serra. Taking a deep breath, she nodded and whispered, "Alright then, I'll go with you."

May faced Padre Serra and glanced into his kind face.

Jacques grabbed May's arm. "We have no time for this," he said, and slung May into the waiting hands of Judanites. Padre Serra stood tall as Jacques moved closer to him. He snatched Padre Serra from behind his neck and pulled him forward. Jacques stabbed a knife with his free hand all the way to the hilt into the pit of Padre Serra's stomach. It almost looked like they were in a friendly embrace. Jacques whispered into Padre Serra's ear then he twisted the knife.

"You fucking monster." May thrashed against her captors, whose fingers dug into her flesh.

Jacques broke away, and Padre Serra collapsed to the ground. A pool of blood moated around him. Tears blinded May, and she struggled harder. Jacques dropped a cell phone next to Padre Serra.

"Let's go."

***

The chilly mist off San Pedro Bay blew against Bernardo. He leaned against the outer wall of the vacated tuna processing factory with his gun in his hand. He used the barrel of the gun to pry open the broken door. A pungent stench of fermented fish guts assaulted his nose, snapping his face away from the door.

He took a fresh breath and crept inside. He tiptoed in the darkness, unable to see anything. Dried fish scales crunched with every step he took. He paused to let his sights adjust to the darkness. All he saw were shadows and more darkness further ahead.

The overhead lights clicked on. Bernardo shielded his eyes with the back of his arm from the flash burn. A mechanical engine cranked on his left. He twisted in that direction with his gun pointed out. His eyes blinked in quick sessions to combat the small square blurs in his retinas. A black conveyor belt rolled on. A swift movement in his peripheral drew his attention. He arched his gun and fired. The bullet ripped into a putrefied tuna, and fish mush sprayed all over him. The smell was appalling. He wiped his face with his shoulder and spit out the nasty taste in his mouth.

Laughter emanated from every corner of the factory.

"You like sushi, Bernardo," Ricky taunted.

Bernardo remained silent.

"What? No answer?"

It sounded like Ricky was behind him. Bernardo wheeled around to a stack of crates.

"What do you think of this stinky piece of fish?"

A motor whined above him, and a green mesh net descended into view. Tessa was hogtied inside it. A gag sealed her mouth as fear screamed from her eyes.

Bernardo's chest wrenched with agony; he had let her down again. A tingle of doubt cropped up that he wouldn't be able to save her. He tensed his muscles. No, he wouldn't fail her for a third time. She depended on him.

Bernardo inched toward Tessa, using his periphery to scan the two-level factory.

"Bernardo, I must say the sushi was pretty filling last night. It was fighting under my touch, alive and raw." Ricky's sadistic laughter echoed through the factory.

Bernardo's heart pounded in his chest as Ricky mocked him. Anger surged through his veins, fueling his determination to rescue Tessa. Ignoring the chilling words, he continued his careful approach, his eyes never leaving Tessa's terrified face. He would find a way to free her from this nightmare. He traced the mesh net cable line that went behind him. He swiveled a hundred and eighty degrees and fired three rounds.

"You did it now, bitch!"

Ricky vanished as the remote swung freely.

Chapter 47

Dao-Ren throttled the gas handle on the street bike. The cool air brushed over his burns from the explosion. He blazed through the cavernous tunnels into the sanctuary. Three headless bodies hung upside down by the stables. "You have honored God," Dao-Ren said in a tribute to his fallen Awakyns.

He rode over multiple footprints in the dirt in the direction of the library. The stench of Judanites was faint. They've been gone for quite some time. The charred glass doors of the library came into view. He squeezed on the brakes and launched himself from the bike, arming himself with his writer's knives.

The street bike crashed into the granite wall. He rushed into the library and surveyed the cave. He saw the two heads of the slayed Awakyns with their eyes gorged out perched on a bookshelf.

"You have honored God." He bowed his head and moved on.

Padre Serra's supine body laid in a pool of blood. The outer ring had started to congeal. Dao-Ren knelt beside him and examined the knife that protruded from his stomach. The knife had been twisted in his gut to keep the wound open. He couldn't pull it out without doing further damage.

Padre Serra's eyes opened. He gasped for breath, his voice weak and strained. "Forgive me… Dao-Ren,"

"Please don't talk, Padre," Dao-Ren said, placing both hands over

Padre Serra's wound. "I'll lay my hands over you."

Padre Serra shook his head. "I'm sorry, I couldn't protect May."

"No, Padre, you protected her with your life," Dao-Ren replied, his voice filled with gratitude and sadness.

Padre Serra's face softened. "Promise me that you'll continue to watch over her, Dao-Ren. She needs someone like you by her side."

Dao-Ren nodded, the weight of responsibility settling on his shoulders.

"Jacques said that he'll trade her life for yours." Padre lifted the cell phone in his hand.

"I will save her." Dao-Ren clasped his hand on Padre Serra's blood-coated hand. "Rest now. You have honored God." Dao-Ren accepted the cell phone from Padre Serra.

Padre Serra smiled, and a little twinkle touched his eyes before his hand dropped on his still chest.

The roar of multiple motorcycles whined. Ariel appeared next to Dao-Ren. He closed Padre Serra's eyes and got up with the cell phone in his hand.

***

Judanites plopped May down on warped floorboards that creaked underneath her. The plume of dust made her nose twitch. *One, two, three, four...* She counted to anchor her emotions to the present moment. Still, the image of Padre Serra's bloody body haunted her thoughts. *Stop, there was no time to mourn.* The urgency of her situation demanded her full attention. With a determined resolve, she pushed aside her grief and focused on finding a way to reach Dao-Ren.

She squirmed on the ground as the plastic restraints dug deep into her wrists and ankles. The duct tape over her mouth made it hard for her to breathe. Someone put a foot on her side to hold her still. The brief movement caused the bandanna around her eyes to shift. She scanned the dimly lit room. The dated wooden interior of a cabin was devoid of any personal items. The place had a strong odor of mildew and mulch. She raised her head and saw a boarded-up window.

All of a sudden, rough hands hoisted May by her armpits and pushed her onto a cracked lawn chair. Someone pulled the bandanna off then ripped the duct tape from her mouth, taking a layer of skin with it. Despite her eyes watering, May held back her shout. She wiped the tears with a shrug of her shoulder, and when she returned her gaze, Jacques stood over her with his men at his back.

"I would've started a fire for you, but I didn't want to create any unnecessary attention." Jacques squatted down to her eye level.

May frowned.

"You look just like Mother." Jacques touched May's cheek.

May pulled her head away.

"Father will be thrilled that I found you." Jacques got up. "But he must wait. I've other goals to achieve first. You'll return to your Awakyns for the time being."

May didn't want anything from him. He was a son of the Lie. Why would they capture her and then let her go? "Dao-Ren will come for me, and he'll release you," May threatened.

"I hope he does." Jacques stared down at her with a smirk.

May's heart stopped, and her stomach tightened. Jacques wanted Dao-Ren for Jacqueline.

"I see that you know Dao-Ren's history."

"I won't let him do that." She shifted in the chair.

Jacques leaned into her face. "What a peculiar statement."

May realized that Jacques' eyes were a similar color to hers but that no light could penetrate them because of the darkness behind them.

"If I didn't know better, I'd say that you've got feelings for Dao-Ren."

His hands suddenly shot up and snatched her cheeks between his fingers and thumb.

May trembled under his hold. The threat of him leaching from her spirit terrified her.

A phone rang.

Jacques released her face and answered the call. He walked away from May, but she could hear him easily enough.

"It's simple, Dao-Ren, your life for hers. We meet and exchange."

"Don't do it, Dao-Ren. They're going to kill you!" May bounced in her seat, banging the chair legs against the floorboards.

Jacques pointed his finger hard at May. A massive hand clamped over her mouth. May thrashed, biting the hand. More Judanites restrained her in the chair. She quickly calmed herself down to listen to the rest of the conversation.

"Give me your word that you won't attack or follow us." Jacques tapped his foot.

May couldn't hear Dao-Ren, but she knew what he would do. She couldn't live with herself, knowing he would sacrifice himself for her.

"I knew you would." He hung up and focused on May.

"It's done."

"What do you believe Judas will do to you when he discovers that you let me go, you idiot?"

Jacques wagged his finger. "I see what you're trying to do." He stood tall. "I'm honored, Malayah. I didn't think you cared much about me. Just know that I'll have you back in my clutches in a day or so."

What did he mean in a day or so? Was it possible that he had a mole? Or was he playing a mental game?

Jacques locked eyes with May. "You really don't get it, do you?"

"Get what?"

"Why is Dao-Ren so willing to give himself up for you?"

May responded with a glare. She felt the heat rise in her face.

"Because you're the key, Malayah. You'll be able to open up the door to Father's greatest dream."

"Never."

"You'll be a mother of nations."

The weight of Jacques' words hung heavy in the air as May processed what he just said. A mother of nations? It seemed unfathomable to her. The idea of it made her stomach churn. She would die before she gave Judas that satisfaction. She took a deep breath, trying to steady herself, but the queasiness only intensified. The room suddenly felt suffocating.

"So don't be so quick to get Father involved."

"You really think Dao-Ren won't try to save me?"

Jacques smiled and swung his head from side to side. "It doesn't really matter, he'll be dead by morning anyway."

"Dao-Ren gave me his word that he would never leave me." May clenched her fists, her determination solidifying. "He'll come for me, and you'll answer for your sins."

"Oh, he won't leave you." Jacques guffawed. "Jacqueline will do that for you."

***

Ariel confronted Dao-Ren. "What did you just do?"

"I saved my wife."

"So, let's go get her. We can put a homing device on you and track you."

"I'm sorry. I promised Jacques I wouldn't do that." Ariel's eyes widened in disbelief. "You promised Jacques? After he killed our brothers and sisters?" she exclaimed, her voice filled with anger and disappointment.

Dao-Ren looked down. "I made a deal with him, Ariel. I can't break it. You know our oath."

Ariel turned away from him.

He touched her arm. "You know who May is. She is the last. Judas will have his way with her until she can't bear any more descendants. We can't let that happen."

"There must be another way," Ariel pleaded, her voice filled with desperation.

"There's no time. We've got to move before the other Judanites clans know of May."

"I can't let you go. You're the only family that I've left," Ariel whispered, her voice trembling.

"You're such a blessing to me. You alone helped save me from my own sorrows. I can't thank you enough for your strength. Just know I had to do what needed to be done to ensure May's safety."

"And you think they'll honor their deal?"

"No. But all of you will come with me and guarantee her safety."

"I'll always love you, my daughter, my sister, my rock."

She spun around and hugged Dao-Ren. "I will miss you dearly, my father, my brother, my shield."

Chapter 48

May's heart quicken at the sight of Dao-Ren striding towards them. She tried to pull away from Jacques, but he had his hand firmly around her upper arm. He squeezed his hand, and she grimaced in pain. Other Judanites set a perimeter around Jacques and her. The reality of the situation dawned on her. Dao-Ren came here to die for her. Death would separate them.

May tilted away repulsed by the closeness of Jacques. He didn't notice as he concentrated on Dao-Ren's approach. She brought her elbow up, jerked her hip, and plowed her elbow into Jacques' rib cage. His grip loosened enough for her to escape.

May ran to Dao-Ren and collapsed into his arms. He wrapped her up in his strong embrace. She felt safe again. She was home. Their lips met in a kiss—a hello and a goodbye. She wanted it to be like that forever, but forever had its end. Dao-Ren pulled back. She knew the time had arrived for them to go their separate ways by the shadow of sadness in his brown eyes.

"I will always love you from the stars and back." He pulled a yellow diamond ring out of his coat pocket and slipped it onto her ring finger.

As he did, tears welled up in her eyes, knowing that this was their final moment together. "No! You don't have to do this. You and I can escape now." May yanked on his arm with both of hers. She struggled to breathe.

He tugged back, and she returned to his arms. "I can't, May. I made a deal."

"You made an promise to me," May said, her body trembling.

"Don't ever doubt my love." Dao-Ren ran his fingertips down her face as if filing it away for the last time.

So caught up in the moment, May didn't see Jacques and his goons encircle them until they were upon them.

"If you die, I will die with you," May said.

Dao-Ren kissed her forehead and pushed her into Omarosa's waiting arms.

"Let go of me!" May fought against Omarosa's grasp. "I want to die with my husband! Let me die with him!"

A Judanite patted Dao-Ren down and took his writer's knives from him. A crowd started to form amid the commotion. Dao-Ren and the Judanites began to walk in the opposite direction from May. Tears blurred her vision.

A car pulled up to the curb, and Omarosa opened the back door and forced May into the seat where Ariel was waiting. She held May tight as the door slammed shut, sealing Dao-Ren and her fate.

***

Bernardo fired two more shots at Ricky, but he missed both times by a wide margin. Ricky moved with such unnatural speed. He couldn't get another clean shot at him. It didn't matter all he had to do was keep Ricky at a distance so he could maneuver closer to Tessa. He was almost to her. If he could set her free, then maybe she or both of them could get away.

Bernardo stood right under Tessa, and their eyes met. The conviction in her expression strengthened his resolve. He would save her.

The net was too high to reach from where he stood. He scanned the factory and saw nothing he could use to reach up and cut through the net. He had to lower the net. He scanned the second floor walkway. Ricky was nowhere in sight. The remote dangled on its cable. Bernardo sprinted up the metal stairs to the walkway.

The remote loomed ahead. All Bernardo could see was the final seven yards. He stretched his arm out. The remote was right there. Unexpectedly, Ricky pounced and clamped his fingers around Bernardo's throat. The momentum banged Bernardo into the railing. Ricky squeezed the breath out of him. He was light-headed. Somehow, he still held onto his gun. He aimed it up to Ricky's heart. Ricky looked down at it. He pulled the trigger. The deafening sound of the click echoed through the air, causing his heart to sink.

Ricky's menacing laughter filled the space. "You're out of bullets." He backhand Bernardo's jaw as blood and a tooth spewed out of his mouth.

Bernardo's vision blurred as the pain shot through his jaw. Blood trickled down his chin. Ricky ripped the gun out of Bernardo's grip and tossed it away, clanging on the ground floor. Ricky snatched Bernardo by the neck and dangled him over the railing.

Chapter 49

Dao-Ren's wrists and feet were bound with handcuffs and shackles. Judanites flogged him relentlessly for the last thirty minutes. His shirt had been ripped off of him. Bruises and cuts appeared on his face and chest.

They hooked chains to his restraints from behind him and hoisted him into the air with a pulley. His torso pointed slightly more upward than his legs. He hung there, suspended in agony, his body weight pulling against the restraints. The pain was excruciating, but Dao-Ren refused to give in. He clenched his teeth, determined not to let them break him. Jacques strode up to Dao-Ren, his eagerness displayed in his countenance.

"Dao-Ren, you're my lucky charm. I want to kiss you. You had killed three birds with one stone for me," Jacques said, tossing his arm forward like he was throwing an imaginary rock. He paused close to Dao-Ren's face on a raised platform.

"I knew the Exorcist murders would draw you here. You had to play the hero. And I was the puppet master." Jacques twitched his finger, acting like he was pulling strings. "Then you and your kind decimated Caiaphas' personal army. The men he sent to try and steal the hybrid virus from me."

Dao-Ren's eyes narrowed as he listened to Jacques' twisted words. The realization hit him like a punch to the gut—he had unknowingly played right into Jacques' hands.

Jacques seized Dao-Ren's face between his two hands.

Dao-Ren matched his glare.

Jacques chuckled. "And the best part is yet to come because when Jacqueline kills you, the thorn in her heart will be removed, and she could love me in a way that you never appreciated." He leaned a few inches closer to Dao-Ren. "But I want you to think about one thing when she cuts you into pieces. Know that Malayah has the potential to become a powerful Judanite. Your death will fan the flames of the hatred she has toward us. This hate will fester inside of her until she is one of us."

Dao-Ren flexed his muscles, and the chains rattled as he rose slightly.

Jacques sneered. "There's nothing you can do. You lost, Dao-Ren."

A pound echoed in the cellar.

"Let the party begin," Jacques said, heading to the steel metal door. He swung the door open to a blindfolded Jacqueline. He escorted her onto the platform.

She laughed. "What is this, Jacques?"

"Your last anniversary gift." He untied her blindfold and kissed her deeply. He pulled away and caressed her cheeks with his thumb. "I love you." He pivoted Jacqueline around to face Dao-Ren.

Whatever trace of excitement lined her face vanished. Malice found its way through her, and she lashed out with her long, sharp fingernails, ripping her nails across Dao-Ren's chest.

Five deep wounds marked his chest. Dao-Ren didn't make a noise. Jacques restrained Jacqueline by her waist and pressed his lips by her ear. "My queen, don't be in such a rush to kill him. Take your time and make him regret every inch of pain he has caused you." He let Jacqueline go and cracked open a jewelry case that displayed the platinum scalpel with the embedded rubies in the handle.

She accepted the scalpel. "You're right, my king. He should suffer."

"And I leave this task for you. Caiaphas is raising hell about his decimated minions. I must calm him down. I'll leave Louis and twenty men outside this door. Just in case Caiaphas tries to do anything stupid. I'll see you when I get back." He kissed Jacqueline and departed.

The wounds on Dao-Ren's chest still hadn't healed. The carnal energy being exposed to him had weakened his spirit. Jacqueline touched the wounds. "Dao-Ren, it's been way too long since we last spent time in each other's company. You know I constantly thought about you. And every time you came to mind, this is how I felt." She dug the scalpel into one of the wounds and carved out a piece of muscle.

Dao-Ren's contracted his neck muscle.

Jacqueline dangled the piece of flesh in front of him. "The thought of you tears little pieces from me." She flung the piece of flesh onto the ground.

She slapped Dao-Ren viciously on the cheek. "What, you don't have anything to say? I haven't cut your tongue out yet."

At his lack of response, anger flashed in her face. She snatched one of Dao-Ren's writer's knives from the side table and jabbed the blade into the cavity of his abdomen. Dao-Ren just shut his eyes. His mouth never moved. She stabbed the other knife into him, to the same result, silence.

"You were always stubborn, Dao-Ren," Jacqueline said, and she started to caress Dao-Ren's undamaged left pectoral. "Maybe I'm using the wrong tactic." She stood on her tiptoes, inches from his face. "Have you ever dreamed of me, Dao-Ren? To lay between my luscious thighs and make love to me again." Jacqueline licked his cheek with her tongue. "I learned many new ways to please a man since we last made love to each other."

She forced her lips against his and kissed him hard. His mouth was clamped shut. She pressed harder on his mouth. His inactivity enraged her. She tore through his lips and bit them off. Flesh hung from her mouth, and ferocity colored her expression. She spat his bottom lip back into his face.

"You never loved me. How quickly do I forget? All you ever told me were lies. You betrayed me more than my father ever did. At least he never told me he loved me." She backhanded him. "You were my last hope! And you denied me. I am what I am today because of you. I accepted this life to be with you, but you didn't want to be with me. You love an invisible God."

Wrath electrified in Jacqueline's eyes. "Do you have anything to say? Look at me!" She raised Dao-Ren's head with her manicured hand.

"Jacques had informed me that you have taken a new Spiritmate, the lovely Malayah. Don't fret, my love, I promise to teach her all that I've learned between the sheets. But first, I must send a gift to her, your heart."

Jacqueline brought the scalpel to his left pectoral and sliced a precise incision. The skin split open. She cut deep into his muscles. The only emotion he showed was the flexing of his body. She dug deeper, chopping chucks of flesh out. The scalpel skimmed over a hard spot. She probed around it until the object popped out onto her hand. She stepped back and stared at the object in her palm. An object she hadn't seen since her youth, the turquoise stone she had found in Mirror Lake.

"What is this?" She shoved the stone into his sight.

He met her with more silence.

"Answer me, Dao-Ren! What's the meaning of this?"

His lips remained firmly closed.

"I hate you!" She thrust the scalpel in and out of his abdomen. The physical exertion slowed her down, and she took deep, laborious breaths. She discarded the scalpel for one of the writer's knives in the pit of Dao-Ren's stomach. She pulled a knife free. "You lose, Dao-

Ren." She fell to her knees and pointed the blade at her heart in a two-handed grip. She extended the knife all the way back.

"No, please don't." Dao-Ren's voice cracked. He couldn't let her do it.

"What's the meaning of this stone?"

"That's the stone Xin-Ji found. I placed the two fragments by my heart after I had become an Awakyn. My spirit must have made it whole again."

"You lie. You never loved Xin-Ji. Your love was only words—a gush of wind. Because if you had loved her, you would be here next to me."

"I loved her, and I still do. She'll always be the flower of my heart. You aren't my Xin-Ji. I came back to life to try to save her one last time. I knew her life had been tainted, and I couldn't protect her from those awful experiences she had to live through." He stared intensely at her.

"I had fought Judanites as a human and witnessed firsthand the despicable things they could do and have done. I couldn't let Xin-Ji's fate stay like that. My mind wanted me to become a Judanite, but my love for Xin-Ji wouldn't submit. Her life had been filled with more pain than love. I couldn't let her burn in hell for eternity when her life on earth was already hell. She deserved heaven."

Jacqueline broke into hysterical laughter. "You may think that you stopped me from plunging your knife into my heart because of your sappy story, but I tell you now that I wouldn't have done it. Your Xin-Ji was too weak and a fool. She believed in goodness, where this world has no such thing. And you could have loved me as you did her. We could've been strong enough to protect each other."

Dao-Ren held her eyes. "I could never love you as I did her because you're nothing worthy of love."

Jacqueline lunged and stabbed the knife into his heart.

Dao-Ren jerked his head back as his spirit was exposed.

"You have failed once again. I'm going to take Xin-Ji to hell with me. But before I go, I'll torture and fill Malayah with so much hate and loathing that she'll go to hell too." Jacqueline dislodged the second knife from his stomach. She examined the turquoise stone in her hand, then squeezed it in her palm. Her knuckles became white. She raised the knife over her head. "Xin-Ji and Malayah will hate you for eternity."

"I'm sorry, Xin-Ji. I forgive you."

Tears formed in the corners of her eyes. She swung the knife across his neck.

***

May returned to the Los Angeles compound and went straight to the command center. Who-Dat worked Thelma into overdrive. He and Rita went against Dao-Ren's wishes and deployed a drone. No luck. Judanites prepared and shot down the drone with their own. He then profiled every known enclave and sighting of Judanites in the Los Angeles metropolitan area in the last ten years where the drone went down. Plus, two hundred Awakyns combed the city for Dao-Ren. So far, no leads have been found.

From the moment she arrived, May cried on Kat's shoulder. Knowing that her husband would be killed tonight caused her unimaginable agony, which she couldn't express. Something had to be done, she felt in her spirit that he was still alive. May shot up to her feet.

Kat stood, her eyes widening. "May, what's wrong?" She moved closer to May.

May wiped her tears with the back of her sleeve and headed out the door.

"Where are you…" Kat's voice trailed off.

She headed down the hallway into the training quarter. From the weapon rack, she selected a small MaNa knife and slid it into her back pocket. She then dislodged a saber by the handle and swung it in an arc. As she finished her swing, Omarosa snatched the saber from her grasp. Fury ignited in her, and she clutched at its power.

"Give that back to me," May hissed through her teeth.

"You need to calm down before you do something irrational," Omarosa advised, her voice laced with concern. May's muscles tensed. The surge of anger pulsated through her veins, fueling her determination to retrieve the stolen saber. Ignoring Omarosa's advice, she took a step closer to Omarosa, her eyes locked onto the weapon in her hand. May heard the rapid thumping of her own heartbeat. "I'm going to find my husband."

Omarosa raised her hand, palm out. "We're working on it. When we locate him, we'll go get him."

"No, I'm going to search for him. It's all of your faults that he's sentenced to death. You should've followed them. You let him walk straight into the slaughterhouse." Indignation burned in the pits of May's being. "His death will be on all of your hands."

"Please, May. This is how Dao-Ren wanted it," Ariel said as she squeezed between her and Omarosa. "I wouldn't have allowed him to do it if he hadn't promised us not to."

"Sometime, promises are meant to be broken!"

"You know we can't." Ariel frowned.

"Yes, you can. You still have free will. Sometimes the end justifies the means," May's voice trembled with anger as she stared at Ariel and Omarosa. She couldn't believe they were justifying their inaction by claiming it was what Dao-Ren wanted. She had trusted them to protect him, to keep him safe, but now it seemed they were willing to let him die. May's heart ached with the weight of their abandonment.

"You're upset. We all are. Don't you think we love Dao-Ren?"

"No, you don't love him. You would share laughs with him, even tears, but not death. I would've died for him. You should've let me die with him," May yelled. "All of you are selfish of doing what's right. I blame all of you for taking him away from me."

"You've got to understand, May. They wouldn't have killed you until Judas decided to. They would have done unimaginable things to you that you couldn't even fathom. I know you love Dao-Ren more than words can define, yet this is how he wanted it and chose to do it. And in my love for him, I'll honor his wishes."

"I need to do something to help him." May pounded her chest. "The ache inside proclaims it."

"You're doing something. Your love is keeping him alive," Ariel sighed.

An invisible force shook May, and the pain of a thousand daggers stabbed into her heart. Something terrible happened to Dao-Ren. She could no longer feel his spirit.

Her legs buckled from under her.

Chapter 50

The MaNa blade streaked through the air, past Dao-Ren's neck, and collided into the upper links of his chained wrist. He dangled freely. Jacqueline shattered the other chains with one strike of the knife. Dao-Ren fell to the dirt with a lifeless thump. He lay motionless.

Jacqueline rushed over to his supine body and knelt beside him. She wrenched the other knife free from his heart. He didn't stir. She lifted his shoulders, scooted under him, and nestled his head on her bosom. "I'm sorry, Dao-Ren. Please forgive me." Her body convulsed, and the hate wrung out of her on the wave of her tears, tears that had been nonexistent since she was a human. The cleansing tears trailed down her cheeks onto Dao-Ren's face and torso. The pureness of her purification riveted into his mouth and into his torn flesh. His wounds began to heal.

Dao-Ren's eyes slowly opened, and he reached up to touch her face. "Xin-Ji."

"Yes, Dao-Ren."

He pulled her into his arms, and they held onto each other. Everything life had thrown at them and all that they had endured had led them to this point of redemption.

"I must get you out of here before Jacques returns from his meeting with Caiaphas. He's not too far away." Xin-Ji moved from underneath him.

Dao-Ren erected with renewed strength. The metal door reverberated with pounding fists.

"Open the door, Jacqueline," someone yelled from outside the door. The barrage of fists continued to bang on the door.

"That's Jacques' right-hand man, Louis. We'll have to fight our way out."

Dao-Ren sighted the camera mounted on the wall. He sprinted toward the wall and scooped up his trusted knife from the floor. He lunged into the air and chopped the camera in half.

The Judanites intensified their clobbering on the door. The metal door began to concave inward. Xin-Ji armed herself with Dao-Ren's other knife and the whip with a MaNa tip that hung on a hook. They regrouped at the center and faced the doorway with their weapons held for battle. They gave each other a quick smile. The door imploded, and the first wave of Judanites rushed in.

"Repent and God will have mercy on you!" Dao-Ren shouted.

***

Ariel gently laid May's inert body onto a bed. Her head sank into the soft pillow, doing nothing to comfort her from what she had experienced. Rita brought her MaNa infused water and assisted her to drink the whole cup.

The MaNa shocked May's mind and body back to life. The memories of the last several hours were unwelcome. It enhanced the emptiness she felt. She wished for death now. The love she had for Dao-Ren was to die for. How could she live on without him?

She pushed herself up and swung her legs out of bed. Everyone in the room studied her with a worried expression. She gave them a reassuring smile. "I have to use the bathroom." She went straight to the bathroom and locked the door behind her.

She stood in front of the sink and stared at the reflection in the mirror. Gloom and despair lined her pale face. She brushed her fingertips on her cheeks, remembering how Dao-Ren caressed them. She touched her lips and grinned as she relived his kisses.

We lived together. We loved together. We would die together. We will always be together. May retrieved the knife from her back pocket. She examined the knife. She rubbed the pad of her thumb over the edge. Blood seeped out of the thin cut. Her heart pounded against her chest. The veins in her wrist bulged against her skin. Could she do this? Dao-Ren wouldn't want her to do this. Her fingers pressed against the almond blossom print.

The loss of Dao-Ren was too much for her to bear.

Chapter 51

J acques had his hand on the pommel of his sword. Caiaphas eyed this movement. He then smiled, crossed his legs, and leaned back in his chair. Caiaphas' personal guards flanked his sides. "What is the cost of betrayal, Jacques?" Caiaphas finally asked.

"You would know." Jacques regarded Caiaphas' guards, their hands gripping their weapons tightly.

"And that's why you are here."

Jacques tapped his finger on the pommel of his sword.

Caiaphas stroked his beard as he observed Jacques. "You sent Awakyns against my men."

Jacques met Caiaphas' glowering face. "I did no such thing."

"You take me for a fool, then." Caiaphas slammed his hand down on the desk.

"Those are your assumptions." Jacques cracked a grin.

The scowl on Caiaphas' face lifted into a smirk. "You've got the most potential out of your brothers and sisters. Yet you only command a few hundred Judanites. This is because you have the biggest weakness. They all see that you worship a devious whore."

The edge of Jacques' sword was under Caiaphas' chin. Caiaphas' guards reacted by pulling on their weapons.

Caiaphas shot his hand up to keep his men at bay. "My point is proven."

"I should kill you." Jacques raised Caiaphas' chin with the tip of his blade. "You don't think I knew that you were planning a coup to steal the virus from me."

"That's my nature. I wouldn't have risen far in life without treachery."

"Your men can't save you this time." Jacques pressed the point of his sword into Caiaphas' throat.

"No, yours will." Caiaphas smirked.

The hangar filled quickly with Judanites with swords drawn.

"What is the meaning of this?" Jacques demanded.

"The cost of betrayal," Caiaphas affirmed.

"Somebody seized Caiaphas' guards," Jacques ordered.

None of his men moved.

"Your men are tired of you running behind that whore of yours. They want someone to bring them riches and glory, not disdain and pity from the other clans. Therefore, I gave them a choice. They could join me and gain their wildest dreams, or they could go nowhere with you. Yet the whole thing still lies in your hands. Your men or your whore?" Caiaphas flicked his hand at one of his guards. The burly guard turned on a television. Jacqueline appeared on the screen, crying and cradling Dao-Ren on the floor.

The muscles in Jacques' body quaked, then tightened by what he viewed. Deceit and rage pulsed through him. He wanted to kill someone. Pierre placed a vial of blood on the table.

"The choice is yours," Caiaphas said.

The choice wasn't hard. He would kill the one whose deceit cut the deepest.

***

Dao-Ren threw himself in front of Xin-Ji as the first wave of Judanites attacked. Dao-Ren maneuvered around them, slashing and thrusting his knife. But these Judanites were tactically sound. He had to act quickly. The advantage was in his favor. The cellar was small. Only one Judanite could enter at a time. The closer they were, the more deadly he was.

Dao-Ren kicked a fallen Judanite's sword up and plucked it out of midair. Dao-Ren sensed that Xin-Ji was close by. He raised his blades. Four Judanites spread out in a semi-arc. The middle Judanite rushed forward, her sword tight against her side. She thrust at his chest, and he blocked it with a swipe of his blade.

Another Judanite attacked from his right. He slipped away from the killing blow. He saw the other two Judanites flank his backside. He parried one strike and ducked the other one. Two bluish-black flashes caught the remaining two Judanites off guard. Dao-Ren struck with his knives and released them.

"You think I'll let you have all the fun?" Xin-Ji said. She scooped up a sword and slung it. It speared into an incoming Judanite's neck. His fallen comrades stepped over him into the cellar.

Dao-Ren and Xin-Ji engaged the next attackers. They found their timing as bluish-black light erupted around them.

"You haven't forgotten a thing," Dao-Ren said.

"I had a great teacher."

Another rush of Judanites barged in. Dao-Ren kicked, blocked, and slashed away, with Xin-Ji protecting his backside with her own lethal combinations. The third group of Judanites burst into bluish-black light.

"Only six remain," Xin-Ji said.

Three Judanites stepped in, shooting machine guns. Bullets swarmed all over. Dao-Ren and Xin-Ji ran for cover behind the wooden platform. Concrete debris and dirt whirled into a dust storm.

Dao-Ren hopped onto the top platform and dove into the storm. One by one, their guns stopped firing, and bluish-black light bolted out of the dust cloud.

As the dust settled, three Judanites attacked Xin-Ji. A mop-headed Judanite stabbed Xin-Ji in the chest all the way to the crossbar. Her scream filled the chamber. He grabbed Xin-Ji by the hair and dragged her out the door as she thrashed. The other two Judanites followed.

Dao-Ren sprinted toward the door and snatched up his other knife off the ground. At the precise moment, he slid onto the ground feet first. Two sword blades stabbed into empty space as he traveled beneath their thrust. The two ambushers positioned themselves in front of the tall, mop-headed one as he freed his other sword from his scabbard. He pressed the blade against Xin-Ji's throat.

Dao-Ren charged at the two Judanites. The first Judanite lunged with her sword and aimed for his heart. He leapt into the air and let the sword plunge all the way through his stomach to the hilt. He slashed his knife through her neck, bluish-black light.

Dao-Ren's feet skimmed the ground before he twisted in a triple-axle and tossed both of his knives, one high and the other low. The Judanite blocked the high one with his sword. The low one speared into his gut, bluish-black light.

With his arms straight out, Dao-Ren landed on the balls of his feet. He dislodged the sword from his stomach and discarded it to the side. He strolled directly at Louis, picking up his knives on the way. He twirled the blades in his hands while he observed Louis. Louis's sword arm twitched. Dao-Ren launched himself directly at him.

Louis sliced through Xin-Ji's throat and let her body shudder to the floor. Dao-Ren jumped head first at Louis. Louis took to the air to meet Dao-Ren.

Their blades collided. They landed on their feet and resumed the fight. Louis threw hard, definitive strikes with his long broadsword, using the distance to his advantage. Dao-Ren parried each blow and felt the vibration pitchforking up his arms. Louis's broadsword blade chipped away at the integrity of his knives—they couldn't take much more.

Louis set off on another offensive charge. Dao-Ren used his knives as little as possible. He ducked and bobbed away from Louis's attack. His spirit was feeling the blow he had taken earlier in the stomach. He would have to take a major chance to get the fight over with.

Dao-Ren spun around and blitzed Louis with a barrage of strikes and thrusts. He kept his blows high to leave his abdomen area exposed. Louis saw the opening and countered with a sawing strike. In the last possible second, Dao-Ren flipped the knives downward and took the brute force of Louis's assault. The left knife snapped at the handle, with the right knife cracking in the middle. The broadsword grazed Dao-Ren's abdomen.

With his back to Louis, Dao-Ren stumbled down to his knees next to Xin-Ji. Louis took advantage of this and charged him. He timed the cadence of Louis's footfalls. At the right moment, he wrenched the sword from Xin-Ji's chest and lunged backward at Louis with the sword pointed over his head. Louis missed him and rammed straight into the awaiting sword. He twisted around and pushed the sword blade all the way through Louis's chest. With his right hand, he jabbed the broken knife into Louis's eye, all the way to his brain. Bluish-black light.

Dao-Ren hurried back to Xin-Ji and folded her up in his arms. "I'm so sorry, Xin-Ji, I couldn't protect you again."

"No, Dao-Ren. You saved me. I'm free again." Xin-Ji's voice came in a heaving wisp from her sliced windpipe.

Dao-Ren brought her close and pressed his cheeks against hers.

"Am I going to heaven?" Xin-Ji asked.

"Yes, you are."

"Give this to May." Xin-Ji opened her hand and displayed the turquoise stone. "Tell her about the life we once shared, so she knows the power of the love she has inherited."

"I will."

She closed her eyes and took a wheezing breath. "Save Jacques for me. Tell him his Black Rose will be waiting for him in heaven."

"I'll do my best."

They sat together for a moment.

Xin-Ji gave a reassuring smile. "It's time."

Dao-Ren swallowed. "I can't do it."

"Yes, you can. Protect me from myself. The hunger and thirst are ravaging my body. I can't fight it much longer. You know I can't die or change back." Xin-Ji placed the broken knife into Dao-Ren's hands. "We will see each other again."

Dao-Ren bent his neck and kissed Xin-Ji goodbye until he tasted the ashes on his lips.

***

Ricky tightened his grip like a noose. Bernardo used his fingers to pry loose Ricky's grasp around his neck. He heard the pounding in his head and felt the pressure building behind his eyes. He would die soon. He forced his gaze to find Tessa. She stared back at him with steel blue eyes. He couldn't let her down.

Bernardo tried to talk, but his vocal cords were too constricted by Ricky's hold. Ricky detected Bernardo's intention and loosened his grip. "You have a final word, Bernardo?"

Bernardo mumbled as he slipped something out of his pocket.

"What?" Ricky brought him closer so he could hear.

"Game over." Bernardo hooked up with the MaNa shuriken blade that he had found at the "House of Angels." He shoved the whole blade up behind Ricky's ear. A bright bluish-black light burst from Ricky's mouth, eyes, and nostrils.

Bernardo snatched the railing with his hand as ashes showered upon him. He hoisted himself over the railing and scrambled to the remote to slam the down button. The motor whined and the net descended to the floor. Bernardo dashed down to Tessa and untangled the net from around her. He untied her hands and feet. She ripped off the gag from her mouth. A word didn't need to be spoken as they hugged and kissed each other between tears.

Chapter 52

"The bodies are ready," Pierre said, his voice filled with anticipation.

Caiaphas examined the five sedated bodies lined up on the table. He ran his fingers along the warm skin of the male subject, a sinister smile lingering on his lips. "Are all of them infected with the virus?"

"Yes," Pierre answered, his eyes gleaming with excitement. "We've successfully infected each of them with the virus, just as you requested."

Caiaphas chuckled, his mind already envisioning the chaos that would soon follow. Each body represented the culmination of his insatiable desire for power and control. With a nod of approval, Caiaphas turned to face Pierre. "Let the men feed on these bodies and release the virus into the population."

"You got it." Pierre walked away, getting on the phone.

Caiaphas brought his sight back to the bodies. He couldn't help but feel a twisted sense of satisfaction as he watched the first group eagerly feast on the infected host. The sight of their frenzied feasting only fueled his appetite for power, knowing that the virus would spread like wildfire through the unsuspecting population to increase the likelihood that the virus would become contagious. He reveled in the thought of the desolation and suffering that were about to consume the city. He, not Judas, would become Satan's right hand.

Armageddon begins tonight.

***

"You're alive!" Who-Dat said with a sigh of relief.

"I'm glad to be," Dao-Ren said, speaking into a cellphone that he found on Louis' remains.

"We've got everyone searching for you. Where are you?" Who-Dat asked.

"I don't know. You'll have to trace this call." Dao-Ren tiptoed cautiously down the hallway with the sword out front.

"I'm doing it now."

Dao-Ren considered the imminent danger that awaited humanity. He needed to quickly figure out Jacques' plan and unravel his sinister plot that threatened Los Angeles.

"I think Jacques and Caiaphas are nearby."

"Why do you think that?" questioned Who-Dat.

"Xin-Ji made a statement that Jacques was meeting Caiaphas close by here."

"…Xin-Ji?" Who-Dat repeated with a slight hesitation.

"Yes." Dao-Ren ascended the stairs, dropping the phone away from his ear. As he tiptoed into the large chamber, he strained his ears to hear for any sign of life. A series of transparent medical tents connected by airtight plastic corridors took up the space. The soft hum of medical equipment filled the air. He saw no one inside.

"Hold on. I think I found something," Dao-Ren said back into the phone.

He approached the tent and pushed aside the plastic flap. The tent held three incubators and a cylindrical sub-zero freezer. As he reached the end of the tent, he noticed a flickering light coming from the corner. On top of a metal desk stood a personal computer with multiple CPU towers and a modem.

He leaned his sword against the desk and sat down on a swivel chair. He moved the mouse, and the screen came alive. A password box appeared. "I found a computer, but it's locked," Dao-Ren said.

"It's okay, I got your location. I'm sending a team now," Who-Dat responded. "But if you can, connect the phone to the computer,"

Dao-Ren searched around the desk and found a USB-C cable. "I'm linking up the phone now." He put the phone on speaker as he heard Who-Dat's fingers flying across the keyboard.

"I'm trying to hack into the system. It might take a minute." Who-Dat exhaled deeply. "I got Thelma searching the property deeds for any known associates to Judanites around your location and Billy Jacob's production company owns a hangar at Santa Monica airport. That's about 15 miles from where you are at."

It made perfect sense to Dao-Ren. The hanger could be an ideal place to stage a covert operation. It would provide ample space to store equipment and conduct operations discreetly. The proximity to the airport also meant easy access to transportation, making it a convenient location to spread the X-virus.

"Alert the other teams to create a one-mile radius perimeter from that location. There's no one here, so Jacques might be planning to release the X-virus tonight," Dao-Ren instructed. He felt a sense of urgency. The stakes were high, and the threat of a widespread outbreak loomed.

"I'm coordinating with the other teams now."

Dao-Ren stood and grabbed the sword. "I'm heading there too."

"Everyone should arrive at the same time as you do," Who-Dat informed.

"One more thing, Who-Dat?"

"What's that?"

"Tell May I'm coming home soon."

***

"I need more bodies." Pierre's words echoed in the open hangar. Unconscious bodies were placed on cots and tables. Each person received a transfusion of blood. "We only had enough for sixty-two Judanites to carry the virus." Pierre's voice carried a sense of desperation, as he knew that time was of the essence. Every second counted in their race to spread the virus.

"Who put you in charge?" Quin said, with his green hair tied back in a ponytail. He crossed his arms and glared at Pierre, challenging his authority.

Pierre straightened his back and met Quin's gaze, his voice steady and determined. "Nobody put me in charge," he replied. "Caiaphas wants everyone out there."

"Fuck Caiaphas." Quinn moved closer to Pierre with his hand on his sword. The other Judanites simply watched, choosing not to get involved.

Pierre raised an eyebrow as he matched Quin's intense glare, refusing to back down. "You forget that we're betrayers now. We've got no clan or name." Pierre's words hung in the air, the weight of their new reality settling upon all of them. Quinn's grip on his sword tightened, his veins popped out on the back of his hand.

"We're running out of time," Pierre exclaimed, his voice filled with urgency.

Quin sneered but loosened his grasp on his weapon.

"Send out the infected Judanites and bring me more bodies," Pierre ordered.

Quin stomped off.

Chapter 53

Jacques squatted low behind the second-floor gargoyle statue, his eyes focused on the front door. He clenched his sword so tight that his fingers felt numb. He kept the rage he felt in check with the flexing of his muscles. His body trembled as the pain of Jacqueline's betrayal weighed heavily on his thoughts. The image of her face flashed in his mind, fueling both anger and sadness within him. It felt as if his body was being torn apart. He couldn't understand why she had chosen Dao-Ren. Her deceit clouded every memory they had shared together. Now, the idea of loving her was poisonous to his very existence.

The front door swung open, and Dao-Ren ran out of the entrance as he pressed a quick-start button on a key fob in one hand and held a sword in the other. A car started, and the headlights flashed on. Jacques leapt from his hiding spot with both hands on the handle of his sword. The blade cocked back and high above his head, parallel to his vertebrae.

Jacques brought his sword downward, aiming for the top of Dao-Ren's head. Dao-Ren spun away in time. Jacques' sword impacted the roof of the car. The blade embedded itself a couple feet into the frame. Jacques dislodged the sword with a hard yank, sparks showered. He launched into a flurry of blows. Dao-Ren parried with his sword.

"Where is she?" Spit flew out of Jacques' mouth.

"She's in heaven."

"You bastard." Jacques attacked more aggressively. His blade swirled all around Dao-Ren. "You never loved her." He thrust for Dao-Ren's heart. "I did."

Dao-Ren blocked the thrust with his sword.

"You didn't deserve her." Jacques swiped for his neck.

Dao-Ren jumped back.

"I just wanted her to love me." Jacques paused to gather himself, his sword out, ready for another assault.

Dao-Ren held his blade high. "She did love—"

Three Judanites sprung out from the tall hedges, swords wielded at Jacques' back.

Jacques saw the reflection off Dao-Ren's sword blade. He twisted around. He blocked two of the sword blades as the third slashed into his arm and chest. Jacques stepped back as they circled him. Caiaphas' bodyguards, that treacherous bastard.

"Repent and God will have mercy."

A sword streaked through the night, beheading one of Caiaphas' bodyguards. Bluish-black light. The remaining bodyguards glanced at Dao-Ren. Jacques decapitated the one nearest to him. Bluish-black light. The last bodyguard angled himself between Jacques and Dao-Ren. Jacques peered out of the corner of his eyes. Dao-Ren vanished as a car sped away.

Jacques swung his sword with fury, parrying the bodyguard's attacks with precision. The clash of their blades echoed through the air, each strike resonating with deadly intent. With a final, powerful swing, Jacques chopped his sword down upon the bodyguard's head, envisioning Dao-Ren's face.

***

A Judanite carried a squirming body out of the van. The victim's mouth was ducked taped and his hands and feet were flex cuffed. His round, wide eyes glistened with fear.

"Bring them over here," Pierre said, standing by the equipment to incubate more of the virus.

Caiaphas observed the scene with intrigue, his eyes flickering with anticipation. He couldn't help but feel a diabolical pleasure at the sight of the restrained victim, knowing that soon the virus would bring him even greater satisfaction. As a Judanite approached with the captive, Caiaphas couldn't contain his saliva-filled mouth from watering, his desire for the virus consuming him. But just as he was about to fully indulge in inheriting the virus into his system, a sudden noise startled him.

One of the captives got loose from her leg restraints from the back of the van. She made it half way to the hangar door before a muscular Judanite knocked her to the ground. She dragged her back by her hair.

Caiaphas glanced at his watch. Time was of the utmost importance. There could be no hitches concerning Awakyns. The sixty-two Judanites who had consumed the virus ought to have begun spreading it among the populace. This virus has a significant chance of shifting the balance of power in Satan's favor. He felt the excitement as he realized victory was within reach. Awakyns couldn't possibly hamper the spread of this virus. It was too aggressive.

The whooping sound of helicopter blades garnered his attention. His body tingled all over. Helicopters usually don't fly this late at night, and there's no heliport here. A fear washed over him, settling in his gut. *Fucking Awakyns.*

He yanked out his cell phone. "Get the jet ready!"

Caiaphas armed himself with the sword on the table and moved in the direction of the others. "Secure the perimeter! We've got company!" Judanites armed themselves with their weapons.

The whine of helicopter blades chopped overhead, and their flood-lights burst through the hangar's glass windows.

"Repent and God will have mercy!" someone said over a bullhorn.

As the windows imploded, the sound of shattering glass filled the air. Awakyns swiftly descended the ropes, shooting. Bluish-black light erupted everywhere. A G6 jet rolled into view and braked. The jet's door hatch lowered. Caiaphas ran for the airstair.

The hangar's aluminum sliding door smashed inward by a speeding car. The car barreled down on Caiaphas. He jumped over the vehicle. The car skidded to a stop. Dao-Ren rushed out with a sword raised high. Caiaphas came to meet him. They traded blows. Dao-Ren sliced Caiaphas' thigh and arm. He circled around Dao-Ren to give himself more room.

"Let's not waste time—my life or theirs." Caiaphas nodded in the direction to his right. Pierre dashed the restrained captives on the examination tables with fluid from a red gas can. Pierre flung the can against a computer screen. He dug in his pocket and produced a Zippo lighter. He struck the flint and dropped the flame onto the ground. The electrical equipment and furniture roared into flames.

"Your time will come," Dao-Ren promised.

"Not today." Caiaphas smiled.

Dao-Ren sprinted to the captives. Caiaphas made it to the jet door ramp as Pierre did.

"Where's the virus information?" Caiaphas asked.

"I couldn't make a copy," Pierre stated, wide eyed.

"How about the original strain?"

"It's within Jacques."

"You fucking idiot!" Caiaphas kicked Pierre dead center in the sternum. Pierre slammed on the ground.

Caiaphas sealed the jet doors.

Chapter 54

"I'll meet you there," Bernardo said, kissing the back of Tessa's hand before letting it go. The EMT lifted the stretcher into the ambulance. Tessa gave him a tired smile as the door closed. Bernardo tapped the back of the ambulance when it pulled away.

Bernardo took a long blink before he scanned the scene around him. Police lights illuminated the chilly night. A mob of news reporters crammed into the parking lot, reporting that the Exorcist Killer had been gunned down and killed.

In San Pedro Bay, a police dive team searched for the remains of the Exorcist Killer. Earlier, Bernardo had made a statement to investigators that the Exorcist Killer had lured him to the factory with Tessa's kidnapping. He thwarted the Exorcist Killer's scheme and chased him down to the bay, where a fight and struggle occurred between them. When Bernardo had the opening, he shot the Exorcist Killer multiple times in the chest as he fell into the bay.

The truth was the least of Bernardo's concerns. His statement matched Tessa's testimony, and physical evidence would confirm it. The degree to how the Exorcist Killer actually died didn't really matter; dead was dead. Nevertheless, Bernardo wasn't totally satisfied by Ricky's demise. He deserved more than death. Still, the case was solved.

"Vega!"

Bernardo cringed upon hearing Graham's voice. Graham stomped toward Bernardo, his eyebrows narrowed in anger, the tip of his nose redder than the rest of his face. "I'm writing you up for insubordination. I should've been notified of your course of action."

Bernardo shook his head and stepped past him.

"Don't walk away from me!" Graham grabbed Bernardo's upper arm with force.

Bernardo tilted his hips forward and flipped Graham over his back to the gravel ground. The people on the scene broke into laughter.

"I'm going to have your badge for this!" Graham threatened.

Bernardo walked towards him. Graham tried to crawl backwards as his hands slipped on the gravel. Bernardo leered over him. "Kiss my ass." Bernardo swung his arm downward. Graham crossed his arm over his face and gave a high-pitched squeal. Bernardo dropped his badge onto Graham's chest.

"I'm retiring."

***

Amy felt his spirit enter her. It was a lot more invigorating than heroin. She let go of the fat biker's neck and rose up from her straddled position off his lap. He sat motionless on top of the toilet seat, sound asleep. He was infected with the virus. She sneered down at him and patted the top of his head.

She straightened her hair and wiped the blood from the side of her mouth with her finger. She turned and opened the stall door.

"Repent and God will have mercy on you."

There was nothing she could do. The sword punctured her heart.

***

It didn't matter whom Tyson fed upon tonight. He just wanted to feed and spread the virus. Earlier that night he broke away from his group. It was always easier to hunt alone in the city. People tend to stay far away from groups dressed in leather clothing in the dead of night.

He squatted low in the bushes. A young couple, hand in hand, promenaded down the pathway. He could handle both of them. As they drew closer, his canines elongated, and his mouth watered with saliva.

A twig snapped behind him, and he twisted around.

"Repent and God will have mercy," she said.

He shuffled backward on his hands and feet. He felt the cold bit of steel on his neck, then immense heat.

***

The hangar's roof crumbled under the roaring flames. The fire's ferocity escalated with each wind gust. The airport firefighters battled the raging fire. Dao-Ren watched from a quarter of a mile away. By the time the airport's emergency response team arrived, Awakyns were long gone.

Dao-Ren had enough time to save all the captives from the burning building. Only time would reveal if those who contracted the X-virus would survive. Awakyns would covertly visit them in the hospital. They would help the infected ones in any way they could.

"What did you discover at the house?" Dao-Ren said as he heard the approaching footsteps.

"Who-Dat initially believes that we've obtained the original research on the X-virus. We'll know more in a day or so," Omarosa said.

"And the containment of the X-virus?"

"We're still combing the streets for infected Judanites. None so far has gotten passed the perimeter we'd set up. We'll just have to wait and see." Omarosa stood next to Dao-Ren and watched the fire.

"Any sign of Jacques?" Dao-Ren said with a hint of concern.

Omarosa eyed him. "He was long gone before we got there." Her eyes lingered on him for a moment before sighing.

Dao-Ren felt Omarosa's hand on his. He peered down at her. Her dark eyes reflected the moon.

"I'm glad you're safe," she said.

"Me too, Rosa."

She smiled up at him and squeezed his hand tighter.

Dao-Ren grinned back. "How's May?"

She glanced to the side.

"What's wrong?" Dao-Ren held Omarosa by her shoulders.

Omarosa kept her eyes away from him.

"I'm sorry, Dao-Ren," Omarosa said. "I told her she should come with us." Dao-Ren's heart sank as he processed Omarosa's words. The worry that had been gnawing at him intensified. "Why would you do that?" he asked, scanning the area with new purpose.

Omarosa's shoulders slumped, and she finally met his gaze. "I thought it would be safer for her to be with us."

"What do you mean safer? What happened?" Dao-Ren took a deep breath, trying to steady his racing thoughts.

"You can ask her yourself."

A SUV pulled up as May stepped out of the passenger seat. Dao-Ren's heart clenched at the sight of May standing in front of him, her eyes wide with shock. She stood there with her hands over her mouth, not believing he was alive. He sprinted to her and gently touched her arm. "May, it's really me," he whispered, his voice filled with a mix of relief and longing.

May's hands fell from her mouth as tears welled up in her eyes. "Dao-Ren, I can't believe it's really you," she choked out. "I felt your spirit leaving me."

"I'm so sorry." He pulled May into a tight embrace. "I never wanted to leave you."

May buried her face in Dao-Ren's chest, holding onto him as if she would never let go. "I thought I had lost you forever," she sobbed, her voice muffled against his shirt. "I couldn't bear the thought of living without you." Her sobs echoed the pain and longing they had both endured during their time apart.

In that moment, they found solace in each other's arms, knowing that their love had conquered every obstacle in their path. Their eyes met briefly before their lips touched. Dao-Ren closed his eyes as tears fell.

This only happened in dreams.

Epilogue

The radiance reflected off the blue glass building from the multiple beams of LED spotlights around the perimeter. The building's exterior gave the impression of being an extension of the sky, and the visitors were entering into heaven. May and Dao-Ren welcomed the guest to the "Heaven's Guardians" exhibit. May couldn't believe her luck that her venue had been changed to the Blue Whale.

May felt a surge of happiness as she glanced at Unc and Tessa, their presence adding an extra layer of joy to the occasion. Unc wrapped his arm around Tessa's waist as they spoke to Omarosa and Willie. Now, he had the time to invest in their relationship since he had officially retired from the FBI.

May focused on Kat in her designer-chic sleeveless silk dress. She looked absolutely gorgeous. Her beauty equaled the company of Gasper, Otis, and Ariel. Kat had matured and learned to love herself. The promise ring she wore on her left ring finger said it all. It symbolized her commitment to herself and her journey of self-discovery. As she twirled the ring absentmindedly, her eyes met with May's, and they exchanged a knowing smile. It was a silent acknowledgment of their shared growth and newfound happiness.

May smiled at Who-Dat and Rita, who were typing away on their smartphones. About what, she had no clue. The X-virus had been contained and isolated to a few individual cases that were exposed to it. Their luck held, and the X-virus had not spread.

Xin-Ji's turquoise stone hung down from May's neck. Dao-Ren

had presented her with the necklace soon after their reunion. She accepted it without envy or jealousy. It was part of Dao-Ren's past. She viewed it as if it were her turn to carry the legacy of the stone and add more meaning to it.

May couldn't help but feel like the luckiest person in the world as they stood there, taking in the ethereal atmosphere of the Blue Whale and starting a new chapter in her life. As the evening continued, the laughter and warmth between the groups became a testament to the beautiful relationships they had all built together.

She let Dao-Ren enfold her in an embrace. "Is my wife enjoying herself tonight?"

She laughed. "It could be better."

"And how's that?"

"It's easier to show you than tell you." May held Dao-Ren's eyes that burned bright with happiness.

"Let's get out of here." Dao-Ren tugged on her hand.

"We don't need to." May drew him towards her and kissed him deeply, expressing what the words, "I love you" never could.

***

Jacques took another sample of blood from the victim he had tied to the bed. He dripped some blood onto a glass slide and sandwiched it with another. He secured it under the microscope and viewed it. His menacing laughter broke the silence. The virus had mutated.

Dao-Ren, I'm coming for you.

Dear Friend,

I am honored to share this story with you. I pray that you found "Awakyns" as entertaining as much as I enjoyed writing it for you. "Awakyns" is merely getting started. Kindly leave a review until the next episode. Thank you for your support.

Always,
KF Lee

www.ingramcontent.com/pod-product-compliance
Lightning Source LLC
Chambersburg PA
CBHW021232310726
48971CB00006B/1787